Lewis Percy

Lewis Percy

by

ANITA BROOKNER

PANTHEON BOOKS • NEW YORK

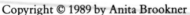

Library of Congress Cataloging-in-Publication Data

Brookner, Anita.
Lewis Percy/Anita Brookner.
p.   cm.
ISBN 0-394-58446-5
I. Title.
PR6052.R5816L49   1990
823'.914—dc20   89-43254

Manufactured in the United States of America
First American Edition

Lewis Percy

————— I —————

Madame Doche, with an air of appreciation no less generous
for being regularly at her command, took the camembert
from Lewis Percy, prodded it with an expert thumb, pronounced it to be good, and ushered him into the salon.
There the regular cast of his private theatre was assembled.
What he thought of as the evening's entertainment, the
evening's instruction, the evening's reward, was deployed
for his pleasure. All he had to do was take his seat.

Sometimes he brought a bag of cherries: something minor
but decorative was thought appropriate to his subordinate
status. In the salon the women, his fellow lodgers, were
eating their irregular refreshments, and as he was the only
man he did not feel emboldened to add a note of robustness,
although he was nearly always hungry and would have
appreciated something more serious than the slices of ham
and the couple of apples that he allowed himself. Occasionally Mme Doche took pity on him and served him a plate of
the thick gruel-like soup which she made for her employer's
evening meal. The soup had usually to go down after the
apples. An equally thick concoction of semolina might
precede the ham. Lewis, being young, could accommodate
these discrepancies. The pleasure of the evening did not reside
in the food, though that was always welcome. The pleasure
of the evening for him lay in the warm and uncritical company of the women, all temporary inhabitants, like himself,

I

of the cavernous apartment of Mme Roussel, the eighty-three-year-old widow under whose roof they happened – for a year, for six months, for two years – to find themselves, for that was as long as their assignments in Paris were to last. While Lewis's contemporaries sighed out their time in meagre student lodgings, Lewis, thanks to a stroke of luck at the Alliance Française and the money his father had left him, found himself in some splendour in the Avenue Kléber. His room was the smallest in the flat, little more than an afterthought to the main accommodation, but the supreme advantage was the conviviality of his fellow migrants. He thought of them as guests, Mme Roussel's guests, although they paid rather highly for the privilege. Mme Roussel herself, being old and rarely completely dressed, was a benevolent absence. Her quarters, entered only by Mme Doche, were separate, at the end of the corridor. Occasionally, on their way to the bathroom, to which they were allowed strictly regulated access, they could hear her playing patience and talking to herself in a loud and surprisingly coarse voice.

After handing over his camembert or his cherries Lewis would take his place with Mme Doche, Roberta and Cynthia, among the Louis XV chairs with their dingy tapestry seats, frayed, in the unseemly way of tapestry, by years of wear, under the twinkling bulbs of clusters of widely spaced wall lights. The salon was dim, its former splendour no longer even a memory. This faded background served only to bring into further prominence the presence of the women. Use of the salon in the evenings was one of the privileges for which they paid so highly. Having paid highly they then put it to their own use. Cartons of Chesterfield cigarettes were placed carelessly on the marble topped iron legged occasional tables, besides packets of smoked salmon and the matzos favoured by Roberta. Working at UNESCO she had access to far greater luxury than the rest of them and thus took further licence: a greasy paper might float down to the nineteenth-century Savonnerie carpet from the card table which she imported for her evening snack, or a riveted

Sèvres saucer play host to the pips of her grapes. Cynthia, a student like Lewis himself, was more fastidious; indeed she was almost too fastidious for Lewis, although he was nearly in love with her. Cynthia, sipping her camomile tea, looked on appalled as Mme Doche sucked out the insides of mussels or tugged on the leaves of artichokes. Mme Doche, being the only one of them who was, so to speak, at home, was also the only one who ate regular meals.

It was 1959. The windows of the salon had perhaps been closed since 1950, when Mme Roussel, then 'cette chère Mélanie', had last played hostess to her busy friends, women like herself of good family and limited interests and outlook. Since then she had declined into vigorous old age, tended by Mme Doche, who was both servant and companion. Mme Doche, however, had never graduated to the position of friend, and that was why she appreciated the company of Roberta and Cynthia, and even of Lewis himself. What prevailed, in that dim salon, in the evenings, was a below-stairs camaraderie, ready money defiantly making weight with the family portraits and the riveted Sèvres saucers, Roberta's salary and Cynthia's and Lewis's allowances cocking a snook at the restrained gentility and the inherited fixtures of a long vanished bourgeois French family. Lewis saw their little group as a temporary encampment in alien territory and was continually and pleasurably divided in his loyalties both to the real if dingy chairs and the Bohemian life those chairs were forced to witness. But then he was writing his thesis on the concept of heroism in the nineteenth-century novel and was forced to dwell on higher things, even when he wished to be free of them.

In this contest between the established and the imported it was the women who won him over every time. To them he owed his lasting conviction that women were a congenial and compassionate sex. As they welcomed him, his camembert and his bag of cherries, with apparent enthusiasm, an enthusiasm that seemed to contain a peaceable indulgence for his youth, his obvious lack of sophistication and his

3

enquiring and anticipatory smile, his heart expanded, and he felt himself to be in a company that had in it something maternal, something undemanding, something even slightly pitying. In later life he was to accept this as the very climate of femininity. It was what he had known in his mother's house, and it never occurred to him to question this. Modest and timid, he looked forward all day to what he thought of as his homecoming. It was not the salon that constituted home. It was the women.

An additional bonus was that after welcoming him they paid him very little attention, but continued to talk among themselves, as he thought women should. The subjects they discussed were nearly always the same: Roberta's day at the office and what Mme Van de Waele, the Belgian delegate for whom she worked, had said, done, and worn – this last being of interest to Mme Doche – and Cynthia's ailments, for which Mme Doche, a former nurse, offered advice and remedies. To Lewis all this represented important material, and as it was discussed conscientiously in French he thought it the height of worldliness. While meekly serving himself with a slice of his own camembert on one of Roberta's matzos, he would in fact be surrendering his daily self, the self that went to the Bibliothèque Nationale and wrestled with the heroes of fiction, to this warm atmosphere of women, who, though largely ignoring him after their initial welcome, were, he felt, kindly disposed, and would muster as a body to protect him if the need arose. Mme Doche, in particular, seemed to him benign: her appreciation of his little contributions never ceased to touch him, and, more important, to make him feel comfortable with his gawky youth, the ankles and wrists that protruded from the sleeves of his tweed jacket and the turn-ups of his grey flannel trousers, the hair that sprang straight up from his forehead and which no amount of water could flatten. Her special softness he put down to the fact that she had a son somewhere: that, and her medical background, gave her a certain importance, a certain authority in the group. She was a large

4

placid blonde woman who had once been a pretty girl and who still had an air of coquetry about her. Yet she too seemed happy with the company of women.

Mme Doche was perhaps fifty, to Roberta's thirty-nine, and Lewis's twenty-two: Cynthia was twenty-five and ashamed of the fact. To Lewis Mme Doche was the most obviously maternal presence, although he could see that Roberta had it in her to be a mother, for she had a vivid and short-tempered kindliness mixed with a ruthless practicality that might, he thought, have suited a houseful of sons. Her natural mode of discourse was a series of gossipy pronouncements; she was an expert on everything, or on everything that mattered. With that, confident, disapproving of poor behaviour, frequently let down, yet with lively trusting eyes. Something a little too operatic in Roberta – her dedication to the office and to Mme Van de Waele, her restlessness, her marvellous greedy appetite – alerted Lewis to the fact that she aimed at higher things. She was the only one of them who did not seem to be cast in a mode of acceptance: Lewis did not know how he knew this. Roberta was usually laughing, head flung back, splendid Jewish teeth in evidence. Nevertheless she had an uncertain temper and would fulminate against a colleague who was also a friend and with whom she was nearly always on bad terms, throwing herself into a vigorous performance of an earlier quarrel, her colour rising, her body releasing fresh waves of scent as its heat increased. She could be laughed out of it, or comforted, but she had to have a full hearing: woe betide anyone who tried to take her to task. She was generous and impulsive, wresting Lewis's plate from him and returning it with a peach or some grapes on it, but she was also outspoken, sometimes brutally so, and was apt to tell Cynthia, who considered herself a martyr to her health and her nerves, that there was nothing wrong with her. This was an obligation upon them all, but Roberta was more caustic. '*Faites de la gymnastique ou faites-vous baiser,*' she would say, and would rock with laughter at the expression on Cynthia's face. There was no malice in her. Simply, she had grown up in the school of hard knocks, and, as she put it, had been knocking around ever since. And as far as Lewis could see she was a vagabond, destined never to reach home. Although she seemed old to him he was not surprised that she had never married.

And Roberta's outspokenness always gave him the chance to comfort Cynthia, who was the only one of the women he cared to think about privately, individually, later in bed at night. Pretty Cynthia, her mouth down-drooping in discouragement at what fate had served up to her: a room in an apartment instead of an apartment of her own, and Lewis, a boy younger than herself, and therefore inferior, instead of the protective and adoring consort her fantasies had led her to expect. To Lewis Cynthia appeared radiant with promise, yet Cynthia herself seemed to think that she was destined for an early grave. Blooming, she gave herself over to headaches, cramps, sore throats, stiff necks, and mild stomach upsets. It was hazardous to ask her how she felt. What she felt, as opposed to how she felt, was disappointment, a forewarning that she might turn into Roberta, without Roberta's robust temperament to sustain her. Placed in this apartment by an agitated mother, given an allowance and registered at the Sorbonne, Cynthia's days were an easy but unsatisfactory mixture of lectures and cultural visits, these last regularly interrupted by a moment of malaise which would secure her escape. She would usually lie down in the afternoon and reappear, washed and changed, for the evening's conversation. This regimen was supposed to prepare her for life ahead, a life without apparent direction, protected by money, already vaguely but hugely let down, taken in, short-changed.

Despite her small tight beautiful face, there was something plaintive and valetudinarian about Cynthia, her dove-like ramblings usually serving as an introduction to tales of illness, her own and other people's, mingled with self-questionings about what she was supposed to be doing.

6

She had persuaded her anxious parents to let her come to
Paris to study French civilisation, since she had shown no
signs of wanting to do anything else, and her French accent
was already pretty. Her mildly punishing appearance, her
fussy self-protective walk, implied a whole world of dignified matronhood. Yet it seemed, incredibly enough, that this
was not to be – or not yet, not while she was a girl. Her age
and status seemed uncertain. Lewis eyed her with respect, as
if she were already a woman, although she was only three
years older than himself. She seemed to have access to a
mature disappointment. Once her mother had come over to
see how she was getting on. Lewis had caught sight of them
from the bus, shopping in the Faubourg Saint-Honoré. They
looked resigned and helpless, stranded by receding waves
of menfolk on whom they trained their batteries of silent
accusation. The resentment Cynthia felt had no conscious
focus yet could be sensed about her like an aura. It was this
aura that prompted Roberta's brutal recommendations. She
would eventually marry, Lewis thought. Some confident and
elderly business man would come along, view her as a prize,
and be hooked; she would sit at the foot of his dining table in
St John's Wood, playing with the pearls he had given her and
vaguely wondering what had gone wrong with her life.
Although none of this had happened – or showed signs of
happening – it was clear that Cynthia possessed a kind of
invalid sex-appeal, which would beguile the sort of man
who was half-appalled by women, half-afraid of them. She
used her fabled delicacy as an instrument of persuasion.
She would become a woman whom men were reluctant to
cross. Lewis saw this as a most valuable lesson in what
he hoped would become his lifetime's quest: the study of,
and love for, women. All information was valuable. In this
way he would arrive at a higher understanding.

   At this stage in his life, and even later, especially later,
in the light of memory, Lewis saw women in general, and
these women in particular, as a beneficent institution. Their
attitude towards himself he divined as merciful, which was

7

precisely what he desired it to be. As to his attitude towards them, it was, given his extreme youth, still unformed, but he looked to his little group, the first representatives of the species he had been given to study at close quarters, with a mixture of love, respect, and innocent enquiry. He seemed to think that all knowledge would come to him in this context. The only son of a widowed mother, tasting independence from her anxious care for the first time, he was grateful, in the midst of the bewilderingly adult city, to be taken in hand and to be thus returned to that silent passive dreaming adolescence which he had so recently left. His days were a mixture of great thoughts and trivial routine. He would rise early, strip-wash himself at the basin in his room, make himself a cup of coffee (use of kitchen allowed at specified hours) and emerge quietly into the grey morning. He loved this time, which made him feel at one with all the workers in the world, although he was only going to the Bibliothèque Nationale to begin his long day's reading. Grasping his new briefcase, his mother's present, and trying to ignore his eternally unassuaged hunger, he would stride out, down the long straight route to the Palais-Royal, where he would allow himself another cup of coffee and a croissant, and a morning paper – *Le Figaro*: he knew he was not old enough for *Le Monde* – which he would, in moments of boredom, read surreptitiously at his desk, giving his fullest attention to the announcements of births, marriages, and deaths. He particularly liked the deaths, the long string of relatives' names, all joining in the *immense douleur* attendant on the decease of their wife, mother, grandmother, aunt, great-aunt, and sister-in-law. Such richness! Such a matrix, he thought, longing to sink into the arms of just such a welter of women, feeling lonely for a while with his lack of worldliness, his ignorance of his own entitlements, and always the thought of his mother at home, even lonelier without him.

It was with a sigh, with a slight lowering of vitality, that he made his way towards the library. Scholarship seemed hedged about with such restraints, such restrictions on the living body. Already his long days of reading were beginning to give him headaches, although he enjoyed his work and could not envisage a future without it. It was just that, at present, he was unsatisfied by his days under the green-shaded lamps. While loving the thick silence that hung like a miasma over the noble room, he was too aware of the incipient mania around him to feel entirely comfortable. Inside every scholar lurked a potential fanatic. From any mild instinctive protest he might have formulated his writers delivered him. They were too epic not to be taken seriously, and too magnanimous. He felt that they had a particular message for him, and that he would learn a particular wisdom from them. This would be his final education, stored up for use in the years ahead. Sometimes he was bewildered by the amount of learning that was coming at him from every quarter, and sometimes it was with a further sigh that he contemplated the burden of his days. Sometimes he wanted to leave the library and run for his life.

What kept him in his seat was a peculiar ideal, all the more remarkable for having been glimpsed so early and at such a young age. What he wanted was not his accumulation of notes but an absence of notes, a holocaust of notes: what he wanted was transparency. He was aware that scholarship – the acquisition of knowledge – brought with it a terrible anxiety. How much was enough? How much more was there? Was there any end to it? If one did not possess enough knowledge how could one be sure of possessing more? And if one called a halt to the process how could one not die of shame? Thus with his love for his books went a certain obscure desire to have done with them, or rather not to have to be an officious midwife to small thoughts about great masterpieces. Let Stendhal, Balzac, Zola speak for themselves! That, after all, was what they were there for. He had even thought, in the days before he had timidly assumed the apparatus of the professional scholar, that one's whole purpose with regard to the arts

9

should be confined to seeing the world as the painter saw it, and reading the world through the books of the masters. Humility, a reasonable respect, were all that was required. He saw himself as having left this stage, even as having forsaken it in the interests of growing up, not knowing exactly what was required of him in the long run. In the short run he had to write and present his thesis, to gain the degree that would put him on the lowest rung of the academic ladder. He had to justify his choice to his mother, to his censorious cousin Andrew, his only other relative, and in euphoric moments – not difficult to come by in this city – he thought it might be a fine thing to expound on great works for the benefit of the eager minds of the young. For he did not doubt that they would be eager. He saw himself quite clearly, in a classroom, holding forth, and was pleased enough with the prospect. Yet at the same time he burned with grateful understanding as Julien Sorel, in his prison cell, pleaded for his ideal life and articulated the great dilemma. '*Laissez-moi ma vie idéale . . .* ' Over and above the life of contingencies was the life of the spirit, the life that many would never know. Real life, dull life, would imprison them, foreclose on their possibilities. Lewis was willing to bet that many people, of every age, woke up in the morning, surveyed the circumstances of the day, and formulated the same instinctive protest. Thus, while initiating his future profession, Lewis already looked ahead to the agreeable prison cell for which he was destined.

At twelve noon, in the interests of his lungs and his stomach, he went out, walked around the stony garden of the Palais-Royal, and bought himself a sandwich in the rue des Petits-Champs. No coffee: that would come later, at the end of the working day. Once the morning was passed, he had little difficulty with the afternoon. In the afternoon, as the light faded, and the atmosphere grew thicker, as the lamps snapped on one by one, a sort of exaltation took hold of him; by four-thirty he thought no other life possible. It was as if his thoughts came more easily in the barely illuminated gloom of the dying day: the mornings were too harsh with rational life to enable him to endure his subdued existence. Also, his thoughts quickened not only with the insights of his trade but with the prospect of his imminent release. He thus rode two horses on which he might gallop in different directions, but was not yet at the point of having to commit himself to either one of them. The high vaulted room seemed to be scholarship itself, putting a finger to its lips, urging silence, but his youthful body demanded movement. After such austerity he desired gratification, simple sustenance, the prospect of adventure. He wanted noise, spectacle, a more than impersonal beauty. Yet in the street it was hard for him to shake off the peculiar thrall of his day, the palpable silence that kept him wrapped in his thoughts, unprepared for, perhaps unequal to, the challenge of real life.

After five or ten minutes he was an ordinary young man again, looking forward to his walk home, his purchase of the cheese that was his passport, his entrance fee to that other world where there was still so much to learn, looking forward even to the privacy of his own thoughts, after listening to the conversation of the women. He was easily, naïvely, simply pleased. The silence pursued him down the ravine of the rue de Richelieu, as if the environs of the library partook of the various silences imposed inside the building, but in the Place du Palais-Royal all was animation. Noise, air, light! He stepped onto this territory as if he were crossing a frontier, and from then on the pleasure was of a different order. He travelled up from the depths to the life of the senses, was happy to know that so many lives were open to him. He took what he thought of as the rich man's route home, passing through great thoroughfares alive with crowds, until he reached the Place de l'Alma, where he sat and allowed himself a cup of coffee. He was always tempted to drink another, to linger and watch passers-by, to increase his anticipation of the evening's further pleasures, mild though they were by the world's standards, but the thought of his widowed mother, drawing the curtains at home in the house in unfashionable Parsons Green, and chafing her permanently cold hands, kept his lips firmly shut, as if one more cup of coffee, drunk in a sybaritic frame of mind, would lower her temperature still further. He missed her: they were too close, and both knew it. Nevertheless the thought of his mother was not unlike the thought of the library waiting for him the following morning, and all the mornings after that, something on which, in this moment of reprieve, he did not wish to dwell.

Conscious now of the dark, of the cold, and of the thin soles of his shoes, worn out with all the walking he imposed upon himself, he proceeded to his next ascertainable treat: buying his food. He bought little, but rehearsed for the day when he would buy much, much more, 'pressed down, shaken together, running over', he thought, remembering that surprising phrase from his Bible of days gone by. Tonight he would present Mme Doche with some superior coffee; that second cup, which he had virtuously denied himself, could not quite be written off. He made his way to the little shop in the rue de Longchamp, where they always gave him a kind greeting, although his purchases were so small. Sometimes, when he was feeling energetic, he would go further afield, curious about the lives of others at this domestic hour. He did not like to go home too early. He had no key: he relied on Mme Doche to let him in, and instinct told him to wait until she had given Mme Roussel her evening meal and was no longer to be seen in the guise of a servant. He liked her to have taken off her overall, so that he need not feel uncomfortable for her. Her position, he knew, was slightly ambiguous. He was solemn in his recognition of such niceties of behaviour, often lurking behind the door of his room when he heard the step of one of the women on her way to or from the bathroom. He hated it for them not to be seen as they would wish to be seen, and was too much on their side to be careless of their appearance or their modesty. They were all modest: their rooms were cells, unvisited. Lewis's tiny room was put at the service of his ablutions and the writing up of his notes, being unequal to any other function except that of sleep. It was also the scene of prolonged calculations as to whether his socks and his shirts would last until the end of the week, when he could send them home to be laundered by his mother. He was aware of the existence of laundries in Paris, but he rather liked the feeling of being constrained by poverty: besides, when the parcel came back, it came back freighted with small delicacies, and smelling of his mother's lavender soap. His youth worried him occasionally, his juvenility more so. He was chaste, and recognized this as a drawback, but did not yet feel the need to overcome it. High ideals, coupled with the need for female protection, had made him a model son, and he did not eagerly anticipate the day when both positions would have to be abandoned.

The writing up of the notes occupied those evenings when the salon arrangements had unaccountably broken down, when Mme Doche took her day off, or Roberta stayed out to play bridge, and Cynthia went to bed early. Then the laborious transcribing into ink of what had already been written that day in pencil brought forth once more his idealism, as he tasted the joy of making connections between images placed like dropped clues, or rounding off a speech that had behind it the force of the author's desire. It was only when he raised his eyes to the thick dull stuff of the heavy brown curtains that he had intimations of subversive thoughts. Then the sound of voices in the street below, or the excited ticking of his watch in the ensuing silence, might make him lay down his pen. On such occasions he allowed himself an extra apple from his budget, although by now he longed for something else.

His parsimony was voluntary. He had some money from his father, but he also had his dead father's injunction to take care of his mother. Actually, he had never heard his father say this, but it seemed to be implicit in the fact that his father was dead. So timorous was his mother that Lewis supposed them to be living on a knife edge. Thus this year in Paris was a risk for both of them, although he did not understand fully just how much of a risk it was. He only knew that in the short time at his disposal he had to lay the foundations for a future career. He also knew that in enjoying himself he must not injure his mother. She, poor woman, had little enough to enjoy on her own in Parsons Green, and sometimes he thought of her looking sadly into the dying fire, making her preparations for going to bed, which she did very early, not with a voluptuous sense of self-preservation, like Cynthia, but in despair at the length of the day.

From thoughts like these, with their dimension of scruple, he was delivered only by the evenings in the salon, which were the equivalent, to him, of the wage-earner's home-coming, the warrior's repose. Already he perceived what he took to be a natural order: female company at the close of a day dedicated to masculine patterns of endeavour. He had no desire to go out, was, in any case, secretly saving as much money as possible in order to buy his mother a stupendous present, a dressing-gown he had seen in the Trois Quartiers store, where he sometimes lingered on his way home from the library. This personal economy he espoused as a justification for all the times he spent not actively thinking of his mother, living her life with her, accompanying her at every moment of the day, as he sometimes thought he should: by dint of some form of self-denial he was granted permission to relax his vigilance, to sink passively into the world of the salon, where the women were kind, paid him no attention, and did not require him for any form of support.

When he had lingered long enough in the cold bright streets, and watched the city firing itself up for the evening, he turned finally in the direction of the Avenue Kléber, longing now only for the sound of Mme Doche's steps in the hall to answer his ring at the bell, longing to hear her invariable greeting, so mannerly, so benevolent: 'Eh bien, Louis, vous avez passé une bonne journée? Oh, du café, comme c'est gentil. Je vais faire chauffer de l'eau. Entrez, mon petit, nous sommes tous là.' And he would be safe; the evening could begin.

14

2

On his return to London Lewis was briefly amazed by the quality of the light, which seemed to him poor, as if the day could not work up enough energy to throw off the darkness of dawn. Used as he was to the fine greyish mist that cloaked Paris on the worst days of bad weather, he had frequently to rub his eyes in this land of what seemed to him ruminative half-shadow. He supposed that he needed glasses. Gradually, imperceptibly, he became accustomed to London's muted tones, and to the wistful noise of a car passing along a street sunk in the slumber of mid-afternoon. For a few weeks he wandered about his neighbourhood, registering new facts or facts which he had forgotten. He was struck by the modest cheerfulness of the people, whose main efforts seemed to go into keeping the business of life ticking over. 'Mustn't grumble,' they said, when asked how they did. 'Can't complain,' as if to complain were to be caught out in an unpatriotic, an un-English activity, an activity that might let the side down. He supposed that the war cast a longer shadow here than in France. And daily life itself was modest, although it was stretched over a larger area: he noticed that new petrol stations were going up on every corner, as if to fuel the heavy lorries that rumbled just out of sight of his mother's house. The lorries themselves were unusual in the city, but, he reminded himself, he was no longer in the Avenue Kléber, a few minutes from the Etoile, but in a suburb, a bus ride away from the centre of things. He felt a certain nostalgia for his previous way of life, yet soon fell into a mood that was indulgent, passive, in tune with his mother's peaceful house, and the dark afternoons, and the uneventful evenings. After a while he hardly missed his former companions. Sitting with his mother in front of the fire, enjoying the comforts of home, and aware of how much he had forgone in the way of comfort in Paris, he congratulated himself on having completed an adventure, some part of him suspecting that he might never stray so far again.

He had brought home the dressing-gown and his mother had been properly appreciative. He noticed that she looked tired, and thinner, but then, he thought, so did everybody else. The bones of her face seemed to press against his as he kissed her, and her hands were a little feverish: he put it all down to the fact that she had missed him, and felt a momentary pang of guilt. Strangely, she did not want to hear much about his great adventure, looked vague when he suggested taking her to Paris to meet his new friends. She cooked him delicious meals, but always said that she had already eaten when he expressed a desire for her to keep him company. Being an only son, he was used to his mother waiting on him, and nothing in this arrangement struck him as unusual.

The unchanging nature of his home life he accepted with a rueful smile: it went, he thought, with the poor light, and the sad sound of a car passing on a wet road. He told himself that when he had finished his thesis he would strike out again, although he knew that his mother would want him to settle down as quickly as possible. Part of him, the peaceable part, the part that had always been attuned to his mother's widowhood, and her fidelity, and her undemanding nature – perhaps in particular the latter – led him to accept the idea of a life that was not all excitement and gusto, but rather given over to what was expected of him, to meditation, and to repose. He had a vision of himself in later years, shopping in the Wandsworth Bridge Road, greeting a neighbour, and replying to his enquiry, 'Mustn't grumble. Can't complain.'

Was this to be borne? In moments of energy, at the beginning of the day, or especially if the pall of cloud ever lifted, he knew that such a life was appropriate to middle age, but not to youth. He felt the same ambivalence when he sat down at his desk in the British Museum, wanting to run, to shout, yet realizing that he was at home and had already taken on the protective colouring of the place. He was, he thought, destined to become a ruminant, a haunter of libraries, and maybe also to live out his life in quiet streets, to look after his mother, as had always been intended, and thus to do his duty as a man. As a man, but not as a hero, not like the heroes it was his present duty to examine. Such heroes had lovers, and he had none. He supposed that lovers would come along in due course, but for the moment his body was quiescent. And perhaps something in his mind was also quiescent, accepting the dim routines, sinking comfortably into blamelessness, where he felt he belonged. His mother had set a pattern which it was easy for him to follow.

While waiting for the next instalment of his life to take place, he devoted himself to his mother's care, and also to her expectations. She asked for so little! Every sortie he proposed – to the theatre, the cinema – she declined, urging him to go by himself or to take a friend. He thought she might be fearful of leaving home, of noise and crowds and unfamiliar streets, all of which he began to crave, and he promised himself that he would soon find a way of doing something to remedy this. Fortunately she was a great reader, and went to the Public Library two or three times a week. He took to accompanying her, and this became a custom; indeed it was the only fixed point in their lives. He was not unhappy, walking with her slowly to the bus stop, by the sodden Common; not unhappy, just waiting.

He could not see what was required of him, other than to ensure that nothing would change. He assumed that this was what she wanted. She said little, and he had no access to her thoughts, nor she to his. They were so used to each other that even conversation seemed unnecessary. Coming home after an absence, he could see that she was a separate person, a fact of which he had previously been almost unaware. She in her turn treated him with her usual solicitude but seemed abstracted, intent on an inner debate of which he could capture no echoes. She was the same, yet not the same; something was different. This something was never explained and Lewis therefore found it easy to ignore. That his mother appeared a stranger he attributed to his own recent preoccupations: she had grown older while he had been away. Smiling at him, she urged him to go out, saying that she was perfectly happy as she was. But he stayed at home, anxious not to leave her, and half sedated by the general mood of the house, which was sober and well-behaved. After a time he thought that she must be all right; he could relax his vigilance. She in her turn professed to be quite well, a fact which he had always taken for granted. Awareness of change he was therefore able to dismiss from his mind. If consulted his mother would have denied that any change had taken place.

Grace Percy, at sixty-two, looked older than her age. She was aware of having been relatively old when Lewis was born, and occasionally she thought that the event must have worn her out. She had to stop occasionally to catch her breath, did not care to be out too long, felt exhausted after cooking his evening meal. Her own she was usually too tired to eat. She was always thankful when it was time to go to bed, for by late evening she could feel the colour draining from her face. She was glad of Lewis's arm when she wanted to change her books; without it, she thought, she might not have had the heart for such an excursion. Sometimes she wondered if she were up to the effort of having him in the house again. She loved him beyond measure, had endured the lonely nights purely in order that he might be free and might return to her because he wanted to, and for no other reason. She could not envisage what his life had been without her, was only thankful that he did not in any way seem damaged by absence from her care. All this, and her adoration of him, she kept hidden, knowing that she must not add to his burden. But sometimes, looking out of the window onto the wet street, she had grieved.

He noticed that she was more absent-minded than usual and thought that perhaps she needed cheering up. His resource in such matters was to buy her a present. He thought long and hard about this and finally settled on a radio. She could listen to it in the kitchen while she was cooking his dinner. He was out all day and began to long for a more lively atmosphere at home, where silence of one sort or another generally prevailed. Six weeks had passed since his return, and now that he had digested the fact that he was back he began to feel as if his unused energies might rise up and overwhelm him. The headaches he had associated with the Bibliothèque Nationale returned, and he went to have his eyes tested. His new glasses, bringing everything sharply into focus, also brought a certain dissatisfaction: what he had previously seen as a benign haze was now revealed as fatally lacking in animation. He bought the radio, but took it up to his bedroom, to dispel the quiet of his studious hours. When he went out in the morning he was careful to return it to its official position on the dresser in the kitchen.

His appearance now began to give him cause for concern. His new National Health glasses, with their pink rims, made him, he thought, look foolish. With the hair that obstinately raised itself in luxuriant waves and his rather large ears, he had an owlish and solemn air, very far removed from the dandyism that he thought desirable. He was not handsome, he knew, not one of those men who attract a woman's glance. Now that he had his glasses he could see all this more clearly, and it made him edgy. He decided to put up with his appearance for as long as it took him to finish his thesis: after that it might prove to be a handicap. He began to think in terms of going abroad again, to a hot country: a tan was always an asset, much prized in this rainy climate. He thought he might teach English somewhere, perhaps take the examinations for the Foreign Service. Without telling his mother he wrote to the British Council. Anywhere would do. He saw himself representing England, coming back a larger, more impressive shape, with a piercing gaze and an aura of experience. His mother would miss him, but she had proved to him that she would survive. And maybe this country was better suited to her way of life than to his.

In due course, his inactive life, and the added weight of his glasses, made him uncharacteristically short-tempered. He was sometimes impatient with his mother: she merely looked away sadly. One evening, as he came into the kitchen, she turned with a start from a curiously crouched position over the table; in turning, her hand swept the radio to the floor. 'Oh, really, Mother,' he cried, exasperated. She looked at him, her face full of fear. 'It's all right,' he said awkwardly, appalled at her expression. 'It's still going.' The radio lay at their feet, emitting a minuscule metallic sound. He replaced it carefully on the dresser, turned a few knobs: it gave forth nothing but residual static. 'I'll have to get it repaired,' he told her, but he was still annoyed. Foolishly, she kept it on. It was no further use to him and he went up to his bedroom without it. When he came down later for his supper it was still giving out its tiny scratchy sound. He switched it off, furiously, telling himself that she had never really appreciated it.

Bad temper made him hungry. Going late at night, long after her bedtime, in search of a glass of milk, he opened the refrigerator and found inside it a plate of stewed steak and spinach. The knife and fork were still on the plate, crossed, as if this meal might be taken up later, when circumstances were more favourable. This must have been her lunch, he thought, since he himself had had the same thing for dinner. Then why had she not eaten it? The incident with the radio could not have upset her: at lunchtime it had not yet happened. He felt disquiet, then more anger, as if she were playing an unfair trick on him, binding him with chains of obligation and pity just when he had devised a programme for his future. He scraped the congealed food into the dustbin, washed the plate, and put it away. Slowly he argued himself into a more robust frame of mind. There was no cause for alarm: she had merely not felt hungry. This was practically incomprehensible to him but he supposed it might happen if one were old. He went miserably and angrily to bed, unable to distinguish between his misery and his anger, but careful to let the anger predominate.

Nevertheless a certain uneasiness remained and he resolved to spend more time with her. Perhaps she was still lonely without him, although his days at the British Museum were hardly a treat or a recreation. His attitude to his work these days was grim, as if it were forcing him into various uncomfortable or untenable positions. He longed for it to be over. Yet it was going well, and his tutor was pleased with him. Much to his surprise, the writing presented him with few problems. It was as if he were programmed to do this thing, in defiance of his natural biology. He came to dread that moment of altered concentration before he actually put pen to paper; he felt an anguish at the prospect of that moment endlessly repeating itself. But when he was writing he forgot himself entirely, raising his head in surprise when it was time for the library to close. At the beginning of the day he found himself longing for a humble job, any job, doing something manageable in the convivial surroundings of an office. By the end of the day he had succumbed once again to the mystery of what he was actually doing, the aligning of words in an apparently logical argument. His recent French interlude fell away from him as he tackled his English sentences. Yet writing, which came easily, also underlined his indeterminate status. Was he to continue to do this? His age had proved to be no handicap: rather the reverse. The life of action, which he could not quite visualize, remained out of reach. He had the disagreeable sensation of signing away his future. Having found that he could do this work he seemed to have sealed his fate. This idea unsettled him profoundly.

His unexpected ability, or so it seemed to him, and the gratification on his professor's face, satisfied his pride but not his judgment. His judgment told him that such competence was at odds with his experience, or rather his lack of experience. He saw himself as an old man in a young man's body. And the body remained very young, subject to the dissatisfactions of its unused state, subject also to the loneliness that had pervaded his adolescence. He thought, perhaps too frequently, of the years he had spent growing up at his mother's side, with no father to take the weight of their survival off his hands. He thought of the unspoken consensus, largely emanating from his cousin Andrew, the civil servant, but present too in his mother's mind, that he must be the man of the family, must ensure the continuity of their little household. This was not how heroes behaved. Heroes left home early, made good, fell in love and died, or, at a pinch, sent for their mothers later. He did not see why he should be denied this opportunity, although the details remained obstinately nebulous.

'Have you thought of the future, Lewis?' asked his tutor, a benevolent man on the verge of retirement. 'I think you might consider some further work; you have managed very well, very well indeed. Of course, I shall be leaving in June. I shan't be able to supervise you any longer. But I doubt if you will need any more supervision; you should be able to see things through on your own. Feel free to consult me at any time.'

To Lewis, June was remote, a sunny upland almost out of sight of this winter landscape. And Professor Armitage, who had always been kind, and whose reference had secured him his scholarship, would, he thought, be there for as long as he needed him. After June, in the revivifying sunshine, he, Lewis, would be free to leave. He saw the whole enterprise reaching a natural conclusion, and this emboldened him. With this end in sight he resolved to be nicer to his mother.

But how to please her, this modest timorous woman

22

who never went out, and from whom, despite his resolutions to the contrary, he had inherited just such a modest and timorous outlook? For as long as he could remember the high point of her day had been his return, from school, from university, from Paris, and now from the British Museum. His most persistent image of her was of a figure at the window, her hand holding aside the curtain, slightly gaunt and abstracted, but warming suddenly into animation as he came into view. Their two arms would lift simultaneously in greeting, as that brief joy of hers showed him the woman who must have existed in the early years of her marriage, before his father died, before he knew her. After the flash of her greeting she would subside into her natural or habitual mood, which was one of silent good nature, offering only lenient opinions, fearful of anything that disturbed the status quo. She was a good woman, he knew, although her fair-mindedness sometimes exasperated him. Of his cousin Andrew's dreadful wife she would simply say, 'Of course, Susan is rather dull. But she means well.'

Meaning well was the paramount consideration. Evidence of malice made her ill, although she rarely noticed it. He sometimes thought that she had chosen so immobile a life in order to protect her innocence. She seemed entirely fulfilled in looking after him, devising his meals, ensuring his comfort. He knew that she would be perfectly happy to act as his handmaiden for the rest of her life.

But he began to wish for her the kind of independence he wished now for himself. He began to see his task – one of his tasks – to be the fashioning of his mother into a different woman, bold, enterprising, viable, able to exist without him, or at least to forget about him from time to time. He wanted her to be smartly dressed: he wanted to take years off her age and to send her away on holiday. The humbly smiling acolyte in the print blouse and the navy blue skirt and cardigan, who spent her afternoons resting in her dark silent bedroom, and who was always at the window to greet him, touched his heart with a mixture of pity and rage. Her sad but merciful smile when he made an unconsidered or harsh remark always covered him with remorse. Through her he had learned a kind of tentative benevolence from which he was trying to break away. And he had learned from fiction that boldness was the thing. Men had to be enterprising. How could he teach her this without wounding her?

He was aware that he loved women in general too much to hurt them, and that his mother's stricture – 'I don't think we want to be unkind, do we, Lewis?' – would always inhibit him from the measure of decisiveness that might be conclusive. And he was also aware that to offer a woman sympathy was not always an heroic tactic. Yet what he felt for women was precisely a kind of yearning sympathy, rather than anything bolder or more straightforward. Unconsciously, he identified with his mother's humility, although he wished that her attention could be deflected away from himself. After all, if he were to marry – and he saw marriage as the sort of alternative to heroic action that he might eventually choose – he owed it to himself to do something manly while he had the chance. A man's education, he thought, was necessarily a rather crude affair; proving one's manhood usually involved some act of destruction. He supposed that innocence would have to go, and even began to square up to the task. But he could not quite bear the thought that his mother's innocence might also have to go. The eternal problem of how to maintain female innocence while accumulating male experience presented itself to him in this novel and startling form. His mother, he saw, was no different from other women, and what he felt for his mother he might eventually feel for the woman he chose as his wife. By the same token, however, he wanted freedom from the strictures that women put upon his conscience. For this reason it was absolutely necessary that he and his mother should part company for a while.

A crucial factor was the money his father had left in trust. He knew nothing of the amount or of its disposition. From time to time his mother saw her bank manager, and between

darkness the sound came again, bringing with it a dreadful fear. The hairs on the back of his neck lifted as he got to his feet and felt his way blindly down the corridor. It did not occur to him to switch on the light.

His mother was on the floor of the bathroom. She had managed to prop herself against the wall. She was wearing the dressing-gown, which was soiled now; the sound was coming from her mouth. She must have been calling for him for a long time, hours, perhaps, and he had not heard her; he knew that he would never forget this fact. In the overhead light, which was still on, must have been on since before he fell asleep, he saw her dishevelled hair, grey wisps stuck to her face by her tears. There was a foul smell, and he realized that she had vomited. He sank down beside her and put his arms round her. They wept together, his mother with relief at his arrival, Lewis himself at the prescience of his dream.

He did not know how long they stayed on the floor. He tried to move her but she was an awkward shape and weight. It seemed to him that she dozed a little, and he held her until the coldness of the night told him that he must get her back to bed. He tried to wake her, but she was not asleep. She even smiled at him and took his hand. He pulled the soiled dressing-gown round her, lifted her in his arms, and carried her back to bed.

Instinctively he went back to bed himself: he turned on his side and willed himself to sleep. To remain awake, with the image of her sickness in his mind's eye, was more than he could bear: he thought he might die of it. He heard no sound from her room, and told himself that it was all over, whatever it was, that she was sleeping normally, and would wake in the morning to another normal day. But an inner trembling kept him awake, and when the window between the curtains turned grey he heard the sound again. By the time he reached her it had changed into a high-pitched and uncensored moan. In a panic he made for the telephone beside her bed and dialled for an ambulance. 'No,' she said. 'No,' and then vomited again.

The ambulance men were very kind. They put her into a folding chair and told Lewis to get dressed. In the ambulance he held her hand, although she did not seem to know that he was there. They sped through the desolate dawn streets, her moaning the only sound he could register. At one point she opened her eyes and whispered, 'Look after my son.' Then they were at the hospital, and she was taken away from him. He watched the trolley being sped along a silent corridor, shot through with brilliant lights.

After half an hour a middle-aged nurse found him and told him to come back in the afternoon with her night clothes and her sponge bag. 'Will she be all right?' he asked, reassured in spite of himself by the woman's competence and the normality of the sounds of breakfast being served. The nurse patted him on the arm. 'We'll see that she's comfortable,' she said.

He walked home, shivering. He welcomed the sight of an early milk float with tears of gratitude. Inside the house he told himself to be practical. He would make a cup of tea, clean up the bathroom, strip her bed and remake it for her return, pack her suitcase, make things pleasant, cancel the previous night. When it was properly morning he would telephone his cousin Andrew and then return to the hospital. He was troubled that he had not thought to ask the name of the ward she was in. They had told him to come back in the afternoon, but he would not wait. He opened windows wide, threw the soiled linen into the linen basket. Then he sat down on her bed to telephone his cousin. On the night table he noticed a box of pills. On the box was written, 'One to be placed under the tongue as required.'

His hand went out to the telephone. At that moment it rang. A voice said, 'Mr Percy? Mr Lewis Percy? One moment, please.' There was a sound of laughter in the background. Then footsteps. 'Mr Percy? I'm sorry, dear. There was nothing we could do. She went quite peacefully. We'd like you to come in some time today and collect the

28

form. Any time today. Are you all right? Mr Percy? Is there somebody with you?'

'No,' he said. 'There's nobody with me.' He replaced the receiver carefully, and sat on the bed, looking down at his large cold trembling hands.

3

Lewis reflected that Andrew's wife's dim personality was entirely matched by her ineffective jewellery. Fixing Susan with a glittering eye, which they thought was occasioned by grief, he saw that today, for the funeral, she had secured the collar of her white blouse with a hand-painted miniature of flowers in a gold frame. On a previous occasion she had worn a brooch in the form of a tennis racquet, with a very small pearl as the ball. Her necklace, of even smaller pearls, was too modest to be anything but real. Her limp brown hair was held back by a velvet Alice band, and she sat, in the late Grace Percy's chair, examining her nails.

Lewis's rage sprang from Susan's occupancy of his mother's chair, and, by extension, spread to cover the whole of her existence. He not only found her annoying; he found her entirely and mysteriously offensive. On her brief and unsatisfactory visits to their house, made when Grace Percy was alive, she was always mute, although he suspected that she had plenty to say to his cousin when they were alone together. She appeared to think that visits to Andrew's unspectacular relations derogated in some subtle way from her own position. She was the sort of woman who only bestowed her full attention when she was talking about herself, and this she had to be coaxed to do if others became too exasperated by her silence. When asked her opinion on any matter, her normal response was, 'I really wouldn't like to comment', or, 'I don't think that's a fair question', thus bringing about a new silence. And yet the triumph of the will was there, Lewis thought; she was the type of wife who would collect her husband from the station, not out of her desire to see him, but so that he should not deviate on the way home to her. With that, joyless, vigilant. Lewis did not doubt that she was the stronger of the two. She had several bizarre and inflexible opinions which she passed on, like a spirit guide, to Andrew, who recounted them to the world at large. She thought there was something untrustworthy about people who lived in flats rather than houses. She doubted the virtue of countries other than England, and, at a pinch, and if she were feeling particularly broadminded, Scotland. She thought it beneath her dignity to enter another woman's kitchen. When Andrew suggested a cup of tea after the miserable ceremony at the crematorium, she turned her attention, studiously, to the pleats of her skirt. Lewis got up furiously and went into the kitchen. Making as if to bang the door, and then securing it quietly, he heard her say, 'Well, why not? It'll give him something to do.'

He knew that his mood was dangerously unstable, that he should not be wasting his emotional energy in this way, should be concentrating on the awful facts of his mother's disappearance and his own impending solitude. But his mother's death was not a matter he wished to share with these strangers – for all who had not witnessed her last hours were strangers to him for evermore – and he knew that he would need the rest of his life to comprehend the fact that she was gone. His mother's death was too serious an event to be admitted to general conversation. He postponed even a consideration of the fact until he should be alone. In those long night hours, sleepless, he would think of her, usually with pain. On this day he failed to remember any episode in their past which could be called happy. And yet he knew that they had been happy, in their largely wordless but companionable lives together. He knew that they had always had undying love for each other, the small boy, then the youth,

31

and the serious faintly smiling woman. Coming back from the funeral he had lowered his eyes so as not to see her absence at the window. His dreadful grief of the past two days had given way to a sort of numbness, as if everything that were to happen to him now were irrelevant, unimportant, unconvincing. Yet through the numbness came random, almost unwelcome flashes of feeling, flashes of dislike for Susan, of pity for Andrew, who managed to be – probably had to be – both pompous and humble, a great man at the office, Lewis suspected, but a poodle at home. Pouring the boiling water into the teapot, he found himself invaded by a rush of pure panic. How would he manage? What would he eat? Who would look after him?

In the two long days that it had taken Andrew to assume his position as head of the family – and he would be everlastingly grateful to his cousin for so doing – Lewis had sat, frozen with misery, on a footstool by the fire, trying to get warm. His lack of experience was terrible to him. He had never arranged a funeral before, had never even been to a funeral. He supposed that someone had kept him at home or taken care of him when his father had died. He could very faintly remember crying for his mother and being restrained by his grandmother from going after her. Even in the matter of building a fire he was ignorant, his experience having been limited to bringing in the coal for his mother. The labour of lighting it, on his first day alone in the house, had left him with smudges on his hands and wrists which he lacked the energy to remove. Higher and higher he had built the fire, piling on coal, unable to get warm, sitting endlessly, with the tears drying to a glaze on his cheeks, his face tightening with the heat which he could not feel. Not daring to go upstairs, past his mother's open door, waiting until it was dark, and late, before forcing himself to bed, leaving the fire to smoulder and to burn the house down if necessary: he half wished that it might be so.

When hunger had finally driven him to the kitchen he had found only some biscuits and a tin of soup, yet he had not

32

been aware that the household arrangements were breaking down. Clearly there had been moments when the weight of the future had been too much for his mother to contemplate. His cousin, coming upon him as he stood in the kitchen, the tin of soup in one hand, tears coursing down his face, had been kind but also severe. 'Be thankful it was over quickly,' he had said. 'Be thankful she didn't suffer like your father. She was never the same after Uncle Jack's death; nursing him like that – for months – left a permanent mark on her.' But Lewis, who did not remember his father, had not been aware that his mother was lonely. And if she had lived for him, Lewis, what was wrong with that? He would have lived for her if she had stayed with him a little longer.

So bereft was he in those two days that his eyes never left his cousin's face, accepting his authority in everything, realizing that at thirty-seven Andrew was a man, likely to know how to pay bills, buy food, and even arrange funerals. He half heard his cousin explain that the house now belonged to him, and that he should get someone in to look at the wiring. Andrew had, after all, known Lewis's father, John Percy, the quantity surveyor, had been all of nineteen when John Percy had died. They were both orphans. Now Andrew had only horrible Susan for company, with her virtuous full skirts, and her small incurving teeth, and her colourless nail polish. Not even a nice woman to cheer him up, thought Lewis, feeling a pang of sympathy for his cousin who had had to be a man perhaps before he was ready, and who had married the ungenerous Susan because that was what men did. He was probably too decent even to acknowledge his disappointment, and had had to get over his dismay at having no family, no context other than work, and only self-effacing Aunt Grace Percy as a relative, with her absent-minded and all but hidden affections. Only Lewis had had access to those affections; therefore he was able briefly to pity his cousin for being so disadvantaged.

Feeling this pity he was glad to accept instructions from Andrew. He attended the funeral because he was told to;

left to himself he would have stayed hidden in the house. His mind was vague, unfocused. It was as if Andrew had dispensed him from all initiative, even the initiative of thinking appropriate thoughts – his feelings he intended to keep to himself. And he was glad to see Andrew sitting in his chair, as if in so doing he were actively substituting for Lewis. It was only Susan to whom he objected.

'You might as well stay in the house.' said Andrew. 'It is your home. But stop lighting these big fires, Lewis; you'll burn the place down. Get yourself one of these new electric heaters. You only need it in the evening, after all.'

'Have you asked Lewis how he's to earn his living?' asked Susan, not deigning or not managing to ask Lewis himself. Obliquity was another of her usages; direct engagement was not willingly conferred.

'Yes, we must think about that,' said Andrew, lighting his pipe. Again Lewis felt a pang of pity. The pipe went with the obstinately soft moustache, went with the office, went with Susan. 'You've wasted enough time, Lewis. What are your plans?'

'I haven't any,' he had been forced to reply. 'I've got my grant until June. Then I thought I'd try the British Council.'

But when the letter had come from the British Council, on the morning after his mother's death, he had thrown it on the fire.

'You should think about the Civil Service,' his cousin had said. 'Your French is quite good, isn't it? There's a procedure to be gone through, exams and so on. But it's a good steady career, and that is what you need. I've never looked back,' he said wistfully, or did Lewis imagine it? 'You'll have to see the bank manager,' he went on, 'and close the account. I can't do that for you. In fact, you'll have to manage, Lewis. Call on me for advice. Don't sell anything,' he added. 'Uncle Jack invested wisely. You should have enough to live on, if you're careful. Of course, you must get a job – that goes without saying. Get that thesis out of the way and set yourself up properly. Work is the thing, Lewis. A man is lost without proper work.'

Susan stirred, uncharacteristically. 'Time we were getting back,' she said. 'Get my coat, would you, dear?' She was full of such requests, deeming her presence alone sufficient to dispense her from further activity. Andrew, still trying to explain to Lewis that he must keep all receipted bills, disappeared into the hall and came back with Susan's coat. 'Have you understood that, Lewis? What? What's the matter, dear?'

'I'm waiting for you to help me on with my coat,' said Susan patiently. Lewis wondered if Andrew hated her as much as he, Lewis, did. But no, he thought, he is afraid of her. What he would really like would be for her to be more of a mother to him. At the thought of the word 'mother' he turned away, faint-hearted, willing them both to be gone.

'Goodbye, Lewis,' said Susan with a tiny smile. 'Cheer up.'

'If you need anything, get in touch,' said his cousin, looking worried.

'But do remember, won't you, that we live rather a long way away,' added Susan.

'I know that,' said Lewis, tired now, and uncomprehending. 'I dare say I could get to you in just over an hour.'

'I mean,' said Susan, 'we can't be dashing up to London every five minutes.'

'Andrew comes up every day,' he pointed out. 'To go to work.'

'Well,' she replied meditatively, pulling on her gloves. 'That's different, isn't it?'

Then he was alone, and on the whole glad of it. He kicked the dying fire, perhaps the last he would ever light, for the coal was nearly gone, and he did not know how to order more. He sank down once again onto his footstool. He was alarmed at the abrasive feelings that Susan's presence had aroused. Such withholding, such resistance as she had manifested signalled a suspicion which he could not begin to comprehend. Yet she was every inch a wife, he mused, every gesture, every inflection proprietorial. How did one avoid women like this? What skills must he develop in order to see through them? Thoughts such as these cast into further urgency the matter of his future life, for there would, he knew, have to be a female presence to comfort his loneliness. Not to replace his mother – the idea was unthinkable – but perhaps to console him for her absence. And he knew no-one. He dimly saw this as a disastrous fault. He had been too wrapped up in his work, in his unpromising idealism, to learn the way a man should behave with a woman. What was worse, he did not yet fully consider himself a man. The idealism he now saw as hopeless, doomed. He perceived with a kind of pity that his lonely evenings, writing up his notes, in careful ink, had precluded him from every other kind of activity. Yet what he would want to feel, with a woman, was something of the idealism he had felt for his work, a self-forgetful ardour that would cancel out his incompetence, his gracelessness, and bring forth a compensating mercy, and also the satisfaction that he had glimpsed when an argument or an explanation had composed itself while in his care. Something, too, of that transparency that meant doing without the argument altogether. Perfect understanding; all effort unnecessary. With that acquired he would be a citizen of the free world at last. That was how the gap would be closed and the circle made whole once more.

Finally, when it was very late, he went up to bed. He stood for a moment on the landing, then, slowly, quietly, he closed his mother's door.

The next day, Saturday, was the day on which he was to begin his new life. He gazed at the heap of ash that had been the fire, then left it and went out. The weather was dull, misty, hazy, damp, as it had been on the day of the funeral, lending the whole procedure an air of unreality: this winter was unseasonably mild. Lewis almost wished for a frost, a snowfall, something that would bring people together, inspire comments between strangers. Yet the street stretched before him grey and featureless, and apart from the lorries in the background, there was no animation. Standing at deserted bus stops he felt a terrible bewilderment, and with it the beginnings of anger. Life should be better than this. It should be splendid, colourful, exciting, not this miserable affair of mortal illness and tinned soup and ashes in the grate. He abandoned the bus stop and began to walk, found himself eventually striding down the King's Road, welcoming the crowds, the air of licence, the greater profusion in the shops, the promise of excess. He bought bread and milk, and, because he could think of nothing better, more soup. Cheese occurred to him, as something that required no cooking, and then, in a Proustian flash, he saw himself buying the camembert in Paris. But that was the solution: he must go back! He could rent his old room again and finish his thesis there, where he had begun it. The thought momentarily excited him. After all, he knew the routine in Paris, knew how to fill his day, and even looked forward to getting back (he did not quite think 'home') in the evenings. Those women, and their indifferent affection or affectionate indifference, would take him into their care, bind his wounds, make him fit once again for this cruel world. He could leave next week, for there was nothing to keep him here. So enabling did this decision seem that he went into a coffee bar and ate the nearest thing to a meal that he had eaten for some days. And now that he was in no hurry he strolled among the Saturday crowds, losing something of his heavy-heartedness, until fatigue came upon him suddenly, and he got on the bus and went home.

Standing at the window, as his mother had done, and feeling grief rising once more to the surface, he was surprised to see Professor Armitage, out of context, approaching him from the corner of the street. Thinking that the man looked diminished without his desk to protect him, and uncharacteristically encumbered as he was with a carrier bag and a bunch of flowers, Lewis realized with alarm that Armitage, knowing nothing of the events of the past week, had come to tea as arranged. This must be prevented at all costs. Lewis rushed to the door and opened it on to Professor Armitage's modest and appreciative smile.

'I'm awfully sorry, sir,' he said precipitately. 'I'm afraid it's all off. I mean, my mother died on Monday.' He found himself in an attitude of defence, almost barring access to the house.

It was Professor Armitage who quailed at this announcement, his smile slowly giving way to an expression of distress.

'My dear boy, I am so sorry. Is there anything I can do? Are you alone? Perhaps if I could come in for a few minutes?'

Lewis led the way to the drawing-room, momentarily ashamed of the empty grate. He was leaving anyway, he told himself; he would clear up before he went. He watched Professor Armitage lower himself into a chair, placing his flowers tactfully out of sight. Why did everyone have to seem to him so unbearably vulnerable? Armitage, he had heard, was a bachelor, had lived with a widowed sister until she died, and since then had soldiered on alone, grateful for any company. A good scholar, but too modest to have made his mark, an excellent adviser, patient and always interested. There had been a wistfulness there too, thought Lewis, who steeled himself to be ruthless. He saw, regretfully, that he must say goodbye to his earlier innocence if he were ever to make his mark in the world. If he failed in this task, innocence – his mother's innocence – would overcome him, and then where would he be?

'You'll go on with your work, I hope, Lewis?' Professor Armitage, Lewis saw with despair, was easing himself out of his coat. 'Of course, I shan't be at the college after June, but you will have the thing well set up by then. And I dare say Dr McCann will look after you if you want any help. I don't think I'm being indiscreet in saying that the university press is always interested in new work. You would have to revise and expand, of course, but that would be a matter for the future. You'll keep in touch, Lewis? I've enjoyed your work.'

Fatal humility, thought Lewis. Yes, he would keep in

touch, but not too frequently. Men like Armitage were obsolete, all but saintly, and thus uncomfortable. He too had enjoyed the work, but, being young, had thought it entirely his own. Besides, it was the company of women that he craved. He did not see, in this moment of discomfort and disarray, how Professor Armitage could minister to him. Of the two barren lives he was forced to prefer his own. Yet how did that help him?

'Have you enough to live on?' pursued Professor Armitage.

Lewis said that he had no idea.

'Well, that is certainly very important. And you will want a job. You might find something in the library to tide you over. That friend of yours works there, doesn't he? If you like the idea I might be able to use a little influence.'

It was to be all libraries, Lewis thought.

'I wonder if I might ask you for a cup of tea, Lewis? It is rather a long way from Muswell Hill. Several buses, you know, and I am not so young as I was.'

It was seven o'clock before he left, after having persuaded Lewis to light the fire again. Even then he seemed reluctant to go. But Lewis was now impatient to telephone the Avenue Kléber, and paid scant attention to Professor Armitage's kind assurances. He regarded the library suggestion as something to fall back on in a case of extreme need, something to be avoided for as long as possible. He felt now that only an investment in his own future could obliterate the grief he felt silently gathering in the corners of the room. He stood at the door, watching Professor Armitage beat his slow retreat, seeing him as a blank silhouette outlined against the fuzzy halo of a street lamp. Only when the sound of his heels had faded and the suburban street was quiet again did he go inside.

The return to Paris he now saw as a desperate act, one perhaps that would not repay him. And yet it was the thing he had to do. He craved the sedative of routine, and here, at home, routine had been cancelled and he did not know how to re-establish it. The untidy grate stared him in the face, ashes scattered over the hearth; the room already had a pall of dust, and in the kitchen the larder was almost empty again. He would go simply because it was impossible for him to stay. He would finish his work – that went without saying – but that was not his primary purpose. What he craved was a return to his earlier self, before sadness had come into his life. Perhaps he would never come home again. He saw himself, an ageing child, living out a bachelor existence in a room in Paris: eventually he would assume the lineaments of a Frenchman, with a trenchcoat and a briefcase and rimless glasses. He would go home in the evenings to Mme Doche and the women. Nothing about this was ideal, he knew, and most of it was illusory, but if he stayed here loneliness would overpower him. He did not like the direction his thoughts were taking. He did not like his situation. And yet he knew that decisions would have to be made, and that now was the time to make them. In so doing he would grow up, grow older, something that he had singularly failed so far to do. He must move immediately if he were not to lose the power of moving altogether.

On the telephone Mme Doche sounded distant, cautious. Mme Roussel was unwell, she explained, was, she feared, going downhill very fast. And she was unwilling to let rooms again, would not want the responsibility. She had not liked those two girls – did Lewis remember them? – and had thought they had made themselves too much at home. She did not want that problem any more, could not in fact even contemplate it. Of course if Lewis were coming to Paris it would be nice to see him. Mme Doche did not see many people these days. But Lewis would understand if she were not free.

'And Cynthia?' Lewis asked. 'And Roberta?'

'Those girls?' said Mme Doche in some surprise. Both gone. They left shortly after Lewis himself had done. And now there was nobody in the apartment except Mme Roussel and herself. It got lonely sometimes. If anything happened to

Mme Roussel – there was a tactful sound at this point – she, Mme Doche, would go home to Brittany. Did Lewis know Nantes? A fine town, and more sympathetic than Paris.

Lewis, encouraged by her growing assurance – her voice seemed to have taken on a new resonance when talking about her plans, although still dipping cautiously at the end of her sentences – promised to telephone when he arrived in Paris, although he was a little disconcerted that she had not invited him to stay in the Avenue Kléber. But if there were illness there he would rather not witness it: his memories were still too raw. Besides, eight months had passed since he had left, and in the summer evenings of the remainder of his stay the winter atmosphere of the salon had been difficult to recapture. He himself, while living through his last days in Paris, had deserted the apartment and had wandered about the city in the brilliant evening light. And now perhaps it was too late, all dark and dim and spoiled by recent events. Something told him that it was a mistake to go back, but his desire for certainty and for the time before things had gone wrong forced him to return to the only set of associations that were still secure. From the depths of his experience he longed to recapture what he thought of as the transparency of that time. By transparency he meant a whole complex of contingencies – his work, his earlier ardour, his singlemindedness, his simple and almost forgotten wish for wholeness. Transparency – or desire – would banish sadness, embarrassment, a sense of failure. *Laissez-moi ma vie idéale* . . . On a more practical level, his work demanded that he revisit the scene, or so he thought. What else could he do? There was no possibility of existence for him with things as they were.

On the following day, Sunday, he made an effort and cleaned the house. He thought of telephoning his cousin, but told himself that Sunday was a day for domesticity, and that Andrew would not welcome an intrusion. Or rather that Andrew might, but that Susan would not. By the evening the house was cleared of his mother's relics. He opened the door of her room, stood inside for a moment, then decided to leave it as it was. He paused only to collect her library books, sober tales of love and loyalty that reflected the moods of women as he wished to consider them. He had often read her books himself, was acquainted with her tastes, which, half-smiling, he acknowledged to be his own. He removed a nail-file from between the pages of *The Song of the Ark*, which the pale girl at the library had put aside for them, with assurances that his mother would love it. A beautiful story, the girl had said: it had made her cry. Lewis supposed that this girl must now be informed of his mother's death. Or perhaps he could just post the books back. He did not think he could stand the words normally offered on these occasions, although he was aware that the sympathy of strangers was often more kindly meant than the sympathy of relatives, of his relatives, at least, and that strangers offered different perspectives onto the lives of the dead, remembered a gesture, a word, that they offered to the bereaved, and that such offerings were sweet.

On the Monday he went to the bank and saw the manager. 'You should be quite comfortable,' said Mr Harvey. 'The portfolio is very conservative and will bring in a small but regular income, as it did your mother. You don't want to diversify, I take it?'

'How much would I have if I sold everything?' Lewis asked.

'Between twenty and twenty-five thousand,' was the answer. 'But I cannot advise . . . '

'Please sell everything,' said Lewis, 'and put the money in my account.'

He booked a ticket on the Night Ferry for the same evening, returned home to pack a few clothes, and went straight to Victoria, where he sat for several hours in the Golden Arrow bar, rising only to buy food. As soon as it was dark he picked up his bag and moved to Platform 1, anxious to be gone, watching indifferently as passengers slowly accumulated, fur coats over their arms, heavy bags consigned to porters' trolleys. Doubting his ability to endure the burden of a sleepless night he had booked a wagon-lit. The thought of the money relieved him enormously; he resolved to go to a comfortable hotel. He remembered seeing such a place in the rue Clément-Marot, on one of his cheese-buying expeditions. He remembered that the bright windows had cheered him, promising pleasure, insouciance. He determined to go there.

He awoke to a dark morning, and an impression of cruel lights dashing through the chink in the blind. He washed and dressed quickly and went in search of coffee. Seated in the restaurant car he felt a sense of anticipation, noting the subtle changes in smells, in sounds. He returned to stand at the window of his compartment, avid now for the sights of France. He was the first person to leave the train.

They gave him a small but adequate room at the Hôtel Roosevelt, one, no doubt, reserved for unaccompanied visitors. He felt disastrously unaccompanied. He unpacked quickly, anxious to be in the street, afflicted with restlessness, and also with anxiety. Suddenly there was nothing to do. He wandered down to the Place de l'Alma, in search of the street market, but it was the wrong day for it. A pale sun broke on the whitish façades of the buildings, and he walked for a long while in a westerly direction. He thought of making for the Bois, but purposelessness overcame him, and he turned back. He caught a bus to the Bibliothèque Nationale, presented his reader's ticket, and sat down at one of the desks. He consulted the notebook he always kept in his pocket, and looked up one or two titles in the catalogue. This, it appeared, was to be the extent of his work, on this occasion, at least.

He must have changed, he thought, in the months that had elapsed since he had last sat in this room. He was no longer content with things as they were, with small pleasures, small perspectives. The thought frightened him, for there seemed to be nothing to put in the place of those perspectives, which, however limited, had always been reassuring. He got up hurriedly, and out of sheer habit, walked round the Palais-Royal garden, and bought himself a sandwich in a familiar café. It now seemed a matter of urgency that he should proceed directly to the Avenue Kléber. He supposed that he should telephone first, but he knew that Mme Doche would be at home. She only went out once a day, he remembered, to do her shopping. She was bound to be in.

He felt a little easier out on the street, walked the length of the Champs-Elysées, dogged only by a fatigue that was more mental than physical. The Avenue Kléber, when he reached it, stretched out endlessly: he suddenly doubted whether he could go much further. He stood for a moment in the dimness of the vestibule, aware of his labouring breath, before mounting the stairs to Mme Roussel's floor. When he rang the bell he heard a faint exclamation, then raised voices. The door opened slowly, very slowly, on to a chain which permitted a limited view of Mme Doche's frightened face. This face, which he remembered as round, blonde, replete, now looked to him puffy and anxious, the hair surrounding it ashy and dry. Stealing through a crack in the door was a strange pharmaceutical smell, mixed in with an odour of stale unchanged air. The door closed in his face, then opened again. He was bidden to come in and make no noise.

He walked instinctively into the salon, where Mme Doche, after another half-heard conversation, this time disclosing an admonitory voice, joined him. He became aware that he should have telephoned, that his visit was inappropriate. Mme Doche seemed to be waiting for him to state his business, but he had a great desire to confide in her, to tell her of his mother's death: a desire, in short, to be comforted. This, he understood, was the whole purpose of his journey. But as soon as he was seated on one of the faded tapestry chairs the hushed and somehow furtive atmosphere was interrupted.

'Fernande! Fernande!'

He recognized the harsh hoarse voice of Mme Roussel, now harsher, hoarser, urgent, a voice that contained anger, even fury. Mme Doche put her finger to her lips, and ran from the room. Lewis waited, heard Mme Doche's voice take up its burden of reassurance, heard the chink of a glass, heard a spoon being dropped. Finally a door closed and Mme Doche reappeared. She put a finger to her lips again and shook her head. Lewis understood that she wanted him to go. He remembered Professor Armitage easing himself out of his coat, anxious to stay, even in that house of the recently dead. And now he was in the same position. He took Mme Doche's hand, pressed it, and went to the door, conscious now of her willing him to be gone. He hesitated for a moment, with all that he had to say unsaid, but then the harsh voice made itself heard once more.

'Fernande! Fernande!'

He stood for a moment on the landing, then hurried down the stairs and out into the street. He all but ran back to the hotel, packed his bag, and made for the station. He left Paris the same evening, catching the same train, or its twin, back to London.

The house was waiting for him, as empty and as silent as when he had left. The house was waiting for him, and he recognized it as the place where he would remain. He picked up his mother's library books, went out, stood at the bus stop by the Common, and began another unmomentous day.

4

Another library, he thought. He felt doomed, irritated, yet
at the same time submissive. Here was destiny staring him
in the face. Not exactly here but somewhere very like, up
imposing steps, through swing doors, into the arched and
silent room, where a timid sun sent coloured refractions
through the lozenge shapes of art deco fanlights, where children sat at one of the two long tables composing essays for
their English homework, and where old men, cloth capped
and muffled, read the *Express* and the *Telegraph* and sometimes dozed until it was time to go home. This was a kindly
place, something of a day care centre for the lonely, the naturally silent, the elderly and the reclusive. The lighting and the
heating were generous, even if the rules were strict: there was
to be no talking, not one word, emphasized Miss Clarke, the
librarian, and although she was well disposed she would not
countenance outright sleep, however frail the sleeper. Tap-
ping across the parquet floor on her military-sounding high
heels, she would shake the offender by the shoulder. 'This is
a library, Mr Baker, not a dormitory! And you were beginning to snore.' This admonition had to be repeated rather
frequently. Mr Baker, white stubble nestling in the folds of
a very ancient, once handsome silk scarf, damp of nostril
but calm of presence, his former bearing resurrected for the
occasion, had once, in Lewis's hearing, replied, 'You make
more noise than I do, you silly bitch,' and had been ordered

to leave. 'Poor old thing,' Mrs Percy had said. 'He probably has nowhere else to go.' 'Oh, he'll be back tomorrow,' said Miss Clarke, with a laugh that was tolerant but a little too hearty. 'I like to do my best for everyone but I can't have the atmosphere disturbed. I feel sorry for him really. But old people can be very tiresome, can't they?' She was perhaps forty-three to Grace Percy's sixty-two. 'Yes,' Grace Percy had smiled in return. 'Yes, I dare say they can.'

'There is something very sad about that woman,' she had said to her son on their journey home. 'I somehow doubt that she will marry. And she knows this. It has probably broken her heart but she is too good a woman to show her feelings. What comes out is a terrible cheerfulness, with no cheer in it.'

Lewis had laughed and pressed his mother's arm. He loved her in this mood. 'Go on,' he said. 'What happened to her? Did some rotter let her down?'

'Oh no,' said Mrs Percy, surprised. 'There never was a rotter, that's the trouble. She's the sort of great-hearted woman who would be magnificent with a rotter. That deep bosom, that high colour. The sacrifices she would have made! The faith in his untested abilities she would have maintained! She would have taken on his parents, his friends, even his lovers. I can just see her keeping open house for all his hangers-on, being decent to the women who ring up, lending him money.'

'Why wouldn't someone like that want to marry her?' Lewis had asked in his innocence.

'Well, he might be a homosexual,' his mother had replied. She thought it her duty, for which she braced herself, to introduce her son to these complexities. 'At any event someone who couldn't tolerate the intimacy of women. And I have to say, although I shouldn't, that Miss Clarke gives the impression of someone whose intimacy might be a little tiring.'

She said no more, thinking to spare Lewis the spectacle, which she had quite clearly in front of her, of Miss Clarke, full-throated, wild-eyed, in the throes of some spectacular but unrequited ardour. It was the sort of thing for which actresses became famous in the theatre. Jacobean tragedy would have suited her, she reflected.

'The sad thing is that many women of Miss Clarke's type never marry,' she said mildly. 'And yet they would make excellent wives. Miss Clarke probably has a chest of drawers full of exquisite linen,' (nightdresses, she thought, but kept the thought to herself). 'She probably still adds to it. And she always looks well turned out, have you noticed? Those very pretty blouses, those high heels. And nice discreet scent. And always well made up. And her hair always immaculate.'

'I suppose she's all right for her age,' said Lewis. 'But I think she's pretty unattractive.'

'She was possibly always heavy in the bust, even as a girl,' said his mother. 'Now, of course, her waist is bigger than it was before. That happens to women in their forties,' she said, giving Lewis's arm a tap. 'You should know that. So that you're not disappointed when your wife gets a little older. The figure loses definition,' she added, although her own had long disappeared into a kind of Gothic sparseness. Contemplation of Miss Clarke's misplaced and unsought abundance always brought her a tiny spasm of personal gratitude for her own good fortune. Although Lewis did not know this, Mrs Percy always reflected at this point, 'After all, I had darling Jack.' But such thoughts were not to be spoken, and after thinking them Mrs Percy felt a little ashamed.

'Remember, Lewis,' she had said. 'Good women are better than bad women. Bad women are merely tiresome. Learn to appreciate goodness of heart. Learn to look beyond the outer covering. Would you like some of those crumpets for tea?'

They had been passing one of the mild small shops that did duty for a bakery in this unworldly district. Two girls in overalls carelessly swathed uncut loaves in tissue paper and swung bags round by corners, varying this activity with sorties to the window to pick out yellow Bath buns and virulent jam tarts with fingers arched daintily for the purpose.

'Remember, Lewis,' his mother had said. 'Never buy cakes unwrapped.'

'I wouldn't buy this stuff anyway,' said Lewis, whose standards in these matters remained haughtily and unrealistically Parisian. 'I could just fancy a strawberry tart,' he added. 'Freshly made.' 'Nevertheless,' said his mother, 'I'm sure you won't say no to the crumpets. Fortunately, they come in packets.'

'Good afternoon, Hazel,' she had said to one of the two girls behind the counter. 'Father feeling better?'

For she had been the genius of the place, he thought, and had somehow made her peace with its lack of pretension, loving its modesty, its uneventfulness, its quiet afternoons. Little ceremonies – the planting of the hyacinth bulbs in the blue china bowls, the drawing of the curtains in the evenings, the bars of soap slipped between the clean sheets in the linen cupboard – all these had kept her happy, kept her attentive, so that with the help of her reading, and with her pride in her son, she had lived a peaceful widowhood, maintained a dignity for which he was grateful. He had had time to reflect on her life, which he now saw as excellent, and which he hoped would always remain with him, and even, when some time had elapsed, cancel out the memory of her death. He would always see her here, against the background of the Common, or else stepping on her narrow beautifully shod feet into the little bakery, the little grocery, exchanging remarks with the shopkeeper, or the girl assistant. Going home to put on the kettle, to build up the fire for the evening, to water the plants. This was a life, thought Lewis, that would always be part of him, although in his mind he longed impatiently to be somewhere else, to be off to a wider, more sophisticated metropolitan setting, one more in keeping with the adult he hoped he had it in him to be, although adulthood still seemed to him to be a long way away. His boyhood, the last days of which he was sorrowfully living, would remain imprinted with his mother's quiet habits, whose decency he would always defend.

His mother's presence was particularly strong on this day when he returned the library books she would never exchange for others. He mounted the steps, pushed through the swing doors, obediently straightened his tie. Once again he succumbed to suburban peace, aware of a rawness round his heart which responded gratefully to the books, to the readers, to the sunlight through the windows, to the smell of polish. Mr Baker was there, he noticed, doing the crossword in *The Times*, although this was forbidden; at least he was not asleep. Miss Clarke was on duty, in a red dress that brought out her high colour; even the lobes of her ears, tightly clasped by large pearl studs, looked suffused. The other girl, the pale one, was searching through the tickets that went back into the books being returned by a very old lady, who drew each one, trembling, from the depths of a woven brown leather bag. Miss Clarke flashed him her famous smile, the one she used to enslave men and reprimand wrongdoers.

'Mother not with you today?' she asked. It was the question he had been dreading.

'My mother has died,' he said. 'I've brought her books back.'

There was a shocked silence. The pale girl turned round, even paler. Miss Clarke, her hand on her heart, paused in her task.

'Well, this has been quite a shock,' she said, after a second or two, lowering the hand to pluck a dazzling white handkerchief from her sleeve. 'This is a sad day for the library, Mr Percy. We've known your mother for ages. Always so kind. Always took an interest. I had noticed she was looking a bit tired, mark you. But I never dreamed . . . '

'It was her heart,' said Lewis miserably, feeling once again the full weight of his misfortune.

'And then, of course, she missed you,' Miss Clarke went on inexorably. 'She once said to me, "I'm counting the days, Madeleine". But she didn't want you to know that.'

50

And now I do, thought Lewis. In order not to prolong the conversation he went over to the shelves to try to find a book that his mother might have liked, hoping to maintain contact in that way if in no other. He found a couple of Edith Whartons, and, feeling lonely and self-conscious, took them to the desk. The pale girl came forward, two spots of red in her cheeks.

'She was awfully proud of you, Mr Percy,' the girl said. 'And she was quite all right on her own, you know. Not weak, or anything. She never complained, never said there was anything wrong. Please don't blame yourself.' She ducked her head in embarrassment at having said so much and busied herself with the date stamp.

'Thank you,' said Lewis.

'I was very fond of your mother,' said the girl. Lewis saw that despite her pallor, or because of it, she had an air of delicacy, or narrowness, that pleased him. Her clothes were asexual: a pale blue sweater and a grey flannel skirt, school-girl's clothes, which made her seem younger than her age. He reckoned she was about twenty-five. What he noticed mostly were her long unmarked slightly upcurling fingers, white as if they had never been engaged in a common or unseemly task. The face, momentarily enlivened by her emotion and the forwardness she obviously thought she was exhibiting, was equally long and pale, and could, he thought, look mournful. The face was framed by thick hair, in a colour midway between blonde and beige, and held back by a black velvet band. Susan had had one of those, he remembered: they must be the fashion. She had large, rather beautiful dark blue eyes, shadowed by long colourless lashes. The skin was fine, the teeth unexpectedly strong, slightly protruding. The chin, he noticed, was a little weak. He wondered why she was not pretty. His mother would have known why the face was so withdrawn, so unmarked. That pose of the head, held slightly on one side, as if listening to an inner voice, those narrow, slightly hunched shoulders, those prayerful hands, set him thinking of pale virgins in stone, the kind he had seen in the Victoria and Albert Museum. Perhaps all virgins had something in common, he thought, revising her age slightly upward. And yet, outside the V and A, he had never seen one so spectacularly virginal. Everything about her looked untouched. Beneath the pale blue jersey the breasts were scarcely noticeable. He felt drawn to her on account of her little speech, which, he supposed, given her shyness, must have cost her an effort. He was grateful to her for telling him what he had wanted to be told. She was the agent of his deliverance.

'Tissy, your mother's here,' called Miss Clarke.

'Tissy?' said Lewis quickly, intrigued by this name, which he had never heard.

'My name's Patricia, really. Patricia Harper. When I was little I couldn't say Patricia, so I called myself Tissy, and the name's stuck. I get called it all the time now. Would you excuse me, Mr Percy? My mother's come to take me out to lunch. I just want you to know I was fond of Mrs Percy, and I'm sorry for your trouble.'

Again she blushed, seemed almost weakened by the effort of speaking. In the face of her alarming fragility he held out his hand, partly in gratitude, partly to reassure himself that she was all right. She clasped his hand lightly with very cold fingers, then turned and disappeared.

'A tragedy, that girl,' said Miss Clarke, leaning her bosom on the counter. Mr Baker, looking up, put his finger ostentatiously to his lips. Miss Clarke took no notice.

'Agoraphobia,' she said, with melancholy satisfaction. 'Says she can't go out alone. Her mother brings her in the morning, collects her for lunch, brings her back at two, and collects her again in the evening. I've tried to talk to her, but to no avail. Apparently it came on with adolescence, although I believe there was some family trouble as well. The father,' she said, lowering her voice to imply discretion, but also comprehension. 'Another woman, I suppose. That's usually the way of it, isn't it? A good little worker, mind you: I've no complaints. But who else would have her?'

'Doesn't she ever go out, then?' asked Lewis.

'Well, I've encouraged her, of course. I've told her she can't stay with her mother all her life. But she turns quite faint if you go on at her. Frightened to death, you see. And it ties the mother down too, now that there's just the two of them. Still, she seems quite happy. And we can't always have things the way we want them, can we? Into each life a little rain must fall. Anyway you don't want to hear about all this, what with your recent tragedy.' She pressed her handkerchief to a ready tear. 'Taking those, are you? Ah, *The Age of Innocence*, my favourite book.' Lewis was ashamed of himself for thinking patronizingly of Miss Clarke. She was a romantic, and therefore an ideal reader, someone like himself. Nevertheless, walking home with the books under his arm, it was Miss Harper, Tissy, whose image stayed in his mind, tiny, chill, eternally distant, like something seen through the wrong end of a telescope. He had thought her quite plain.

She might be somebody he could marry, he thought, quailing at the prospect of his mother's empty house. The thought, though idle, was sudden yet not surprising. And then he could cure her, and she would be able to go out again. Or else she could stay indoors, waiting for him to come home. It would be nice to be expected again.

He raced through *The Age of Innocence* and *Ethan Frome*, and was back at the library two days later. This time he was disappointed: no sign of Tissy Harper, or even of Miss Clarke. No sign of anyone, and only a large indolent girl he had never seen before at the desk. He took out an Elizabeth Bowen and a Margaret Kennedy. He found himself drawn to the books his mother had loved, as if in reading them he could get in touch with her in a way of which she would have approved. In any event such reading seemed to him salutary. He began to think that his official reading, which involved him in grown-up theories about heroism, and nineteenth-century heroism at that, might have led him, not exactly astray, but perhaps a little too far from normal concerns. He whiled away several evenings with what he thought of as his mother's type of book, and for a time he was soothed and charmed, although the moment at which he was forced to emerge from these tender fictional worlds was always harsh and painful. He began to long for a female presence, something shadowy, beneficent, something that would bring health and peace back into his life, which he perceived as threatened. The desire for such a presence was infinite, although he saw little possibility of its being satisfied. He thought how sad it was for a man of his age to be reduced to loneliness, with only his books for company. At the same time he began to realize that he could not spend his life reading. The British Museum was his refuge, but it was also his prison. He felt mildly distressed when the library closed, but once that moment had passed he strode out down the steps with a feeling of liberation. As the year stretched once more into spring the days perversely got both longer and chillier. Walking home, he could hear sad bird song under a darkening sky. In the gardens crocuses were already splayed and untidy, past their best. Timid buds showed on bushes; even the cheerless privet seemed brighter. In a moment of depression he turned out again one evening after his supper and took the Elizabeth Bowen back to the library. He had left it late and arrived just as the lights were being clicked on and off to signify closing time. But he was rewarded by the sight of Tissy Harper, this time in a pale pink twinset, one arm already inserted into the sleeve of a grey jacket.

'Take your time,' she whispered. 'I won't put the lights out until you go.'

'I just wanted to return this,' he said, placing the book on the counter, near her hand. 'I'll come back another day.' He hesitated, and then asked, 'Can I walk you home?'

'Thank you,' she said, 'but my mother's here.'

Her mother was in fact looking at him rather insistently from the vantage point of a seat opposite the one Mr Baker would have been occupying had he not been

54

turned out earlier by Miss Clarke. Ah, but the mother was a surprise. The mother, thought Lewis, was a beauty, a bold strenuous-looking woman, with a curiously out-of-date sexual appeal. She was heavily made up, her mouth a dark red, her eyebrows arched in permanent astonishment, an artificial streak of white inserted into her upswept dark hair. She had exactly the same look of disdain that he remembered from the screen goddesses of his childhood. For all its apparent and carefully nurtured perfection the face was discontented, with an incipient puffiness round the mouth and chin. Lewis could see no resemblance at all between the mother and the daughter, but then he remembered Miss Clarke hinting that the father had gone off with another woman, and he supposed this renegade, this ingrate, to have had the same fair looks that his daughter now possessed.

But why had the father gone off? What sort of a woman did a man go off to, when he had this red-lipped smouldering creature at home? For she was still in the prime of life, not much more than fifty, he supposed. She looked tricky, hard to please, and also capricious, exigent, the last person to be the guardian of a pristine semi-invalid daughter. A fur coat was flung back from a plumpish compact little body; her skirt was short enough to show fine legs in fine stockings. He could see no sign of conjugal or maternal disillusionment in her face, but simply impatience. Mrs Harper looked like a woman whose husband had left only a minute before, to perform some necessary but unimportant duty, and who would return immediately once the duty were out of the way. Mrs Harper, in fact, looked like a woman invisibly accompanied by a man. Yet here she was, tied to her daughter, clocking in at the library four times a day, without any possibility of release from this obligation until the daughter resumed her autonomy.

Lewis felt a pang of pity for them both. He felt too that if he could wean Tissy away from her mother he might effect the happiness of three people. He still retained a sense of chivalry towards women. He was aware of his lack of experience, and ashamed of it, but he was even more ashamed of certain publications bought in Paris and hidden beneath his sweaters until they could be safely deposited in public rubbish bins. These texts had left him with a sense of surprise and disappointment, and he hated the idea that the getting of wisdom involved both. For himself he envisaged something more chaste, if that could be managed: it could be brief, but it must be perfect, heroic. He would be prepared to lose all, but only if at some point he had gained all. Although Tissy Harper, with her prayerful hands and her downcast eyes, might not provide the promised sins of the flesh, she still represented a quest and a safeguard. She would be kind, would not mock or disregard him, would care for him studiously and with gratitude. And her mother could go back to whatever society she had been forced to abandon – he imagined hotel terraces, bridge games, cocktails – when the girl, her so unsuitable daughter, had become her only occupation.

The problem now was how to divide the mother and the daughter for as long as it might take him to pursue his plan. For he had to emancipate her from her tutelage before he could do anything else. The project appealed to him: it had the requisite altruism. He had an obscure feeling that a man must perform an act of nobility before claiming his prize. This, he knew, was ridiculous. But he had never felt comfortable when he had been merely lewd and selfish. He supposed that in later life, in remote middle age, perhaps, these attributes might be sufficient to motivate him, but by then he would have sunk far from grace, as old people did, his mother excepted. For the time being he knew himself to be not only young but powerless. His powerlessness was reinforced by his virginity, which he felt to be tardy and shameful. In Paris nothing had happened to change his hopeful self. With his abundant hair, his short-sighted smile, and his respectful expression, he had attracted no predatory gaze. And he suspected that he would not have been equal to such a situation. The prospect before him now promised a certain equality, if only of inexperience, and vouchsafed him, at the same time, a quota of generosity, of honour, even. He needed these feelings not only because they were pleasurable in themselves but because they were required to offset certain censorable images that crept back to him from his unofficial Parisian readings. He had no sensation of being attracted to Tissy Harper. What he felt was a mixture of respect and charity. He would rescue her and take his reward. Or, if circumstances permitted, he would take his reward first and leave her with a legacy of freedom, waking her, like the Sleeping Beauty, from the strange enchantment that had kept her a prisoner for so long. For how long? Since the father had left home, Miss Clarke had implied. When would that have been? There was no clue to this. The key to the whole enigma was the mother, he thought. And if he could free them both they could thank him by performing various domestic duties about the place. These were becoming urgent. No matter how many times he changed the sheets he habitually forgot the day on which the laundry was collected and delivered. He was, as always, extremely hungry. If they would look after him, he thought, he would take them both on. He would marry them both.

Yet initially they must be separated. This looked to him to be a virtual impossibility. Stealthily he followed them out of the library, studied their backs, as they walked, arm in arm, down the lighted street. The mother walked elaborately, in the manner of one throwing out physical hints to passers-by, hips in movement, legs thrust forward, small feet turned outward, like a dancer's. Beside her her daughter appeared awkward, apologetic, large of foot, meek of gesture, head dipping in obedience or in fear, beautiful indigo eyes cast downwards. Lewis saw that they walked on decisively, disdaining the bus stop, and he did the same, thinking that at least he could find out where they lived. This did not seem to him underhand: he was in any event going in the same direction. Having no strategy at his disposal he merely said, 'Hello, again, Miss Harper. Or perhaps I should say good evening. Good evening,' he added, in the direction of Tissy's mother.

'Oh, Mr Percy.' Miss Harper was not unduly surprised. 'I don't think you've met my mother. Mr Percy, mother. You may have seen him before. In the library, I mean.'

'No, I don't think so,' said Mrs Harper, tonelessly, in a voice that contained chest notes but was harshened by cigarette smoke. 'How do you do?'

'We seem to be walking in the same direction,' Lewis hazarded.

'We live in Britannia Road,' said Miss Harper. 'And you?'

'Further on. Opposite the Common,' he replied. 'May I walk along with you?'

So the meeting was effected. But it was only to be a meeting, that was clear. He sensed a powerful indifference emanating from the mother; he felt her deliberately withholding her interest in him. And why should she be interested, he thought humbly. She was obviously a woman of the world, a woman of some experience. The daughter must take after the absent father, the father who had so inexplicably left home. He imagined the mother trapped, baffled, chafing at the legacy of that useless husband, inwardly raging at the chore that fell to her lot four times a day. Lewis, in his mind's eye, saw Mrs Harper raising a cigarette to her lipsticked mouth, stroking her hair up from the nape of her neck, appraising herself in a glass. He did not see how there could be any room for a Miss Harper in Mrs Harper's life. Mrs Harper, he thought, gave out all the signals of a woman accustomed to playing for high stakes, rather than of merely being a pawn in the game. And Tissy, poor Tissy, must represent to her both burden and sacrifice. In the light of Mrs Harper's dead-eyed acknowledgement of his presence, Lewis crept nearer to Tissy, wondering if he dared to take her hand.

He saw them to their door. Their little house looked trim, immaculate, at least so he judged from the outside. Clearly he

58

was not to be invited in. He watched the mother extract a key from a powerful handbag, while the daughter stood politely to one side, like a guest. Desperately he sought to prolong the encounter. Ask me in, he thought, ask me in. Ask me to share your meal: be pleasant, be merciful. He felt all the desolation of one who goes home to an empty house. Above all he was a little shocked by their exclusivity. Surely it was within the bounds of normal politeness to express an interest in a new acquaintance? Yet he could hardly go on asking questions, with their own attention to him so minimal. They were too used to each other's company, he supposed, and the routine of their days was so deadening that they had lost their manners. For a moment he felt intensely sorry for himself, could hardly face the short distance that separated him from his own house. But I know no one else, he thought sadly. This will have to do.

'Miss Harper,' he called. She turned back from the door. 'I could walk you home, if you like,' he said, feeling himself blush. 'I mean, it would give your mother a break. And we live so near each other.'

It was to be concluded that he knew all about her disability; he thought it better to make no reference to it. And she seemed quite tranquil in the knowledge that she had no explanations, no excuses to offer. Looking back on this later Lewis wondered whether he should have challenged her at this point, brought matters out into the open. He could see, past her, through the open front door, a hallway papered in brilliant red. This shocked him; such colours were unknown in his milieu. All his mother's rooms were white. He saw the dark blushing cave into which Miss Harper was about to be subsumed in womb-like terms: this was to be a birth in reverse. Every night, when the lights were on and the walls glowed red, Miss Harper would become the property of her mother all over again. The creature of her mother. He promised himself that he would examine this thought when he got home. For the time being, whatever reservations he felt about their hospitality, he had to have

59

an answer to his offer, his request, his plea.

'Well, I'm not sure,' was her reply. But she lingered; that was a good sign.

'Do you always walk home?' he went on. 'I do, every evening. The evenings are so long now that my mother's gone.' He felt a charlatan, introducing the subject of his mother into this simulacrum of a flirtation. But it is time, he told himself. I am lonely, and why shouldn't she know it? Why shouldn't she take account of me for a while? After all, I'm not going to frighten her. She has nothing to fear.

'We only walk the whole way in the evening,' she said conscientiously. 'We usually catch the bus in the morning. And we have lunch out, near the library. I really don't think . . . '

'Tissy,' came her mother's voice, to be followed by her mother's outline, solid black against the brilliant red hallway. She was smoking a cigarette.

'Mother, Mr Percy has very kindly offered to see me home one evening. But I've told him . . . '

Lewis was aware of the mother smiling, albeit a little sourly.

'Tell Mr Percy that you're very grateful for his kind offer,' she said. Lewis detected a certain sarcasm in the remark. 'I don't mind the walk. But you could ask him if he'd like to come to tea one day. Saturday would do. He can walk home with us then.'

Lewis blushed again, and thanked her, and promised to meet them at five o'clock on the following Saturday. Having accomplished his mission he was anxious to be gone. It seemed to him that he had worked too hard for the minimal concession she had made, and he disliked the feeling. He could not quite make out this couple, he thought; he would need his mother to decipher them. A great wave of misery broke over him. He trudged along the street, away from the false promise of that lighted hallway, back to the dark house that it was now so difficult to think of as home. He stood for a long time at the window, staring into the empty street. Then he let the curtain fall and went upstairs to his room. On the landing he opened his mother's door and watched the moon stream in over her bed. This, strangely, comforted him. If his mother were present, in however dematerialized a form, he could proceed. And the future was there, after all; it simply had to be filled in. He went thoughtfully to bed, thankful, at least, to have so many new reflections to keep him company.

5

Across the table Mrs Harper watched him with the stillness of a lizard. She signified her detachment from the common business of eating and drinking by placing her chair at a slight angle and smoking a cigarette. The room was snug but joyless. Its walls were as red as those of the hallway, as were its curtains, but those curtains were half drawn against the tender blue of a late spring evening. The effect was of a consulting room where secrets were the currency. Small though it was the room contained a handsome though over-large dining-table and two equally sizeable armchairs placed beside a minuscule hearth. The unsuitable nature and appearance of the furniture, which looked as if it had come from a more commodious house, countermanded the intimacy of the red walls, and it began to be apparent to Lewis that a quite foreign existence, of a variety with which he was unfamiliar, might be lived here, that meals might be taken at that grandiose table and impenetrable comments exchanged between the occupiers of the two armchairs. Were it not for the half-drawn curtains, and Mrs Harper's insistent gaze, Lewis would have felt alert to receive information, signals, codes to be decoded. As it was he felt shabby, far from home. This effect was enhanced by the fact that he had thought to wear his best suit.

Nor was he eating the innocent food, to which he had been accustomed in his mother's house. Mrs Harper, like Marie

Antoinette, believed in luxury above necessity. He had been presented with a coffee gâteau crowned with whipped cream and a ginger cake with a melting base of pear and crushed walnut. Clearly he was expected to eat both. Tissy, whose appetite was remarkably steady, offered him further dishes of tiny macaroons and small but abundant iced biscuits. Even these revealed themselves to be dangerously emollient. Feeling slightly sick at the drenching sweetness of these offerings Lewis remembered to compliment his hostess: he thought, correctly as it turned out, that she was a woman to whom many compliments must be paid. And he was genuinely surprised at the sophistication of the table, and indeed its festiveness. These cakes, and Mrs Harper's distant expression, made him feel as if he had been translated elsewhere. He could see no connection between this afternoon and his ordinary life, which seemed to him to be lived on a different plane of reality. He felt, and not quite agreeably, out of his depth.

'Did you make all this yourself, Mrs Harper?' he asked. 'It's very impressive.' He felt he had struck the wrong note, particularly as no answering comment was forthcoming. He felt uneasy, eating this luxurious food, in this impenetrably strange setting. His heart grew heavier, and he registered the effect not only mentally but physically as well. Mrs Harper's diet, though profuse, was also upsetting. 'Delicious,' he murmured again, although to his ears the word had a slightly desperate ring.

'Mother makes everything herself,' said Tissy. 'She's a wonderful cook.'

Throughout this exchange Mrs Harper continued to gaze at him indifferently and to smoke. Tissy did the honours of the tea-table, but under her mother's supervision or protection. Conversation was sparse, owing to the almost palpable withdrawal of the mother, who had, Lewis noted, dressed herself up for the occasion in a rather tight black coat and skirt, with a silk blouse open to show the beginnings of an opulent bosom. The discrepancies between the appearance of mother and daughter could not have been more pronounced. Yet Tissy, timid pale Tissy, seemed entirely at ease under her mother's watchful yet abstracted eye, and the presence of Lewis, far from making her nervous, seemed to add to her sense of security. He was surprised to see her eating so freely of the rich food, which appeared to have no connection with the frailness of her body. He supposed that in this little household all sorts of cossetting and cherishing went on. He imagined days spent in just such a restricted setting, curtains drawn, beyond the sphere of male influence: ample shopping, self-indulgent meals, fires in bedrooms, routines that might have descended from a grander establishment altogether, as this afternoon's delicate confectionery seemed to indicate. And Mrs Harper's noble bust, swathed in a spotless butter coloured blouse, her tight black skirt, and her endless cigarettes, seemed better suited to an afternoon at the bridge table than to this nursery occasion. It occurred to Lewis that the half-drawn curtains were there to reassure Tissy, neither entirely open, to frighten her, nor entirely closed, to send her regressively back to where he sensed she was happiest: at home, in a very small room, with her mother.

Lewis, whose appetite could not match that of Tissy, drank his tea and studied Mrs Harper. No attempt had been made to welcome him, and yet he had the feeling that he was already accepted as a suitor. This thought did not displease him, although part of him was a little disappointed at how dull he was finding the experience. Dull and intimidating. Surely a feeling of conquest should be more liberating than this! For it seemed to him impossible that he should now back down: Mrs Harper's still beautiful eyes, set in deep shadowed sockets, informed him that he was on probation. Yet if he were not to be seamlessly drafted into this household, as appeared likely, he must reassert his own independence, his own claim to existence. The trouble was that he was uncertain how to proceed, and knew no one who could advise him. Their hospitality, though lacking in any sort of charm or grace, was nevertheless superior to what he

64

himself could offer. Such cakes as he might provide would not match these in splendour. Yet there was an oppression in the air which made him long for his own much larger house and the untouched memory of his austere mother about her tasks within those white walls. Here, a brazen electric fire, with simulated orange and black coals, added considerably to the heat and weight of the occasion. After a fairly long silence Mrs Harper's hand reached out to pick up a macaroon. Her fingers, he noted, were stubby, her mouth, as it closed on the tiny cake, prim. Both mother and daughter had this in common, that they made eating look like an act of virtue, far removed from bodily appetites and the secretion of gastric juices, distasteful matters with which they did not appear to concern themselves. Mrs Harper drank cup after cup of watery milkless tea, and with each fresh cup she lit a new cigarette. She seemed entirely uninterested in Lewis, yet he knew that nothing escaped her.

'Do you like to cook?' he asked, again desperately. The cake theme was beginning to sicken him, as was the fire, as were the curtains, but he thought this was the limit of the kind of question he could legitimately ask.

'I learnt to cook when I was at school,' was the reply. 'I was at school in Brussels, for two years, when I was seventeen, then eighteen. I liked the Belgian cooking, so I took lessons.'

Yes, he thought: despite her appearance there was something about her that spoke of a Belgian pension. Her high colour, her brutal appeal, seemed reined in, restricted by strong conventional beliefs. She was animated more by a righteous sense of obligation than by anarchic feelings and desires. Yet she seemed never to have enjoyed what was due to her. Someone, somewhere, had defaulted.

Tissy turned to him earnestly: obviously she was willing to be forthcoming on the subject of her mother.

'Mother's family comes from Jersey,' she said. 'We often talk of going back there one day. She's never really been happy here.'

65

'And your father?' he ventured, powered by the need to know all that had happened to the deserter.

At this she dropped her gaze. 'I don't really remember him,' she said. 'I haven't seen him since I was very little.'

'Tissy's father is in Canada,' said Mrs Harper. 'We don't expect to hear from him again.'

This utterance seemed to leave her undisturbed: its finality told Lewis that further questions would not be welcomed. He felt indignant on behalf of Tissy, that she should be deprived of a broader, more robust influence in her life, one that would fling back those half-drawn curtains and let in some much needed fresh air. And how did a woman like Mrs Harper manage without a man? She was well built, even voluptuous, to some tastes a handsome woman. Not exactly discontented with motherhood, but unfitted for the role, uninterested. Despite all this wealth of *pâtisserie* she seemed absent, distanced from the task of providing it. Sitting there, slightly at an angle to the table, to which she lent rather than gave her presence, she was dressed for another occasion, markedly different in this respect from her daughter, who appeared to belong in a more juvenile context. Tissy, in her pale blue sweater, was too much of a schoolgirl to be at home in this red room, whose half-drawn curtains revealed a thin white moon in a remote darkening sky. Yet Tissy herself seemed obedient, even docile in his presence. Tissy appeared to acknowledge, tacitly, his right, even his duty, to be there. And Lewis felt himself to be identified with her in a process which he had only inadvertently brought about. To extract Tissy from this room suddenly seemed beyond his powers. Tissy and her mother had not been drawn to him; rather, they had been unaltered by his presence. He could impute no unkind action or inference to the mother, although he sensed in her a detachment which affected him almost with embarrassment. Yet when Mrs Harper's eyes rested on him, as they so frequently did, they were calm, thoughtful, appraising. It was their lack of curiosity that he found so disconcerting.

Perhaps she wanted to be free, he thought. Perhaps she

wanted to give her daughter into safe keeping so that she could be off to the world that suited her, a world of hotel rooms, steamer trunks, new friends. Perhaps she wanted to go back to Jersey and whatever life she had led there before the arrival of the unsatisfactory husband and the restricting daughter. Off to sunny afternoons and male companions and night clubs. There was something perfunctory about the furnishings of this room, with its bold walls and its haphazard and out-of-scale contents, as if no attempt had been made to integrate the two. As if she would sail out and leave it all behind before the disagreeable necessity of making it into a true home imposed itself. Yet she was devoted to her daughter, as that daughter's shining appearance and healthy appetite averred. Lewis would have felt sorry for Mrs Harper, trapped as she was, had it not been for a reserve in the woman, a silence during which she so obviously entertained her own thoughts, indifferent to the thoughts of others.

And Tissy? Tissy now appeared to him to be composed of the same fondant yet friable material as the cake she was so dedicatedly eating. Tissy, in this setting, seemed to him to be composed entirely of cake. If he nibbled her ear it would break off and melt in his mouth like marzipan. Her pale delicacy almost invited assault; making love to her would be like violating a nun. The thought intrigued him but made him uncomfortable. To lay a hand on Tissy would be both necessary and forbidden. She already had the appearance of a victim, with all of a victim's innocence, yet there was something about that innocence, that virtue, which invited thoughts of assault. An approach to her, on this level at least, presented itself as a question of taste. Her many fears would have to be allayed; he did not think she had it in her to be anything but trustingly passive. Part of him felt lonely at the idea. Love should be strong, if not necessarily decent. Love should be eager and unplanned, not an affair of exorcism or therapy. He had before him a vision of sunlight, of peace, of maturity, which seemed very far removed from this dark hot room. And Tissy was not included in this vision: that much was clear to him. He could also see that she was blameless, unprotected, and part of him, the other, better, half, knew that he matched her in this, that they were both novices, and that no one else could teach them what they wanted to know. For to the inexperienced certain degrees of experience in others are almost unacceptable.

His male conscience still reserved and clung to a vision of innocence for himself, although he was well aware that he had passed the age at which innocence was appropriate. Yet here he was, a relatively honest man, or one who liked to think of himself as relatively honest, apparently accepted, apparently absorbed into the curious wordless dialogue of this strange couple, with its wealth of meaning not made clear. There was even a sort of peace in the knowledge that he did not have to present his credentials, that in being in this house for the first time he was regarded as part of the set-up, however alien that might appear to be. And he liked the idea of having a girlfriend. Surely with an accredited girlfriend he would have passed one of the many tests awaiting him, for he did not doubt that there were many tasks ahead, many stages to be passed through on his progress to true adulthood, and if possible heroic stature. Maybe he was being asked to undertake this task as an act of unselfishness, as his first trial on the way to a just reward. What that reward might be he had as yet no idea: he simply saw himself far from the final result, the right true end. He saw the future through a diminishing lens, a camera obscura that revealed little. He knew that he would always strive towards a final recognition of his place in the world. And yet he saw Tissy Harper as an ineluctable part of his quest. He thought of her again as the Sleeping Beauty, whom he would awaken with a kiss, and once more the thought commended itself to him. But could he reconcile himself to the massive preoccupations of her mother, from whom Tissy, either consciously or unconsciously, took her cue? Must he go through this entirely unaided, unsupported, without encouragement or enthusiasm on the part of what he could not help thinking of as the main beneficiaries?

68

Their house suddenly seemed intolerable to him and he wondered how soon he might leave. But he could not leave without some sort of a sign from them as to how he was to continue. He knew that he would come back, yet he also knew that he would want to be a welcome guest, not merely tolerated, but gladly, excitedly, anticipated. It seemed to him that he could rise to fulfil any expectation, if only that expectation were to be indicated. Without that he would turn away in disgust, yes, disgust. He had come so near to beggary that he was indignant on his own behalf. He thought how differently his mother would have behaved in a similar situation and longed to be at home again, away from these people with their enormous reticence, their absolute lack of desire, their basic powerful refusal of life. Their indifference alone made him want to insist that they pay more attention to him, yet at the same time he had a feeling of impatience, as if he were in two minds about the whole affair and might easily be persuaded to call it off. He lacked a champion, a spokesman, an advocate, someone who would tell him what he wanted to know, that he should opt for the wider, fuller life. Something called to him beyond his present circumstances, beyond anything he could logically see, yet here he was, entrapped in this small room as if it were his destiny, as if his course were already chosen for him. The effect of Mrs Harper – and of her daughter too – was to deprive him of initiative. He longed to be gone, but curiously doubted his ability to free himself from their spell.

And that saturation of sweetness, overlaying an immoveable core of opacity. He saw a trace of melting cream on his plate and felt a qualm of nausea. Tissy's plate was clean; as he glanced at her her cup came gently and finally to rest in her saucer. She turned then to look at him, and smiled. He smiled back, vastly relieved. His strategy now, he saw, was to get her out of this room, preferably without her mother, and into his own house. In those astringent and much saner surroundings he would get to know her, and get to know her on his own terms. After all, this meeting was only a rite of passage, one that they had all been obliged to perform, and one that they probably found to be as discouraging as he did.

'I must be going,' he said. 'Thank you for this splendid tea, Mrs Harper. I wonder if you'd both like to come to my house next Saturday?' Harrods, he thought. They sell cakes, don't they?

Mrs Harper stubbed out her cigarette. 'One of these days,' she conceded. 'If Tissy is not too tired.'

With this he had to be content. 'I'll see Tissy at the library,' he said, 'and fix something up with her. Would that be all right?' For by now he was determined to persevere, and, more important, to get his own way.

As he was rising to go the doorbell rang.

'Tissy, let Ralph in, would you?' said Mrs Harper, piling dirty plates on to a papier mâché tray, another relic of former times, he supposed, and of a more commodious house. 'The doctor,' she added, for Lewis's benefit. 'He looks in once a week to see how Tissy is getting on.'

For a moment he had thought he might have a rival and was surprised to notice how alarmed he felt. For he seemed set on his course to become Tissy's husband, even if she had given no sign that she was to be his wife.

He was reassured, too, by the visit of a doctor, as who is not, when there is no illness in the house. The presence of a man had seemed to him to be lacking, and he wondered if the mild depression he had felt throughout his visit was due to the fact that however sympathetically he felt towards women their unadulterated company made him feel uncertain, at a loss. Fatherless, always seeking a home among women, reading their books in an effort to love and understand them better, he nevertheless looked to them to love and understand *him*, and it occurred to him that this was true of most men. Men were banded together not simply as hunter gatherers but rather in sheer bafflement at the behaviour of women. Looking for a mother, they nevertheless longed to escape the commitment that such a search required, and tended to fall back on easier stereotypes, women of lesser importance, who would not exact emotional tribute money. But if the love of any woman were not forthcoming, who could describe the hurt of a man who might find himself scorned, rejected, laughed at? And why did women make such a fuss about not being loved and understood? Surely they could see that it was far more serious for a man to be in this situation, for who could understand him if not a woman? At best a man had to fall back on the unspoken sympathy of other men, who would shrug their shoulders in comradely bewilderment. The doctor, thought Lewis, must understand him, and might, moreover, hold the key to this establishment. If he called every week he must know a good deal about the Harper ménage; he would certainly be able to tell how damaged Tissy really was, and when and in what circumstances she might be held to be cured. The doctor's visit he saw as a kindness, a formality, for it was obvious at a glance that no cure might be undertaken unless the curtains of this red room were symbolically drawn apart and the full light of day admitted. He was thus reminded of his own part in this hypothetical cure and the inherent difficulty of his role. For this reason alone he would be glad to see the doctor.

The doctor, as if to fulfil Lewis's expectations, entered like an old friend, a familiar, an habitué. Surely nothing less than friendship would explain the informality of his appearance, which was rumpled, untidy, unprofessional, thought Lewis, who had anticipated a dapper figure in a black coat and striped trousers. This man wore a creased grey suit with a white chalk stripe, the straining waistcoat of which bore the traces of a fall of cigarette ash. He wore, in addition, a grey overcoat, which seemed to be sliding off his shoulders, as if he had not entirely decided to put it on, and a grey Homburg hat pushed to the back of his head. He carried an attaché case which he put down beside one of the overstuffed armchairs, removed the coat and hat and hung them over the top of the door, to which he could reach quite easily. He was a tall man, but a tall man gone to seed, for there was a large rounded stomach beneath the chalk stripes. He had also lost the original fresh colouring which might have gone with the intensely waved, now grizzled, hair. Formerly fair, the doctor had become empurpled: a heavy shadow of beard darkened the lower half of his face which was now equally divided into areas of red and blue. His most striking feature was his mouth, which was full, pouting, babyish; the lips, which were violet, had the thin sheen of grape skins. He looked tired to death.

'Well, Thea,' he said to Mrs Harper. 'Well, Tissy. How's our girl this week, then?'

'Tea, Ralph?' queried Mrs Harper. 'I'll make some fresh, if you like. This is a bit cool.'

'No, leave it,' he said. 'I like it cool.' He received a cup and saucer in a large fatty hand.

'This is Mr Percy. A friend of Tissy's. Dr Jago.'

'Well, young man,' said the doctor. 'How do you come to be in this neck of the woods?'

'I know Tissy from the library,' he responded, thinking that he might state his business to this man and get something like a sensible hearing. 'I was wondering if she could come out with me? Nothing too arduous, a walk in the park, perhaps. The weather is so gorgeous now. Would you like that, Tissy?'

'Would you like that, Tissy?' echoed the doctor in a fair imitation of Lewis's eager voice. The doctor's adherence to his cause, Lewis saw, was not to be taken for granted.

'Well, I'm not sure,' said Tissy, as Lewis had known she would. 'I usually go out with Mother.'

'But if you got used to me,' urged Lewis. 'If you got to trust me and if I didn't leave you alone, wouldn't that be all right? It doesn't have to be tomorrow,' he added, seeing that he was committed to this thing, and backing down slightly now that the opportunity presented itself. 'I could try walking you home from the library, to begin with. Wouldn't that be the thing? And when you got used to me we could try something else. What do you say?'

Tissy looked instinctively to her mother. 'Up to you,

72

Tissy,' said Mrs Harper. She was nothing if not impartial, Lewis thought.

'What do you think, Doctor?' Lewis asked. Dragging himself forward in his chair the doctor seized Tissy's wrist, a gesture which surprised Lewis until he saw that it was made in order to feel the girl's pulse. The man's movements were undisciplined, awkward, yet it was cunning of him to feel Tissy's pulse at that particular moment.

'Can't do any harm,' he said. 'Give it a try.' He exchanged looks with Mrs Harper, then put his feet up, discarded the *New Statesman* from a small table at his side, picked up *Woman's Own*, and immersed himself in an article on how to brighten up the bathroom with a really stunning blind, special offer, see coupon on page 49. All this Lewis could see over the doctor's shoulder, since the doctor had moved centre stage and tended to ignore him. Once again he felt ousted from what should have been his natural position.

'More tea, Ralph?' asked Mrs Harper. He held out his cup without relinquishing his magazine, and when it was placed once again in his waiting hand took a deep and audible draught.

'Well,' said Lewis, a little stiffly now. 'I must be going. Nice to have met you, Dr Jago. Goodbye again, Mrs Harper. Tissy, I'll . . . '

'And what does Mr Percy do with himself?' asked the doctor, *Woman's Own* now folded back on a column of make-up tips for the over fifties.

'I'm just finishing my Ph.D. thesis,' he said eagerly. 'I should get my degree very shortly.'

'And what will you do then?' murmured the doctor, the crumbs of an iced biscuit nestling in a womanish cleft in his chin.

'I don't know. Get a job, I suppose. I really haven't thought that far ahead.'

'And what will you live on?' pursued the doctor, taking another biscuit.

'I don't know,' said Lewis. 'But my father left me some

money. Quite a lot, in fact.' For he thought £20,000 a great deal of money, more than he could ever earn. And he had so few needs that it was bound to last a very long time. Having delivered this information, which appeared to fall on deaf ears, there seemed to him to be nothing more to say.

When he finally made his escape from the house, which he found inordinately difficult, although no one made the slightest effort to detain him – indeed their indifference as to whether he came or went seemed a positive obstacle to his doing either – he raced down the street, taking enlivening gulps of fresh air. The impression of having been among aliens was hard to dislodge. He had never encountered such obliquity. And yet Tissy had smiled at him, and had, finally, when he reached the door, put her hand in his. This cheered him slightly, although he reflected that the gesture was minimal. He had the impression that the afternoon had been immensely difficult, not what he had hoped at all. But, he thought sadly, he had been too eager, too needy; this was always an unfortunate tactic. And he had made it too easy for them to behave badly. For he thought that they had behaved badly, even very badly. Perhaps they were naturally deficient in courtesy, as some people are born colour blind or tone deaf. And they had told him nothing about themselves. The mystery of Tissy's disability remained unsolved, nor were there any clues as to how it might be cured or what had induced it; at the same time it seemed to cause little concern. The doctor – who was obviously Mrs Harper's boyfriend, he thought, in a flash of intuition – had not given him the help he required, and required rather urgently. And yet the existence of this man, his weekly visits, argued that Tissy was becoming a charge, preventing him from doing whatever he wanted to do with Mrs Harper. Lewis turned from the idea with distaste; he thought that anything between the doctor and Mrs Harper would be disreputable, based on secret understandings that should never see the light of day. He thought it quite in order that they should eclipse themselves, seek exile, and not outrage more sensitive eyes with their unattractive alliance. To Lewis, a middle-aged liaison, out-side marriage, but with all the trappings of a settled affair, seemed deeply unheroic, not to be visited on the young. Clearly Tissy had been affected by what she might have guessed at. Except that with Tissy it was very hard to know how far she had progressed in adult understanding.

She was transparent, he supposed, remembering her long cool fingers lying in his, and transparency had once been his aim. Faced with the existence of it in another human being he was forced to think again. He had not come out of the experience too well, he reflected, remembering Mrs Harper's opaque gaze. Neither had they. Maybe they simply found it difficult to be pleasant. Tissy, he knew, was different because she was unspoilt. Nothing had occurred to mar the spotless record of Tissy's conduct. It was with some surprise that he had learned that she was twenty-seven, a few years older than himself. Such arrested innocence affected him painfully, as did her large eyes, which had looked up into his face with every expression of trust. He would simply try to see her outside the confines of that house, he thought. He retained a disagreeable after-image of the red room, the heat, and the melting sweetness of the food. He would in fact seek Tissy out tomorrow, before her mother turned up. And he would insist that they come to him next time; politeness demanded no less. That way, he felt, he might have the upper hand.

Unable to face supper, he ate a banana, hunted out his mother's copy of *The Constant Nymph*, and took it up to bed with him. It was all easier in books, he thought, especially in books written by women. They knew their feelings so well. He was more than ever unsure of his. But he supposed that it had been an experience, and one, moreover, which had had the advantage of making him feel very tired. He found that *The Constant Nymph* had nothing to say to him, so immersed was he in the difficulty of his position. He put out his light and was asleep almost immediately.

6

As the year slowly turned into summer the prospect of a major change began to fade. With his grief gradually losing its edge Lewis sought a way of life that would be appropriate without imprisoning him in false expectations. The long days and the light evenings bred in him a restlessness that he attempted to turn to his own account. He discovered that the way to deal with this life of his, in which everything was unresolved, was to behave as if he were a tourist in a foreign city. Even the house, in which he spent as little time as possible, gave him the impression that it belonged to somebody else. He escaped from it at an early hour, enjoying the effervescence of the morning streets with their air of hopefulness, purposefulness, promise; he viewed the workers with approval, although he was only going to the British Museum, and sometimes not even there. He ate all his meals out, drifted from one bookshop to another, returned home when he was too tired to stay away any longer. He felt guilty and free. But once back in his house, looking out of the window at the still intense sky, he might feel a darkness fall on him: he was lonely and could no longer ignore the fact. He would leave the house and go out into the garden, with a book and a cup of tea. Sometimes he would sit there until real darkness made reading impossible. Then he would get up with a sigh, wander round the now unkempt flowerbeds, incline his head to the magnificent yellow rose that flourished in spite of his neglect, and make his way regretfully indoors. Moving from the back to the front of the house always caused a sadness. Mounting the stairs to bed, he moved like a much older man.

This life lasted for perhaps six weeks: he no longer counted the days. He had virtually forgotten Tissy. He was aware that this was ignoble of him, but the memory of that red room and its secrets weighed too heavily on him, and was too much at odds with the life of semi-vagrancy that he seemed to have adopted. With this mood went a desire to be free of obligations, and although he knew that such a way of life was impossible he clung to his freedom, while knowing that at some point it must be relinquished. Through the incredibly hot days of July and early August he wandered, shabby now, and dazed with irresponsibility and also with anonymity: whole days passed with only minimal conversation. The hot weather imparted a sense of emergency: no serious behaviour could be undertaken in such conditions. 'Hot enough for you?' people said to each other, as they watered their gardens. Bare-armed, the population shrugged off gravity until the weather returned to normal.

The summer ended with disconcerting suddenness one evening. Thunder cracked and waves of rain sent Lewis running for cover. Regretfully he closed the doors that led from the drawing-room into the garden. He awoke in the night aware of a new chill in the air. The following morning he put his jacket on again, and turned his gaze reluctantly back to the matter of his life and its difficulties.

Eventually, a search for bracing certainties led him back to his work and the refreshingly clear-cut – or at least clearly stated – problems of masculine aspiration. Not that he had any definite ambition himself: he saw his path in life as eager and inexpert. Sometimes, in these days of early September, when he awoke in the morning, it was with a feeling of sadness and surprise that this mole-like existence was all he was to be allowed, this permission merely to continue. He put the feeling down to the isolation imposed by the final stages of his dissertation, and the long hours spent in the college library, to which he had returned out of a sudden sense of urgency. A certain trustingness saved him from anything more serious than the mildest form of despair. He made promises to himself that he hoped others might fulfil. Next summer, he thought, not noticing that the weather was still balmy, although the evenings were now dark. Indeed those very evenings, which he promised himself as a reward after a long day's reading, were in fact a torment to him, for it was then that he became aware that there was nothing in life that was close to his heart. He took to staying in the library until it closed at nine, and eating a sandwich in a coffee bar. That way, all that remained for him to do when he got home was to go to bed and try to summon his courage for another day.

His work was the only innocent area of his life, for in all other respects he felt guilty of multiple derelictions. He was aware that the house was grimed and dusty, and that his mother's plants had died. Sometimes he could not be bothered to make his bed. He invited no-one home, although he would have liked to have done so. A notion of hospitality pursued him but remained abstract. When I have finished the footnotes, he promised himself, but he could no longer ignore the fact that they were virtually complete. Anxiety and discomfort kept returning him to the body of the text, which he read with amazement. Had he done so much, thought so clearly, felt so deeply? When had this happened? He was reluctant to let the work go, for what would come after it? He already felt much older than the man who had undertaken the research, as if a naïf and sentimental self, a humble and dedicated self, were slipping away from him, leaving him only with a dull residue. His friend, Penry Douglas, with whom he sometimes ate his evening meal, told him that he was pushing himself too hard.

'Scholarship isn't a route march, Lewis,' he would say, lowering his glass coffee-cup and delicately dabbing his upper lip. 'It isn't a religion, either.'

'I thought it was,' Lewis said gloomily. 'I thought it would fill my life. As it is, there seems to be a lot left over. Life, I mean.'

'Scholarship', said Penry, 'is an occupation for gentlemen.'

'All very well you for, Pen. I'm neither a scholar nor a gentleman. I probably won't ever qualify for either position.'

'Don't be an idiot, Lewis. You're perfectly capable of doing what you are doing. The word is that you're brilliant, you know. Did you know that? But I see what you mean: you're not having a good time. You come trudging in with your briefcase every morning as if you've been turned out of your own house. You ought to be enjoying yourself more, getting more out of what you're doing. How's your girlfriend, by the way?'

But Lewis, having dropped Tissy's name rather ostentatiously in earlier days, could not now claim to have furthered her acquaintance. He considered Penry Douglas too good a man to be misled, and he rather wished he had never mentioned Tissy at all. He felt in many ways closer to Pen, whom he had known as a student, and who now worked in the library for which he, Lewis, was destined, than he thought he ever could to Tissy Harper and her enigmatic mother. He wondered what impulse of chivalry had ever made him want to rescue her. He believed that he would need to be rescued himself before he could contemplate so quixotic a course. And when he thought of Tissy he felt distress that he had set his sights so low. Only, with the distress went a feeling of constriction round his heart, as if the two of them were identified in some way, as if he felt sorry for them both, seeing them as equally vulnerable, equally endangered. And as if only with someone as undefended as Tissy Harper could he confess to his various feelings of shame and sorrow, and to the loneliness that sent him to bed as soon as he returned home in the evenings and kept him blackly asleep until dawn, when loneliness gave way to fear. How could he explain all this to Penry Douglas, a man of means who lived very comfortably and went to the opera and believed in God? The very real affection Lewis had for Pen he showed quite simply in not burdening him with these womanish sentiments, but in keeping friendship light and graceful, as Pen liked things to be, and not seeking him out as a confidant. The ultimate friend, the secret-sharer, he knew, must be a woman. And yet he also knew that the very act of sharing secrets would bind him and weaken him. Thus while valuing Pen for his optimism and good spirits Lewis kept his innermost thoughts to himself, wondering if they would ever be known, and, if known, accepted and validated.

The state of the house could no longer be ignored. He tried clearing up at the weekends, but the sensation of being a caretaker, or even his mother's ghost, frightened him so much that he usually gave up and went out. He was extremely confused as to what was expected of him. One day, tracing the smell in the kitchen to an ancient bottle of milk which had sent up a stalagmite of ice and coated a shelf of the fridge with a thick odorous deposit, it came upon him with the force of a revelation that he needed help. Not spiritual help, which was the sort that Pen always offered him, and not the sort of help that the promise of an eventual marriage held out, but plain practical help in the kitchen, a nebulous someone who would rinse out milk bottles and change beds and generally look after things while he was absent all day at the library. Someone whom he would not necessarily have to know, someone to whom he need have no commitment other than a certain amount of money to be paid each week. The idea that such a person might be available, that help might be forthcoming as soon as he put a card in the newsagent's window – for he did not doubt that there would be a rush to fill the post – inspired him to the extent of sitting down there and then to write out his requirements and to set out for the shop on the corner, where Mr Fisher, one eye closed against the smoke from his cigarette, scrutinized it and said, 'My sister-in-law might be able to help you out.'

'Really?' said Lewis. 'But I'd want someone local.'

Mr Fisher removed his cigarette, pinched it out, and laid it carefully on a ledge behind the counter.

'Lives upstairs, doesn't she? We had to give her the room when her husband left her. My wife's brother, that is. Can't say I blame him, between me and you; she's a bit of a misery. She's not afraid of work, mind you; anyway, I reckon she needs every penny she can get. We could have let that room for good money, but when it's your family . . . ' He made a large noble gesture. 'Name of Joliffe. Mrs Joliffe. Of course, she's got the boy, but he's no trouble. And then you're out all day, aren't you?'

Lewis wondered how Mr Fisher knew this but supposed that he was not entirely invisible, and reflected that his mother had known, and was no doubt known to, everyone in the neighbourhood. The fact that he did not like this man, he told himself, had nothing to do with the case. He had decided that all his feelings were unreliable. And the prospect of a Mrs Joliffe starting right away was enough to dispel any residual feelings of hesitation.

'Could you ask her to come round and see me?' he said. 'I'll be in this evening.'

'Well, Friday night, you know,' said Mr Fisher. 'She's entitled to a bit of relaxation, isn't she? Tell you what, I'll send her round first thing tomorrow morning. Then if you sort things out she can start the following week.'

This negotiation had proved to be mysteriously easy. Lewis set off for the library in a state of excitement, as if he had done something immensely significant. His unaccustomed vigour powered him to seek an interview with Professor Armitage, whom he found clearing his desk, and to announce to him that he had finished his thesis, that he was sending it to the typist, and that as soon as it was typed and bound, he would, with Professor Armitage's permission, and if possible his blessing, present it to the examiners.

'Excellent, Lewis, excellent. And I think I can promise you a favourable report. Did I mention the university press? Yes, well, something may come of that and I hope it will. Of course, it will soon be out of my hands, but I think my word still carries a little weight. What is your title, by the way?'

'I thought, "The Hero as Archetype".'

Professor Armitage pursed his lips and shook his head. 'Your other examiner won't like that, I'm afraid. Rather a sober-sided fellow, you know. Save your archetypes for the book, if there is one. Gravity should be your watchword for the time being. What about "Studies in behaviour in the nineteenth-century novel in France"? Or the nineteenth-century French novel. Whichever you prefer. Then give your dates. I think that should do. And of course you can always expand it later. You have a good subject there. Now, have you thought any more about what you are going to do in the future? I believe they are still looking for someone to help in the library. Would you like me to have a word with Dr Goldsborough?'

'Not yet,' said Lewis, who could not contemplate breaking so soon with his self-imposed routines. 'I'd rather wait until this is settled, if you don't mind.'

'As you wish, as you wish. You have some money to tide you over? Yes? Well, don't wait too long. We shall meet in due course, Lewis. And I shall always be pleased to hear how you are getting on.'

To Lewis the major event of the day was not Professor Armitage and his good-natured encouragement but the prospect of meeting Mrs Joliffe on the following morning. When he got home he submitted the house to a rigorous cleaning, sweeping the dust in wide arcs before him. He succeeded in defrosting the fridge, and pressed dirty laundry into two bags which he took to the launderette. The ironing he would leave to her, he thought, although he could have done it himself. But he had found the labour so exceedingly uninteresting that he vowed to pay Mrs Joliffe whatever she asked in return for his freedom. Saturday morning found him up early, breakfast cleared away by eight o'clock. At nine, as if in answer to his wish, the doorbell rang.

Mrs Joliffe looked like a woman who had suffered multiple

privations and had not come out of them too well. Gaunt and watchful, she was nevertheless powerfully made up; auburn hair with dark roots framed a face that reflected disgust with her lot, but sported a variety of colours. One of her legs was hampered by the clasped hands of a small boy of about two and a half, who still bore about his mouth the remains of a hasty breakfast. Their business proved to be mutually advantageous. It was quickly agreed that Mrs Joliffe should come in for three hours every morning, Monday to Friday.

'General duties,' said Lewis vaguely. 'Things have got a bit out of hand since I've been on my own. Would that be all right, Mrs Joliffe?'

'I reckon so,' she replied, without enthusiasm. 'Only I have to bring Barry with me. He's too young to start school yet. He's no trouble – if he's got his toys with him he'll play for hours. Would it be convenient for me to give him his lunch here? I could do the shopping on the way in and leave you something for the evening, if that's all right.'

'But that means you'll be staying longer than three hours,' said Lewis.

'The longer I'm out of that place the better,' was the heartfelt reply.

'Well, old chap, what do you say?' said Lewis, squatting down to meet Barry Joliffe's gaze. The child looked so sad that he could not bear to deny him a kitchen in which to eat his lunch and a garden to play in. He rather liked the idea of having a child in the house. And the little boy's bleak expression moved him, as did the thought of his being shut up in one room over the tobacconist's all day. 'Would you like to come here, Barry?' The boy removed from his mouth the corner of a toy truck he had been sucking and nodded.

'Splendid,' said Lewis. 'Well, I'll see you on Monday, Mrs Joliffe.' He handed her the spare key and they parted on good terms. She was not quite what he had envisaged, Lewis reflected. Not quite the spotless cheerful independent paragon on whom he had set his sights. He supposed that the services of such superior women were hotly contested, and the advantage of Mrs Joliffe was that she lived only five minutes away. And in any case, having made the initial effort he rapidly lost interest in the whole affair.

Mrs Joliffe turned out to be competent if unenterprising at preserving Lewis's household from further decay. But the novelty of finding a note on the kitchen table stating 'Fish pie in oven' was so overwhelming that Lewis was inclined to overlook Barry's toys left on the window sill. As the days passed, and as food was always left for him, he closed his mind to the fact that Mrs Joliffe and Barry occupied his house for most of the day. Now that he had surrendered his thesis Lewis found he had little to do and tended to come home earlier. On one occasion he saw Barry's face staring at him impassively from the window; on another he found Barry sitting in the middle of the drawing-room floor with his favourite toy, an egg cup containing a marble. Once, coming home later than usual, he found the house empty but inadvertently trod on the marble, stumbled across the room, and bumped his head on the mantelpiece. None of this bothered him greatly, although he took to buying small educational items such as picture and drawing books, which he left modestly on the kitchen table. He returned to find them stacked on the window sill, with the truck and other paraphernalia. He told himself that he liked this evidence of occupation. It was when he returned one evening to find the bathroom full of steam that a doubt crossed his mind. But 'Lamb chop under grill' enabled him to silence whatever qualms he was beginning to feel, and he decided to ignore the whole business until such time as he might have the energy to think about it.

There was no doubt that she was a vigorous cleaner, although she did not seem to be very clean herself. Surprisingly, she appeared to like the work, and applied herself spasmodically to what she was doing, although as far as he could see there was absolutely no method in it. Days of energy would be followed by intervals of torpor, when she apparently limited herself to the washing-up. But it

84

was good to see the polish restored to Grace Percy's fine round Victorian table, and her silver tea service gleaming once more. This emboldened him to invite Pen over one Saturday. They would have tea, he said, and go to a film.

'I like this house, Lewis,' said Pen, pulling a dark green handkerchief from his sleeve and honking into it. 'A good size, marvellous stuff in it. All late Victorian; such a relief after this modern rubbish. Terrific crewel work on those footstools. But look here, there's a scratch on this table. Do you see? That's very bad news. What have you been putting on it?'

'Barry must have been playing with his truck,' said Lewis glumly. He hated to see his mother's belongings so treated. He had never accepted the fact that they now belonged to him, and the thought made him sad. But the idea of coming home to an empty house after so blessed an interval dismayed him even further. Pen, however, was a householder who took a pride in his job.

'And there is his truck,' he said. 'And his ball. And his stuffed – what is it? Dog? Are you sure you couldn't get somebody better, Lewis? A regular house-keeper, for instance? This house is too good to be left to mercenaries.'

'I suppose it is a good house,' said Lewis. 'It belonged to my grandfather. He was a dairyman in Fulham. He bought this place when it was new. Everything here belonged to him originally. Then my grandmother lived here and eventually my father. My mother took to it and refused to change a thing. I like it here. But then I've always lived here.' Stealing quietly into his mind came the image of his mother, head on one side, with her book, by the fire. But he was not yet able to bear such images, and, starting up, poured Pen more tea.

'Don't let the house go under,' said Pen. 'Get someone else. Or better still, get married. Why don't you do that? Lots of people do. Not me, of course, but you could. And then there'd be no argument.'

'I'm afraid Mrs Joliffe might want to stay on,' said Lewis.

'A woman can deal with that sort of thing better than a man. Can't you get a woman to live with you? It's done all the time, I understand. After all, we're living in the 1960s. And frankly, you need a bit of looking after. That jacket, Lewis . . . You'd better let me take you to my tailor. You're not strapped for cash, I hope?'

'Oh, I've got plenty of money,' said Lewis.

He did not resent Pen's advice, but once he was left alone again, with the prospect of Sunday to get through (the Tate again, he supposed), his thoughts turned with some reluctance to Tissy Harper. He had behaved very badly, he reflected uncomfortably, in not going back to see her again, as he had promised, at the Public Library. To tell the truth, he had felt a certain distaste for all those women's novels with which he had comforted himself, and was at present immersed in *The Eustace Diamonds*. But that was not the point. What was needed was not an excuse but a reason. He had had no reason to seek out Tissy Harper again because he had managed to bury the part of him that ached to be consoled, sought out, preferred, in the more masculine excitement of finishing his work. And because he had become aware of the discrepancy between his work, so exalted in tone, and that awful red room, between the part of him that consorted with words and the inarticulate communication that passed wordlessly between Tissy and her mother, and that fearful doctor. He knew that he was destined to seek his home in language. But he also knew in his heart that he could not remain forever without a companion. Some restlessness in him – and maybe it was this feeling that he mistook for loneliness – informed him that the day would come when he would renounce everything and begin in earnest his real life, his true life, the life that at present somehow escaped him. He smiled as the thought came into his head. People did not seek their fortune any more, or at least not outside the covers of a book. And yet he thought that in time he might do so, although he knew that the hour was not yet come. Not yet, he thought; not yet. For to take that step he must be on his

86

own, unencumbered. And that was what he could not quite bear to contemplate. First he must be understood, accepted. Later he might seek his freedom.

Until that day came he could not live in an empty house. As if he had opened the doors of his mind to the idea of a woman, and of Tissy's large sad eyes, his desire woke him in the night. He was so startled by this, after a long period of quiescence, and so impressed by the programming of his body, that he determined to go back to her, the following week, if necessary. If only she weren't such a girl, he thought despairingly. If only he could get rid of her mother. And yet the thought of her in his house did not sit oddly with him. He liked her quietness, her delicacy. She was undiscovered; he liked that too. With her he need not be afraid. He smiled sadly to himself in the dark, for he knew the step was as good as taken.

Most men married because it was convenient, because the time was ripe. So he reasoned with himself, still aware of an old, old longing to be comforted. Passionate love affairs were not compatible with marriage. Marriage was a reasonable partnership, one that enabled a man to get on with his work. Still he felt sad, and his sadness extended to Tissy, who must be wondering about his defection and who did not yet know of his decision. Suddenly, after so long, so shameful a delay, he could not bear for her to have been hurt. His face burned in the darkness as he thought of her drooping head, her great eyes. She was blameless in all this! The life she lived was terrible, not to be endured! And he had been cruel to her, following her so clumsily, and then ignoring her for weeks. If anyone ever needed him it was Tissy, who would in return be faithful unto death. Who knew what she was thinking, what she had felt in the weeks when he had drifted away from her? Would she even speak to him again? His throat ached as he thought of her, and he took this for a form of love. It was the best he could do. Poor little girl, he thought.

Only it was not quite what he wanted, that was the

trouble. He had wanted to find his everything, his right true end. To have his house filled with a peaceable presence, and to feel a rightness, a oneness, a glow of good conduct. Never again to have to seek what he could not find at home, or to spend his leisure hours wondering how best they might be filled. This house, with its large windows and its bosomy furniture, was made for domesticity. It had a settled rather than a nuptial appeal: it would take his wife to its Victorian heart. There would be a minimum of adjustment. It was just that he had desired more, a coming to life . . . Not merely the declining sun, seen through the house's wide windows, but the blaze of noon, incandescence. No doubt such things were not easy to come by, he told himself; they probably only happened in books. Ah, but that was what he wanted to be, he thought: a character in a book. And when he had formulated this thought (and been very glad that he had not confided it to anyone else) he measured both his disappointment and its unwisdom. He was not to have a legendary life, he told himself. He was Lewis Percy, and he would probably take that job in the college library. The time had come for the shedding of illusions and the making of sensible decisions. He could no longer fill his house with the company of the Joliffes. He could not let them have the run of the place until they took root there and regarded it as their home. He had no family; that was what had to be taken into account. Therefore he must found a family of his own. He liked children and identified with them. Even Barry's unresponsive little face seemed to mirror something in his own. He would have children, many children. Maternity would free Tissy from her bonds. Together they would have some kind of real life, even if it were not the one he had always wanted.

The next morning he bathed, shaved, and dressed carefully. Pen was right; he was getting shabby. All that must now change. Out in the street he was aware that autumn, his favourite season, was well advanced, and he determined not to let another year pass without some semblance of normality in his own affairs. He felt a sense of acute displacement, and yet his steps seemed to be taking him in the direction of the Public Library. He was the first one there, and he was glad there was no one to witness the scene in which he had to take part.

It was all easy, easier than he had imagined. Tissy came over to him, gliding in that way of hers that he remembered. He heard himself apologizing for his long absence, heard her polite acceptance of his excuses, heard her say, 'I knew you'd come.' What she was thinking he could not begin to guess. She had, he thought, something of her mother's disconcerting lack of curiosity; he might never know what she was thinking. But she heard him out, and the reserve in her manner made him more and more determined to overcome it. He issued his invitation to tea for the following Saturday, and she promised to convey it to her mother. 'The only thing is,' she said, 'the doctor usually looks in on a Saturday.' 'Well, he can come and pick you up,' said Lewis firmly, for he did not see why he should have to entertain the doctor as well. It was arranged, with dreamlike ease, that Tissy and her mother should walk themselves down to his house at four o'clock, on the following Saturday, and that Dr Jago should collect them at half-past five. The thing was taking on the aspect of a military exercise, but then he supposed that was how it had to be done. The thought did not please him, but he managed to suppress it.

It was Mrs Harper who took care of the proceedings. Lewis found her neither more nor less intimidating than she had appeared at their first meeting. She was just as elaborately accoutred, and just as indifferent. In her company Tissy became a shadow of her always shadowy self, although he was pleased to see that her appetite was unimpaired. Mrs Harper, once provided with an ashtray, let her gaze roam round the room quite peaceably, possibly took an inventory, but evinced no opinions. She managed to call him 'Lewis', which was a good sign. He knew, however, that she would always make him uneasy, and he wondered at her peculiar power. When the bell rang he was quite surprised, for he did not see how so much time had passed when so little had happened. He counted the afternoon a disappointment, and got up to let in the doctor with a feeling of failure.

The doctor sank into a chair, still wearing his ill-judged hat and coat. As before, crumbs descended from his plate onto his burgeoning stomach. But the doctor made up in amiability what Mrs Harper lacked, and soon Lewis found himself discussing his future, or as much of it as he thought might interest him.

'And what about a job, Lewis?' asked the doctor, still amiably. Lewis registered the fact that he had become 'Lewis' to the doctor as well.

'I've been offered a job in the college library,' he said, with a slight sinking of the heart. (But that was to be expected, he told himself.)

'Quite a coincidence,' mused the doctor. 'You and Tissy both being in the same line of work.' After that there was a short silence, until Mrs Harper expressed a desire to see the rest of the house.

When he saw them out he felt a curious relief. Their presence, he reflected, was onerous, yet it left him with a desire for Tissy's unsponsored company. If that could be arranged – and he had mentioned a play, a film, not knowing what she would like – he foresaw no great difficulty in finding out more about her. She was limpid, he thought. And the very enigma of her deeper feelings was beginning to obsess him. She had shown no very great excitement, keeping her beautiful eyes modestly lowered, but there was colour in her cheeks. 'I like to look at pictures,' she had said.

'Tissy has always been artistic,' said her mother distantly.

So he would take her to museums, to galleries. That suited him very well. He would suggest this as soon as . . . As soon as what? There was no reason to delay. He wandered out into the chilly garden. All this is less than heroic, he said to himself quietly, very quietly, so as not to disturb his resolution. But then for a man life is a desperate business. One must seek what refuge is available. All this makes sense, and yet it is a disappointment. The worst thing – and I must face the fact now – is that happiness simply doesn't come into it. Tissy must never know. She must think I love her, which I almost do. Not too much: it would break her. Terrible, terrible half-measures, for which I shall surely pay. But she must not be hurt, she must be happy. Raising his face to the empty sky, he murmured, Please let me do well.

7

There are those for whom the performance of a duty, however tedious or unpleasant, is a reward in itself. Such people are rare, although one comes upon them from time to time. Tissy Harper, once she had become Tissy Percy, seemed to find fulfilment in the role of being married, and of performing like a married woman, although Lewis was never quite sure whether or not this entirely satisfied her. This he put down to his false expectations of happiness: both great literature and unpretentious fiction had taught him that he would experience some kind of apotheosis, which would leave him dazed but mysteriously matured once its effects had died away. He had been encouraged to think of the first months of marriage as a kind of saturnalia, a permitted period of extravagance, after which he would be summoned to join the ranks of the adults. But if he had expected folly and licentiousness for however short a time he was to be disappointed, or perhaps less disappointed than surprised, for Tissy at once assumed a grave air of maturity that accorded ill with all his prognostications. Within thirty-six hours of marrying him her demeanour changed: for the better, he was forced to admit. Ranging round his house, which she accepted in its totality, she discovered treasures that his mother or even his grandmother, when widowed, might have put away for ever, thinking they had no place in a reduced life, a life without men. Thus Lewis would return in the evening to find silver trays, polished and refulgent, bearing decanters with silver throats and labels, or elaborate china tureens and sauceboats on the sideboard, waiting, with the huge platters that had once borne gargantuan joints of meat, to be reintegrated into the fabric of their married life. The excavations and the renovations undertaken by Tissy, the care she devoted to what he supposed were his belongings, and in some way his inheritance, the dynastic seriousness with which she made inventories, impressed upon him that he had married a more substantial woman than perhaps he had intended to do. While he had seen in her the frail companion whose intimacy he need not fear, the secret-sharer of his imaginings who would come to grateful life in his embrace, she had possibly had no such insights, and simply regarded being a married woman as occupation enough. Such duties as a married woman might expect to have were construed by her with a narrowness that accorded with her narrow face, her narrow frame, and although Lewis would wistfully try to detain her in the early mornings before they were both dressed she would break away almost sternly, as if he were asking her to infringe certain rules. These rules were not rules of propriety – for she assented to his overtures without demur – but rather rules of employment. Her curatorial role seemed to leave her little time for leisure or even for conversation, although she never failed to enquire after the progress of his work or of his day. 'And where did you have lunch?' she would ask. 'Did you see Pen today?' She had only met Pen briefly at the wedding but had taken him on as part of her husband's furniture. 'We must have him to dinner soon,' he suggested, while wondering if it would be in order to invite Pen's friend, George Cheveley. But the problem was shelved as Tissy revealed further programmes of restoration. 'Wait until I've washed the curtains,' she might say. 'And a lot of the bedlinen needs replacing. Wait until I'm straight.'

He supposed that she was happy enough. But how much happiness was enough? He had expected, for himself, an almost mythological state, a metamorphosis, and it was true that on some mornings he felt his feet virtually skimming the pavement. He liked, too, the sensation of returning home to what was in fact becoming a small marital museum, virtuous with household tasks punctiliously performed. He thought of Tissy sentimentally, as his child bride, yet she was in effect shedding her childishness; even her disability seemed to constrain her less, although her mother still collected her every morning and took her shopping. As her expression was always grave, even in the intimacy of their bedroom, he often wondered, with a touch of uneasiness, what she was thinking. She had assumed that maternal air of women who regard men as children, to be kept clean and fed, and disciplined out of unruly thoughts. Such women look on the activities that captivate men as nonsense and men themselves as fantasists: their calculating and repressive gaze establishes members of their sex as persons possessing a more mature understanding of the world and its priorities. Tissy had such a measuring look, while her responses remained soft and dutiful. Her voice was never raised, but the great eyes, which were basically without expression, sometimes ranged beyond him, as if preoccupied with weightier matters, as if the infinite were no longer contained in what he had to offer her; they would return to rest on him with absolute and dispassionate calm. He began to see a resemblance to her mother, and was almost amused.

He had no time for Mrs Harper and was reassured by her absence. One of Tissy's more discreet achievements was to confine her mother's visits to the mornings. She was willing to go shopping with her but not to keep her company as before. Very occasionally Mrs Harper was allowed to visit at the weekends, but such visits were in the nature of a favour conferred. Reduced to pointlessness, and possibly loneliness, Mrs Harper (and to Lewis she would always be Mrs Harper, although he conscientiously addressed her by her Christian name) had utterly lost her ability to offend him. He supposed too that Tissy, who, although good as gold, was only human, rather enjoyed this reversal of roles. Through the agency of her marriage she was at last permitted to view her mother from a position of equality.

Of course his feelings were impure. Whose feelings are not? He had thought to subdue her and to release her simultaneously, whereas he now found himself taken for granted. He loved her for her wifeliness, which told him where he stood, established him as a man with a social position, yet felt a little dismayed at having his romanticism brought so impassively to heel. He supposed her to have been mysterious all along, and, despite himself, thrilled to the long-term prospects of loving an enigmatic woman. She was not what she seemed: that was his most tentative conclusion. She had, despite her mild appearance, something like authority. That this authority was entirely passive gave it a curious additional weight. As to her inner thoughts and reflections, which were hidden from him, he had no idea of how to gain access. He tried not to dwell on what, for him, amounted to a disappointment which he knew to be inappropriate, for he felt gratitude and devotion when he saw her sitting in his mother's place, filling what had been to him an intolerable void, and serving him his soup with the great silver ladle which she had found, black with tarnish, at the back of a cupboard in the kitchen. He loved the orderliness of his home, the shining windows, the laundered sheets, the smell of wax polish. She had even subdued Mrs Joliffe, who now only came on two mornings a week and took her bearings accordingly. Of the little boy there was no further sign. Lewis rather missed him, but had to acknowledge Tissy's mastery in the matter.

All these tasks she performed as one called to higher service. When he would telephone her during the day, having been visited by an amorous thought, she would say, 'I can't linger, Lewis. I'm washing the paint. What time will you be home?' He supposed that she was old enough to behave like this, although he himself felt frivolous in comparison. It was as if the few years' difference in their ages had been multiplied by two or even by five. When he returned in the evening he would greet her ardently, willing and even anxious to delay dinner, and she would usually disengage herself without much more than a smile. This smile, he sometimes thought, was directed at him, or over his head, to an unseen crowd of witnesses, and he wondered why desire should have to be postponed so often. When, however, postponement was no longer in order, she was acquiescent, competent, even intelligent. But she was not silly, not the mindless grateful creature he had occasionally entertained in his imagination. He gained the impression that she was prepared to accommodate him as part of the arrangement, but that she would not be much put out if they settled down together as brother and sister. Her hitherto excessive shyness and timidity he ascribed to the influence of her mother and the regular visits of the odious doctor. Together they had kept her subservient, childlike – in her shape, her movements, her air of concentration – but she was no longer timid. His embraces were permitted and even indulged, but she allowed no passionate exhibition to derogate from her dignity. He sometimes felt ashamed of his own insistence, in comparison with which she displayed a propriety which disconcerted him. This merely intrigued him further, although it sometimes made him feel downcast. He felt, obscurely, that she lived on a higher plane than he did, and therefore considered himself to be at fault.

Her status, which had been augmented by marriage, was precious to her. To see evidences of her in his bedroom, to see her wide-skirted dresses hanging in his wardrobe, her pale stockings rolled in the drawer of the tallboy, sometimes gave him a pang of longing for her but also revealed a shocking loneliness. It was not exactly what he had wanted. His acquiescence at the reasonableness of her manner and at the life that she denied him – and that he would now never have – he disguised as a sort of jaunty tolerance which nevertheless had something tired about it. He longed for her to overwhelm him, to seduce him, or even just to surprise him. But nothing came, and he was too puzzled ever to allude to this disappointment and too good-natured ever to complain about it. He supposed that men talked to other men about these matters, but he swore to himself that he would never betray Tissy, or indeed his own desires. He blamed himself for not loving her properly, but knew that he lacked the courage to live alone and wait for the woman whom destiny had reserved for him, if such a woman existed. And if she did not? He would always seek the company of women, and, if permissible, their love: his own, he felt, was simply waiting to be engaged. How, then, could he have ignored Tissy, when she had languished within his reach? How could he ignore her transformation into contented housewife? For he supposed that she was contented, having escaped her thraldom, having graduated to the adult world. What she felt for him he did not quite know. There was something obedient about her that saddened him. Yet she seemed perfectly happy.

He sought to make her understand that she could now express herself. He was still beguiled by her innocence, to which his physical response was never lacking. He loved to adorn her. Fashion now dictated that the wide-skirted dresses should be put away. He bought her the new short skirts, which gave her a bewitching air of juvenility. With her thin legs and her slightly knock-kneed stance on view, she lost some of her dignity, and with it her ability to repress him: he was correspondingly grateful. He watched entranced as her long beige hair was cropped into a geometrical shape which made her eyes look even bigger. No longer dowdy in her matronly clothes, she began to attract glances in the street. When they walked down the King's Road on a Saturday afternoon – for she waited for him before doing the weekend shopping, still a little uncertain about her ability to go out alone – he felt a glow of pride and told himself that he was now in truth a married man. His reward would come later, when his wife was confident enough to shed her wifeliness. At the same time he warned himself not to frighten her with his ardour. He had waited so long that he could wait a little longer before coming into his own.

He was also beguiled by her fastidiousness. She was as

neat and as silent as a cat. After a day spent putting his house to rights she would devote much time to her own upkeep, spending what seemed like hours in the bathroom while he lay wistfully in bed waiting for her. He sometimes had the feeling that she was the cleanest person in the world, and felt coarse and gross in comparison. He teased her, but she was so absorbed in the problems of her hygiene and her appearance that his teasing had little effect. He supposed that she was used to thinking of herself as frail, yet he could see that this was not entirely the case. Bottles of lotion began to accumulate on her dressing-table, and when she finally entered his bed various tonic scents came with her, as if the whole human organism had been swept and garnished. He was proud of her and amused by her in equal measure; he was even impressed by her, although he was forced to wonder what went on in her heart, or even to wonder whether that heart had not atrophied during the long years of her claustration. He still waited for her to come to life, and was forced to regard the many ways in which she performed her marital role as a long and brilliant form of delay. He had acquired, simultaneously, an excellent wife, whose competence he could only value and admire, and a sort of artefact, which, like the automata in *The Tales of Hoffmann*, came to life when he was not there. For it seemed impossible to believe that he knew all there was to know of her, and that what he did know was enough to last him for the rest of his life.

He was not unhappy, far from it. But sometimes he felt a sense of relief in leaving for work, for that library in which the rules were so clear, so reassuring, and so manifestly without guile. He had of course accepted Professor Armitage's offer as soon as he had contemplated marriage; once he had received his doctorate he could no longer postpone a sort of career, the only kind for which he was fitted. Just as his glasses precluded anything of an athletic nature, he thought his scholarly pursuits ruled out higher ambition, or indeed ambition of any sort, as if he had taken a vow of mental chastity. He sank into the routines of the library gratefully rather than otherwise, glad to be in familiar surroundings, glad to see Pen's head and shoulders at a distant desk, glad to be so virtuously employed. If he was also a little disappointed (here too) he had no grounds for complaint: the job was modest but intellectually respectable, and after all doctorates were two a penny these days. He was allowed one free afternoon a week for research, and this time he devoted to the labour of turning his thesis into a book, for he had been encouraged to submit his material to the university press. The rest of his time he spent cataloguing articles in the many publications that were allotted to him. This subject index kept him in touch with work in his field and even with work outside it. It was not uninteresting; it had a certain dignity. He was aware that he needed a dignity of his own, and was glad to find it in his work. As time went on he became thankful for the humble tasks that fell within his competence, grateful for the rite of passage that had turned him from a student into a wage-earner, grateful for the very books in the stacks. But he was still surprised to find himself on the bus every morning, with his briefcase, and again at lunchtime, drinking a half of lager with Pen; he was surprised to be taken seriously as an adult when he felt so much in need of care and concern. Sometimes he thought back to his time in Paris as if it were half a lifetime ago. He still unconsciously sought that glow of protection which had enabled him to sustain his indeterminate status and thus, in an entirely mysterious way, get on with his work. Now he felt falsely grown up, masquerading as an adult, a working man, in fact, part of the labour force. He worried that his brain might suffer. And yet, as far as he could see, his brain had not registered the change and continued on its course, indifferent to the circumstances that hedged it about.

The one irritant in this atmosphere of false serenity – for he was aware of, even bemused by its artificiality – was Arnold Goldsborough, the chief librarian and his nominal boss. Florid, large, shapeless, with rosy curls blossoming above his collar, Goldsborough's welcoming appearance was undermined by his cautious eye, which was oblique, like that of a halibut. He bore, like an oriflamme, his elaborate name – 'Goldsborough!' he would announce, holding out a comradely hand when meeting a new acquaintance: no one escaped. He was something of a true scholar, but, like many a scholar he needed the plaudits of the crowd, was shrewd, an entertainer, not good on his own. It gave him pleasure to hear his witticisms – of which the most famous was 'Only deconstruct' – quoted by students. Officially, in his capacity as practitioner of the new criticism, he was a marauder, a manhandler, busy taking the text away from the author and turning it into something else. In Goldsborough's hands no writing was safe. He trembled on the verge of intoxicating double meanings, inadvertences, involuntary confessions. Most of his time in the library was spent corresponding with colleagues in France, sacking the temple of language and redistributing the spoils. Feet of clay were discovered everywhere. Yet he was essentially a simple man, genuine, naïf, even timid, one who advanced his cautious sideways eye with suspicion, ready to resist any infraction of his code. Code was another of his favourite words. He was currently applying his technique to an anthology of artists' letters, a bold move which combined colonizing ingenuity with, he thought, valid enquiry. The delicate and seductive language employed for this task took up his entire attention, and it seemed unfair to ask him to settle more mundane matters; indeed, Lewis owed his position to Goldsborough's pre-occupation. Yet he was adept at reinforcing his seniority, while at the same time dismissing it as an obstacle to the higher thought. A show of exaggerated patience would be combined with a suspicious look from his small glaucous eye. Since requests for his authorization were never more than formal, the intrusion into his private thought process was not serious. Nevertheless, petitioners came to expect the moment when his pencil was flung down and the phrase 'I cannot take the responsibility' was uttered.

'Why does he say he can't take the responsibility, when I am merely asking him an entirely reasonable question that affects nobody but myself?' Lewis asked Pen one lunchtime.

'I suppose he thinks you're showing too much initiative. *Point de zèle*, Lewis. Unbecoming in a newcomer. Just remember that although you could do this job with both hands tied behind your back, your official apprenticeship will last for several years. To Goldsborough you will always be a tongue-tied juvenile.'

'But I merely wanted to start giving the index to Hilary to type.'

'You don't mean to say you've brought it up to date?' said Pen, scandalized. 'Don't you understand? You're supposed to be doing that for the rest of your life.'

'Don't joke; this is too serious. Of course I haven't brought it up to date. You were joking, weren't you? I only thought it would be easier to read if it were typed and on larger cards. There's nothing to stop me adding to it. In fact it would be easier if the cards were larger. But he said he couldn't take the responsibility. I rather thought it would be mine. Responsibility, I mean.'

'Maybe that's what he didn't like,' said Pen. 'He's the anal type. Don't take it personally. He really only wants to be left alone to get on with his work. I can't blame him; neither should you. You want to get on with yours, don't you?'

Lewis brooded. 'Of course I don't object to his work, far from it. It seems eminently respectable. But does he have to dress up for it? I thought Bohemian life went out with the nineteenth century. Long before, in fact.'

'Oh, come on, it's all quite harmless. Why shouldn't he strike a pose if he wants to? He's quite a sound man, I believe, or so I hear from people I more or less respect. Not my field, of course.'

'But the clothes!' said Lewis. 'The Aristide Bruand hat. The long red scarf. The way he's always explaining his theories to nubile girls over a drink.'

'Ah, well, that's a common weakness. The thing to remember about Goldsborough is that he's entirely harmless. At the same time, and probably for that reason, he likes to think of himself as a seriously Rabelaisian character. Actually, he works quite hard. Many's the time I've come past late at night and seen his light still on.'

Lewis still looked worried; in truth he was shaken to find that he had doubted another's innocence. It was, he thought, the first time he had done this, and he did not like the idea.

Pen ordered another round. 'The trouble with you, Lewis, is that you're a prig. Cheer up, old son. It can be our secret.'

'Yes,' said Lewis sadly. 'I daresay you're right. But in the meantime I've got to do the whole index by hand because he can't take the enormous responsibility for the consequences if Hilary starts typing it. Oh, come on, Pen. Is this serious?'

'Only if you let it annoy you. It's not bad work, you know. We're not making munitions or anything. It's a decent place, decent people. And he's probably right about those cards, as you'll very soon agree. I thought you'd be less restless by now. Everything's all right, isn't it?'

'Oh, yes,' said Lewis. 'Everything's fine.'

He spent the afternoon going through the papers of a learned symposium and took an article on Delacroix to Goldsborough in a spirit of penitence. He was greeted by the flung-down pencil. 'If it's about changing the cards, Lewis . . .'

'I thought you might like to see this,' said Lewis. 'I thought it might be in your field.'

'Oh, my dear fellow, I was there. I heard that paper. I thought it was quite inadequate. Still, I'll glance at it again, just leave it there, will you? Good of you to notice it. Off, are you?' He glanced at his watch. 'Yes, I suppose it is six o'clock. I'll have to stay on for a bit. No time off for me, you know.' 'Come!' he sang out to a timid knock on the door. 'Yes, well, if that's all, Lewis, I'll see you tomorrow.' Lewis left, nodding to a girl in a very short skirt, with an official-looking notebook in her hand. 'Pippa, my dear, where were we?' he heard as he closed the door behind him.

Leaving the building he hesitated, unwilling to sacrifice the beautiful evening so soon. The idea of the bus was distasteful to him and he decided to walk home. What was wrong with him, he reasoned, was that he did not take enough exercise. As he thought this he became aware of a very slight residual sadness which he decided to put down to the effect of a day spent in the drugged atmosphere of the library, to the silence, and the fiendish radiators. Whatever the reason, he was not anxious to get home without some kind of an interval for rumination, some time to call his own. The idea of covering a long distance appealed to him. Gentlemen in Trollope, to whom he was devoted, even more than to his early heroes, covered vast distances and were thus able to sustain their noble thoughts. Mr Wharton, in *The Prime Minister*, was said to do his round of the parks every Sunday, whereas he, Lewis, merely trudged from his house to the bus-stop every morning, and from the bus-stop to his house every evening. He resolved to walk home regularly, and to tell Tissy to expect him an hour later than his usual time.

He walked through the clamorous Strand to Trafalgar Square, down the Mall to Victoria, and then into Pimlico Road and Sloane Square. Then it was merely a matter of following the King's Road until he got to the Common. He found himself energized, even excited by the movement of his feet, and began to formulate thoughts as to how he could recast his introduction. Unwittingly, and even unwillingly, he made a connection between the freedom of his thoughts and the freedom of his temporary respite. Free! But he had never wanted to be free, or had not thought he did. He took off his glasses (now horn-rimmed and more professional) and registered a blur of lights. So doing, he managed to recapture some of the rhythm of earlier evenings, when nothing much awaited him except the little ceremony in the salon, during which he could give himself over to attentiveness and his own thoughts. But that was nothing, surely, to what he had now. He put on his glasses again, and the queue outside the cinema sprang into relief. Now he had everything that was appropriate to a man of his age. Only he was not quite at ease, and this he did not understand. I should have waited, he thought, and suppressed the thought. His life with Tissy, with Goldsborough, was a reasonable life, even an enviable life. And yet he was lonely. The sight of an almond tree just coming into blossom moved him beyond measure, making him aware of a zone of vulnerability round his heart. It is only the season, he thought, this fag-end of winter that makes me yearn. It happens every year. But again came that desire for gratification, for more blossom than this modest tree could afford him, acres of blossom, nature in abundance. He wondered if he might take Tissy to Provence for Easter, so that they both could witness such things. But she remained reluctant to go away. Her agoraphobia, now minimal in London, tended to return when he suggested going further afield. He saw that he might have to defer to her on this, for at least as long as she still lacked confidence, and that he would have to put in more patient work before she would be free enough to take her strength from his.

And his strength? He was still not a hero, never less. Just a man walking home from work, guiltily aware that he had not telephoned his wife to tell her that he would be late. This life, this moderate life of his, seemed to close in on him, as did the lights in the windows, glowing prudently behind drawn curtains. He felt circumscribed by the decency of his surroundings. Once, not so long ago, he would have wished to be safe inside one of those houses, behind those drawn curtains. Now he felt a dull ache of longing for something else, something that he could not identify. Speak to me, he thought; tell me who you are. But he did not know to whom this plea was addressed.

He passed the awful post-war flats, the Texaco station, the fly-blown newsagent's, above whose premises he imagined Mrs Joliffe to be sitting glumly with Barry. Nearing home, his steps imperceptibly slowed down. The rest of the evening stretched before him: dinner, a little conversation, of the kind he could easily anticipate, then his book, until it was time to go to bed. Tissy read less now that she had left the library. She seemed quite happy to sit with him, or to watch television, but he was aware of her silence, and felt obliged to look up on occasion to ask her if she wanted anything. It was time they invited some people round, had a dinner party. Her cooking was up to it, though it was not exciting; the liquor in her stews and casseroles was always a little too thin. He had more feeling for food than she did. He always enjoyed the shopping expeditions, urging her to buy more. Every fruit, every vegetable seemed to have within it a promise of earthly delights. But she usually demurred. 'Someone has to watch the money,' she said.

The cleanliness of the beautiful evening died on his skin as he shut the front door behind him and sniffed the familiar aroma of his mother-in-law, the Messalina of the suburbs: cigarettes mingled with slightly stale *Vol de Nuit*. Something expansive, even unbuttoned in the atmosphere told him that the doctor was also present, a fact which he found particularly unwelcome. A spasm of dislike for these people who had fashioned his wife into the sort of companion he feared she would always remain shot through him with the speed of lightning, a visitation from the unconscious, which, like all such visitations, gave no warning. Forcing himself guiltily into a good humour he sang out a greeting, lingering as he examined the letters on the hall table.

'At last,' he heard Mrs Harper remark.

'Well, Thea,' he said. 'This is a surprise. Hello, Doctor. Hello, darling, sorry I'm late. I decided to walk home.'

Tissy rose to greet him, kissed him on the cheek, then returned to her chair, as if anxious not to offend her mother.

'I've been so worried,' she said. 'I didn't know what could have happened to you. I was so upset that I had to ring Mother.'

'Fortunately I was at home,' said Mrs Harper. 'Ralph had just looked in, so we both came round. I hope you won't go in for this sort of thing, Lewis. Any kind of strain is bad for Tissy. She's not strong, you know.'

He saw that there was a tray of tea on the table and he helped himself to a cup. The cups were frail and pretty, from a service long since put away.

'I only walked home, you know. I'm going to do it regularly, so don't worry if I'm later than usual, darling. I should have telephoned, I suppose. I'm sorry. But there was no need to disturb your mother. Or the doctor,' he added, seeing that the doctor, lying supine in an armchair, was all set to remain for the evening. He had removed his hat and coat, which now lay on the sofa. His creased grey eye was focused on Tissy and came only briefly to rest on Lewis.

'We don't want our girl upset,' he said judiciously, re-removing a fleck of something from his tongue. 'We don't want her under a strain.' He heaved himself out of his chair and took Tissy's wrist between his fingers.

'She's not under a strain,' said Lewis, deeply annoyed. 'She's perfectly well. Good Lord, I should know. She never complains about her health.'

'Ah, but she wouldn't,' sighed the doctor, replacing a lock of hair which had fallen over Tissy's forehead and fondling her cheek. 'Come on, Thea. They don't want us hanging around. They want to be on their own.'

Lewis smiled grimly, determined to say nothing. But, seeing them about to leave, he relented, pressed Mrs Harper's arm, and said, 'Don't worry. I'll take care of her.'

Mrs Harper's voluptuously lipsticked mouth trembled a little, but she looked at him with disdain. She must be very lonely, he thought, while Tissy helped the doctor on with his coat. She would never forgive him for taking her daughter away. And yet he felt sorry for her, in her sad middle age, with only the doctor to care for her. For the doctor himself he felt hatred, steady and mounting.

'Tissy,' he said, later in the evening, when they were washing the dishes. 'What was your father's name?'

'William,' she said without hesitating, but her eyes rolled round like a doll's.

He let her go to bed first and sat in his old place, staring at the unlit fire. Not her fault, he thought; not her fault. He resolved to make it up to her. But in the corner of his mind, along with that surprising, even shocking gesture of the doctor tucking away Tissy's wayward lock of hair and taking her face in his obstreperous hand, came the sensation of freedom that he had rediscovered on his long walk. Again, with that unwelcome lucidity that was the curse of this particular evening, he thought that this might be the only freedom he was in future to be permitted to enjoy.

8

Tissy allowed her fashionable hair to grow long again. Within a remarkably short space of time she had reverted to her original appearance. Her virginal gentility, which had mysteriously survived marriage, disconcerted Lewis but left him without a valid reason for questioning its persistence: he supposed it to be innate, something akin to the odour of sanctity. Sometimes, despite her rigorous exertions and her still watchful housekeeping, she seemed like a ghost around the house. He said nothing. The only sign of his own evolution was to be sought in the breaks and tremors in his hitherto regular handwriting, which now ran faintly but persistently down towards the corner of his catalogue cards. In the library the silence was intense, broken only by the unconscious sigh of a student oppressed by a particularly weighty volume, or the rattle of Goldsborough's tin of blackcurrant pastilles as he moved bulkily towards the index: his progress, despite his hushed step, reminded Lewis of an animal in a dry watercourse. Across the greenish expanse he could see Pen, elegant even in shirtsleeves, head bent over the booksellers' catalogues he was marking up for Goldsborough's final inspection. Hours passed slowly, the clock, like God, sometimes an ally, sometimes, more frequently, an enemy.

He always walked home now. It would not have occurred to him to make an excuse for this stratagem, which was one of delay, and yet he could not bring himself to give the true reason for it. Tissy had ceased complaining; he sensed a with-drawal in her. Her earlier timidity had hardened into a kind of refusal to engage which was in fact a sign of strength rather than weakness. Her silences were loaded with criticism, yet they were maintained as silences, and they became more elo-quent than the words they suppressed. There was no open disagreement between them. Their routines were so estab-lished that they moved with an automatic accord through their daily lives. Sometimes it seemed to Lewis that their value to each other was as a foil for what was essentially an individual experience of solitude, which, borne alone, might strike either one of them down with intolerable perplexity: with the other there neither could feel totally abandoned. Yet for each of them a peculiar loneliness was an older, perhaps a more natural experience than companionship, and perhaps there was a recognition of the inevitable, even a rapture, in succumbing once again to this experience, which was felt to be archaic, predestined. Down they sank, through all the pretences, through the eager assumption of otherness that each had sought in marriage, down to that original feeling of unreality, unfamiliarity, with which they had first embraced the world. With this, a recognition of strangeness between them, as if each were puzzled by the continued presence of the other. From time to time there was a coming together; afterwards they took leave of each other, like partners at the end of a dance. Neither blamed the other, for there was no specific cause. But Lewis began to feel that his life was a dream from which he would presently awaken to reality.

Even this state he found useful, predetermined, neces-sary, for it was powerfully conducive to the elaboration, and even the justification of his book, which was now recognizably a book, and no longer the raw vehicle of his youthful enthusiasms. He seemed to be writing it in a life parallel to the real life he lived with his wife, yet he found them both to be profoundly mysterious, even enthralling, and occasionally antithetical. Sometimes he felt himself to be more truly authentic when contemplating a shift in the fortunes of a fictional character than when talking to Tissy, or attempting to talk to her, for when he got home in the evenings she was usually watching television, and, not considering himself entitled to disturb her, he would go to the kitchen and there eat the dinner which had been left for him on a plate in the oven, like a message in a tomb.

He thought that it was nobody's fault that they had become so imperceptibly estranged, although Tissy, in one of her rare moments of eloquence, blamed his work, towards which she entertained feelings of hostility. At first this reaction seemed to Lewis so primitive that he refused to take it seriously. Her mother, he knew, shared it and even encouraged it, as if *The Hero as Archetype* were the equivalent of an infidelity. Mrs Harper was openly censorious and assumed an air of pinched indifference whenever the work was mentioned. He had noticed something of this on the occasion of their first meeting, at the tea party which had seen the launch of his marital plans: as to who had launched them he was still unclear, and preferred to remain so. But the mulishness of his wife whenever it was a question of his authorship or his ambitions was quite clear, overwhelmingly so. She saw his book as an insult to herself, and little by little he learned not to mention it. He felt guiltily aware that she was right, that it *was* an infidelity, for when he was writing it he no longer thought of her, and if he had it would have been to consider her as an unrealized character whom the author had failed to develop. The writer in him would have tried to devise for her some enlightening experience which would cause all the inhibitions to disappear, yet the husband knew that he had intended this all along, hoping that marriage itself would perform the miracle.

It now seemed to Lewis as if his wife would remain for ever within the tight small circle of her limitations, and even that it was policy on her part to reject anything or anyone outside the circle. Her disability had left her suspicious: what he had originally seen as pure timidity was in effect an act of retrenchment. She proclaimed to the world,

'You may come so close and no closer.' Therefore the wider world, and all that pertained to it, was viewed as disruptive, annoying, unnecessary. Lewis's refusal to accept her standards, her parameters, she regarded as threatening. Even his desire to walk home was perceived as a kind of insult, an action personally and potentially damaging to herself.

She saw no need for him to write a book. She had an idea that this not only excluded her but cancelled her, and in this she was right. Lewis could see no way of convincing her that she occupied one part of his life and his book another. He was not comfortable about this but he was genuinely unable to see what he was supposed to do about it. He still had desires for greatness, openness, some kind of apotheosis: sometimes, even walking the city streets, his heart would expand with joy at the beauty of the world and its possibilities. He had learned to see eternity in a grain of sand, or rather in the simplicity and the beauty of a tree in a suburban garden. He still hoped for some kind of transforming experience, of translation to another place, even another country, where nature was more beneficent, more prodigal than even he could imagine. His little book was to him part of this upward progress. And Tissy would come with him. He had never thought of leaving her behind. She would come with him and he would teach her to be happy. Or rather he would try again, hoping that this time she would shake off her restraints and her apprenticeship. It did not even occur to him to wonder why this process was taking so long, for he had patience enough for both of them. Occasionally he might feel melancholy, but he told himself that this was tiredness, or that he was getting a little dull, and once more, mentally, he promised them both a holiday, just before remembering how impossible it was to dislodge Tissy from her iron habits and from the boundaries which she drew around their lives.

He bought her flowers, chocolates, not in an attempt to win her favour or her approval, but rather as symbols of the more rewarding life he would have liked her to enjoy. He was still fascinated by her, although now it was as a stranger that she exerted her fascination. He loved to watch her as, pensively, she allowed the taste of the chocolate to melt in her mouth, her long tapering fingers poised over the box, descending slowly but without hesitation. She appeared to derive no active physical enjoyment from this appetite, but rather a calm sense of replenishment, as if sugar were her natural and only diet. It was her unaltered and abstract expression as she ate her fill that struck him as singular; it went with her pale face and her large eyes and her glistening, very slightly protruding, teeth; it went above all with her assumption of virtue. If he thought of her at any point during the day his thoughts presented him with an image of Tissy, sitting in the sunlight, beside the big window of the drawing-room, and slowly but purposefully filling her mouth with chocolate. Sometimes, when he kissed her in the evening, her breath was as sweet as honey. She began to put on weight.

It was a different matter when he purchased and brought home the typewriter and installed it in his old room. This she regarded as an affront, seeing, quite correctly, that he would spend less time with her, not physically, but mentally, once the means of typing the final draft of his book were actually present in the house. By an enormous mischance Mrs Harper was paying her daughter a visit when Lewis came home with his new Olivetti.

'I'm surprised you want to bring your work home, Lewis,' she said. 'I should have thought you'd want to spend your spare time with Tissy.'

'But this is my book,' he attempted to explain. 'I told you all about it. And the sooner I get it finished the happier I'll be.'

'I wonder you don't do it in the office,' she said.

'I work in a library. They don't use typewriters in libraries. Look,' he said, turning to Tissy with some impatience. 'If it's going to upset you I could apply for a carrel in the university library. But that means using it at the weekends and in the evenings. Would you prefer that? I know I wouldn't.'

Tissy, who usually let her mother speak for her, merely said, 'I wonder you can't give it to somebody else to do. Leave it here if you like, but don't expect me to dust that room.'

'Good God, no,' he said, alarmed. 'Don't even go in there. Just leave it entirely to me.'

Mrs Harper brought her prodigious gaze back from her contemplation of her daughter and observed, 'I would never have allowed separate areas in my house.'

'Ah,' said Lewis. 'But, you see, this is my house.' And was immediately aware that he had said a fatal thing.

Thereafter he was eternally nervous that they might disturb, even tamper with, his work. The tension became so great that he took his typewriter to the library with him, borrowed the secretary's office, and typed through the lunch hour when she was out. Pen complained that he never saw him any more.

'Come to dinner,' said Lewis recklessly. And then, even more recklessly, 'Bring George.' He had no love for George Cheveley, a rascally-looking antique dealer whom he had met with Pen in the Burlington Arcade, and, subsequently, at Pen's house in Notting Hill. He had disliked the man's tight smiling face, his longish fair hair, his too correct tailoring. He always greeted him cheerfully, but he was aware of Pen's discomfort at seeing one side of his life intrude into his altogether innocent friendship with Lewis, which was doubly valued precisely because it was innocent. But Lewis, who had infinite love and tolerance for Pen, merely wanted him to be at ease, whatever he did, and if that meant accepting George, whom he suspected of being a bully, he was perfectly willing to do so. At the same time he was aware that he might have a hard job persuading Tissy to be equally tolerant. But the die was cast and on the whole he was glad of it. Pen was his friend, and it was time that Tissy learned to be more forbearing. Her views sometimes shocked him by their languid ruthlessness; he derived a perverse thrill of annoyance when Tissy and her mother discussed anything of wider import

113

than their immediate concerns. Calmly, even judiciously, they condemned out of hand any moment of untoward sympathy. 'Hanging's too good for them,' was Mrs Harper's usual comment on a wide range of people, from Communists to drunk drivers. Unfortunately, in her eyes, quite a lot of men fell into one or the other category. Lewis was pretty sure that George would rank very high on her list. Nor did he doubt that George, who was a cruelly excellent mimic, might have something to say on the matter himself.

Pen's smile was swept away by a slight frown.

'The thing is,' he said, settling himself on the edge of the desk. 'George is not with me at the moment. My sister's staying in the house. She's all set to stay indefinitely, or rather until she finds a flat of her own. Well, she can't keep coming up from Wales, can she?'

'What does she do?' asked Lewis.

'She's an actress. She gets tiny parts on television. Actually, she's too lazy to do any real work. But she's a great girl, you'd like her. Quite mad, of course.'

'Bring her,' said Lewis. 'Tissy would be thrilled. She watches television all the time.'

'She'd have to, to catch a glimpse of Emmy. Emmy's always the painfully upper class woman in a queue complaining about something. Or some mogul's snooty secretary. She only does it for a laugh; nobody at home bothers to watch her. But she's an entertaining sort of character, and we've always been close. She's the only one who knows about George.'

'Come on Saturday,' said Lewis. 'I'll tell Tissy.'

He prepared himself for the further indoctrination of Tissy, who expressed great anxiety whenever he proposed to bring someone to the house. This had reduced their social life to nothing, or rather to the visits of Mrs Harper and the doctor, both of whom preferred to come when Lewis was absent. Susan and Andrew, at the beginning of their marriage, had been invited as a matter of course, and had been, on the whole, a success. Susan and Tissy had not so much looked each other over as taken tiny sideways glances at each other. Evidently reassured by this examination, they had nevertheless not fallen into a friendship, as Lewis had hoped. Equally, at the outset of their marriage, Professor Armitage had been invited. He had been tolerated, but Lewis had not felt comfortable; as Tissy's cooking had never progressed beyond little girl accomplishments he had been aware of the inadequacy of the entertainment. And when Professor Armitage had taken up the subject of Lewis's work Tissy had abruptly risen and begun to clear the table. Lewis had felt deeply hurt, both for himself and for his guest, although Professor Armitage had talked on, seemingly unaware that anything was amiss. Now he was going to require of her something more difficult, since Pen and this Emmy presumably had a run of sophisticated entertainments at their disposal and would be disconcerted if Tissy betrayed incompetence, thus plunging her into further confusion. Walking home, Lewis shook his head at his own folly. But it was done, and he had known that it had to be done.

Tissy took the news of his invitation – already given and accepted – as if her husband were announcing something conceived solely as a personal threat to herself. He could hardly believe his eyes when she shrank back in dismay. Taking refuge beside the cooker, she busied herself with the knife drawer, her whole back registering grievance and panic. Hanging, he reflected, would be too good for him when the news reached Mrs Harper. The dreadful embarrassment to which this marriage was subject almost overwhelmed him, until he realized that Tissy, in her frailty, was even more susceptible to its insufficiencies than he was.

'Darling, darling,' he said, putting his arms round her and cajoling her into the centre of the room. 'You must stop being frightened. There's a great big beautiful world out there, and sooner or later you'll have to discover it. I'm not asking you to do anything exorbitant. I've simply asked a couple of friends to dinner. We can't go on living as we are. At least, I can't. It makes me sad sometimes to just sit here in the evenings and wait for it to be time to go to bed. And you're not really happy, are you?'

'I'm perfectly happy,' she said, startled.

'But you could be even happier if you'd only open out a bit. If only you'd let me take you away somewhere, anywhere. We could go to Paris.' He felt a nostalgia for those grey mornings and for his earlier self, free as a bird, savouring his solitude as he walked the broad avenues that would take him to his daily task. He saw it all now as blameless, innocent. With what zeal he had lived his poor little life, and how he recognized its benefits, yes, even now. He felt eternal gratitude for his own apprenticeship. But as a married man, and a householder, he felt nothing but dryness, interspersed with spasms of desire. He longed for one real upward flight. He longed for his wife to join him. He could hardly believe that she was perfectly happy, as she claimed to be. He was beginning to see that she confused happiness with respectability, and was ready to believe that it was the duty of the married woman to express happiness, for how else could she feel superior to the unmarried?

For Tissy, appreciation of status and possessions constituted happiness, or rather represented it. Not for her the flight or the aspiration: she could not feel safe unless tied to the earth, her feet literally on the ground. How many times she had repudiated him, deflated him! She was at one with her mother there, although she lacked her mother's generalized hostility, just as she lacked her mother's vicious prettiness. He realized that his wife considered him to be a specimen of an unfortunate but necessary race, and that, far from there being any personal charge in this, she had absorbed the attitude from her earliest years, environmentally. The shambling doctor had not been cast in a mould heroic enough to break the spell; his failure to do so must be added to his other vices. Tissy had in fact done sterling work in purging herself of cruelty, hatred, and the desire for revenge that such an attitude might have fostered, but in this work of abnegation, of studious refusal to take sides, to accuse or to blame, she had rendered herself inert, colourless, without ardour. Lewis knew that she trusted him because he had never hurt her, had treated her gently, had loved her. For this she was willing to do her best, to play her part. He realized that they might have kept this bargain for life, faithfully but joylessly. It took something as minor as this announcement that he had invited a friend to dinner to shock her out of her lethargy, the lethargy which she found so necessary. When he saw her expression of fear he knew the extent of her malady.

'You must ask your mother to help you,' he said gently, releasing her. 'She will tell you what to do. And it will be nice to use those Crown Derby plates for once.'

On this level she was at one with him, although he knew that she preferred to enjoy their possessions on her own. Passing him a plate of food, she would be visibly waiting for him to hand it back again, so that she could wash it and put it away and close the cupboard door on it. For once she was going to have to share her belongings, and to do so not merely with a good grace but with a good heart. He saw that this might be too much for her, as it was nearly too much for him to have to watch her. Yet he felt that the test was timely; more, that it was crucial. The dinner party was almost lost from sight. He winced with disbelief when he remembered it. As an occasion for pleasure it was already doomed. He began to dread it almost as much as his wife seemed to do.

Contrary to all reasonable expectations it was his mother-in-law who saved the day. Along with her general implacability and her spoiled expectations, Mrs Harper possessed a certain taste for splendour which her life had refused to gratify. The Belgian convent had left her with a sense of formality with regard to the preparation and presentation of food which Lewis found commendable and impressive. He was always loud and genuine in his praise when he and his wife dined with Mrs Harper, although he suspected that there was something unresolved in her attitude to her own cooking: enormous appetite had to be masked by enormous

117

indifference. Translated, this meant that Mrs Harper would serve them a perfect leg of lamb with flageolet beans, and watch them, smoking, while they ate it, dousing her cigarette only to bring in the salad, the cheese, and the melting almond flan to finish. This effort at self-domination would exhaust her. 'Tissy, make the coffee,' she would sigh. 'But you've eaten nothing, Thea,' Lewis would protest. 'The cook eats all the time,' Mrs Harper would tell him with her usual reluctant smile. 'That's why she never sits down to dinner. Did you enjoy it?' Even this query would be ground out of her, an unwilling concession to the male appetite. 'Superb,' Lewis would say. 'I've never eaten so well in my life as I do here.' The smile would be repeated, only to sink away into the usual mask of imperturbability. Another cigarette would be lit and the case would be closed.

On this occasion Mrs Harper decreed a menu of spinach soufflé, roast poussins, and her almond tart. There would be salad and cheese; Lewis would choose the wine. He considered this excessive, but decided not to interfere. The question of whether Mrs Harper would join them was settled by Mrs Harper herself, who wished her daughter to take credit for the entire performance. Mrs Harper would remain in the kitchen until the chickens were served and then invisibly take her leave. Lewis saw this as generosity, even nobility on her part: his mother-in-law and not his wife would be the heroine of this occasion. On the Saturday afternoon he stood respectfully in the doorway of his kitchen, where Mrs Harper, plump elbows flashing, was already directing operations, emptying cupboards of china and glass, assembling pans and kitchen cloths. Under her mother's supervision Tissy docilely laid the table, and then went upstairs to have a rest. Lewis, unequal to the task of instructing his wife in her duties, went out, ostensibly to buy the wine, in fact to get away from Tissy. His mother-in-law, he was surprised to note, was, in her present mood, entirely tolerable.

Nevertheless he breathed the rainy spring air with a sense

of relief, feeling the burden of his marriage lighten some-
what in the general lightness of the atmosphere. Narcissi,
iris, and tulips stood in buckets outside the greengrocer's,
and he bought lavishly of each of them, inhaling their cool
earthy delicacy. He walked a little way, with his armful of
flowers, feeling fatalistic, as if any further worrying must
be done by somebody else. He had no desire to go home.
He was not sure whether he would ever want to go home
again. Left to himself he might have slipped away, unnoticed.
But so much drew him back, so many possessions, so many
accoutrements, and his wife palely presiding over all. Both
host and guest in his own house, Lewis no longer felt at
home there. He loitered, drifted, strolled in the weak sunshine, nodding to neighbours whom he rarely saw, until
consciousness of the tasks ahead returned him to himself.
Then, as the light began to fade and the coolness of the day
became more noticeable, he sighed and went home to have
his bath.

In another part of London, Pen told his sister, in a moderate tone of voice, 'Tissy, I believe, is a little nervous.' 'Oh
Lor',' his sister replied. 'Then I suppose I'd better play the
fool.' Nevertheless she dressed with her usual extravagance
in a garment brought home by her from Mexico, with much
Mexican turquoise jewellery. Holding the material of her
dress away from her body, she tipped her usual half-bottle
of mimosa cologne into the well of her bosom. Disdaining
a bag, she tucked a handkerchief into her brother's pocket
and urged him to hurry. 'The sooner we go, the sooner
we can come back,' she said. 'Be kind, Emmy,' said Pen.
'Lewis is my friend.' 'Oh, I am always kind,' she threw
out contemptuously, already on her way to the door. Pen
said nothing, although he knew that this was not altogether
true.

Pushed forward to receive her guests, Tissy appeared
calm, even uninterested, although Lewis knew that under
the pink blouse her heart was beating painfully.

'Well, Tissy,' said Pen, kissing her on both cheeks. 'This is nice of you. And it's good to see you again, looking so well, too.'

Lewis poured champagne for them all into the beautiful glass flutes his wife had found in the attic. While Pen engaged Tissy in gentle conversation, guaranteed not to discompose her, Lewis studied Emmy, admiring her long brown hair, her round face, and the rosy stain of her cheeks.

'I hear you're looking for a flat,' he said.

'Oh, I've found one,' she replied. 'Near to Pen. Isn't that lucky? Tissy,' she called. 'You must help me furnish my flat. I'm hopeless at that sort of thing. And you've done wonders here. I love this room.' But she was looking at Lewis as she spoke.

'What is that marvellous scent?' he asked, inhaling.

'Mimosa.' She pulled down the front of her dress and took a deep breath. 'It's good, isn't it? A boyfriend brings it for me from Tahiti.'

A boyfriend, he noted. Not my boyfriend. He filed the information away for future investigation, then went over to his wife and put his arm round her waist. 'Shall we eat, darling? Bring your champagne,' he called to Emmy. 'Will you have some more? There's only a perfectly ordinary white wine to follow.'

He stood while she rose, admired her long waist and legs. Beside her Tissy looked like a child. Yet at that moment he felt a painful wave of love for his wife, whose weakness he so clearly felt. He would defend her to the death, he thought, not knowing why he felt her to be under threat. He took her hand, willing her to enjoy herself, but merely registered the extent of her nervousness. Her peculiar gift, he reflected, was to turn pleasure into mere absence of pain. Sometimes this worked. On a domestic level it ensured calm and order. But there was a defensiveness that militated against high emotion. Not that high emotion was called for on this occasion. But Lewis wished that something a little more active than her usual manner could be demonstrated. She had refused champagne, saying that it gave her a headache. He knew that she would refuse the wine as well.

The perfectly risen soufflé awaited them on the dining-room table, as if by magic. Emmy ate enthusiastically; at one point a large Mexican ear-ring fell with a clatter on to her side plate. She looked at it indifferently, and then removed the other one. 'This always happens,' she said. 'I've left ear-rings all over London. Put them in your pocket, Pen, I haven't got a bag. Evening bags are so goody-goody, aren't they? Don't lean back, you'll crush them to fragments. Have I said something funny?' she said, surprised, catching Lewis's grin. 'Yes, I'd adore some more, if there is any. Gosh, Tissy, you must give me lessons. My cooking is nowhere up to this standard.'

At this point the figure of Mrs Harper was to be seen crossing the hall. The peculiar showiness of her gait had not diminished since the first time Lewis had seen her stroll out of the library, her daughter on her arm. Age had, if anything, increased it, made it heavier. She was slower now, more elaborate, more declamatory. At some point in her girlhood she must have expected roomfuls to rise at her entrance. There was still something of the proud beauty about her, but spoilt now, diminished, disappointed.

'Oh, look,' exclaimed Emmy. 'Your cook's just leaving. Do stop her. We must tell her how good this is.'

'It's my mother,' said Tissy, tonelessly.

'Thea,' called Lewis. 'Come and join us. This food is wonderful. My mother-in-law is a brilliant cook,' he explained to Emmy.

'I'll say she is,' said Emmy, 'Oh, do come in, darling, and tell us how to make this heavenly stuff. Pen is getting so tired of beans on toast.'

Pen poured Mrs Harper a glass of champagne, which she drank with her normal lack of pleasure. Lewis sensed that she was tempted to stay, and would have done so were it not for her daughter's honour. Suddenly he felt entirely relaxed. But,

'Enjoy your meal,' said Mrs Harper, as soon as her glass was empty.

'If you stay I can walk you home,' Lewis urged, but she was determined to go. 'Nice to have met you,' she said to Pen. 'We've heard a lot about you.' Pen lifted his glass to her. Emmy blew her a kiss. All the while Tissy sat immobile, a faint pink colouring her cheeks.

The four roast poussins nestled in a deep bed of parsley-speckled greenish rice. Their arrival was greeted with a cheer. As Tissy lowered the heavy platter on to the table Lewis reached for Emmy's plate. Between two silver spoons a poussin slipped inexorably downwards, landing on the table-cloth. The platter was abruptly relinquished, a chair pushed back. 'Look, darling,' said Emmy busily, wiping a fleck of rice from her cheek, as Tissy burst into tears. 'I do this all the time. At least it didn't land on the floor.' She appeared to think of this as an extenuating circumstance. Lewis took a deep draught of wine. Emmy ladled the chickens untidily on to their plates, went round to Tissy, and put her arms around her. 'It's your tiny wrists you ought to blame. Look at mine! Like a navvy's! Don't let it get cold, it looks too delicious. There's a good girl.' She wiped Tissy's cheeks, went back to her chair, and ate, again enthusiastically. 'Nothing is better than food,' she pronounced beatifically. 'Not even sex. Well, not all the time.' Pen groaned and shook his head. 'I must ring your mother and ask her how she cooked these. You are lucky, Lewis. When I think what we put up with at home.'

Suddenly Lewis felt reckless. Destiny stared him in the face; he knew it must be resisted, but he thought he might offer himself a few moments of reprieve.

'Dear old thing,' said Emmy. 'You've done us proud. I shall have to lose weight before I go on camera.'

'I've seen you on television,' offered Tissy.

'You'll see more of me in the autumn,' said Emmy. 'Oh, this tart! Divine!' Her fork poised in mid-air, she closed her eyes in ecstasy. 'It's only a small part but we're shooting it in France. Near Dijon. More lovely food. Well, lovely everything.' Her face took on a look of sly reminiscence: she seemed older, greedier. She was not young, Lewis thought; about his own age, thirtyish, a little more. She was not slim, careful, elegant, virginal. She was the opposite of all those things, very much the opposite. He was surprised to find himself evaluating her in this way, and wondered mildly at the brutality of his thoughts. Even his fantasies, it seemed, must always be censored. Besides, he told himself, he did not appreciate this sort of carelessness in a woman. He was, for better or worse, attuned to something in his wife's mould, even if not always to his wife. He watched Emmy covertly, as her face loosened, coarsened. Then he looked at Tissy, who, under Pen's gentle tutelage, was now talking prettily and happily.

'Coffee, darling?' he said, feeling once more well-disposed, benevolent, but also guilty.

'Of course,' said Tissy. 'Coffee, everyone? Would you like to go into the other room?'

It was at this point, hearing his wife utter these appropriately wifely sentences, that Lewis realized that the evening had been a complete success.

'You did very well,' he said, later in bed, meaning it, but stifling a yawn as he said the words. 'Did you enjoy it?'

There was no answer. He knew she was not asleep.

'You like Pen, don't you?' A silent nod, in the dark.

'And Emmy? Did you like Emmy?'

There was a long pause, so long that he wondered if she had gone to sleep. He felt his consciousness drifting. 'Tissy?' he said, coming to himself with a jerk. There was another long pause, this time apparently definitive. Suddenly Tissy turned over violently, presenting her back to him. He knew what that meant.

'I thought she was rather rude,' she said.

'Peace, Lewis,' said Goldsborough, raising a pontifical hand.

'Good morning,' Lewis replied.

This new airy yet solemn version of Goldsborough made him feel staid, impossibly old hat. What was his excuse for not joining in what Goldsborough referred to as the 'effervescence'? The trouble was that it had reached the library rather late, too late for any sustaining ideology, and Goldsborough, now wearing a flat black leather cap, was forced to preside over empty desks and only rare disruptions. These, however, were enough to rejuvenate him. The new criticism had been cast aside, and the hapless artists and their letters temporarily discarded. It was the sociology of television that now claimed his attention, his devotion, even. He saw a brilliant future for himself at very little capital outlay: when not watching television he could be on it. He had jettisoned dignity as being of little use to him in these exciting times; voluptuously he threw in his lot with the lowest common denominator. And who better to deal with the culture of the masses than the universal man he knew himself to be? Life, to Goldsborough, was infinitely more genial once he had abandoned his hard-won academic solitude. Like a man who has been on a stringent diet for too long he surrendered himself to popular entertainment, popular music, popular food, popular beer. He had found a new use for deconstruction. Best of all, he had rediscovered the simple pleasures of his adolescence, of that time before he had learned to strive and to discriminate. 'Identifying' was how he thought of this process, as if he were on an eminence which permitted him to view the world with enormous yet enlightened sympathy. Tucking into a manly meat pie and chips in the canteen, he was assured not only of solidarity, not only of pioneering a new study, but of the satisfaction of appetites he had discarded with his naïve and hopeful boyhood. He characterized this feeling as 'relevance'. Sometimes, to distinguish himself from his material, he would smoke an articulated futurist chromium pipe. This he confined to his leisure hours, in the pub. Inside the library he felt he was taking on a new intellectual lustre. At lunchtime he could address himself to the further delights of jam roll and custard with a clear conscience.

Lewis was aware of the effervescence only in the form of odd-smelling cigarette smoke in the corridors, and on one occasion in the open doorway of the library itself. His own anger, once he had traced the stale vanillic odour to its source, astonished him, as did the vigour with which he seized the offender's arm in one suddenly giant hand. Manhandling him out into the corridor, he listened grimly to the man's whining protest.

'Jesus, man, this is 1970.'

'Too late,' said Lewis, tight-lipped. 'You missed the bus in 1968. And probably before that too. *Nobody* smokes near the books. Is that clear? Only barbarians smoke in libraries. The last person to misbehave in a library was Attila the Hun.'

The power of his feeling was both surprising and puzzling to him, since of recent weeks he had been aware only of a vast and almost terminal calm. He was inclined to shrug mentally at the damping down of his hopes, thinking this to be consonant with maturity, or if not with maturity then with growing older. Yet his dreams told him of his disappointment, and even of his displacement into an alien environment. Lying there in the dark, beside a wife who was no more distant in sleep than she was when she was awake, helpless with the need to protect her and to instruct her, he longed for freedom. On one occasion he dreamed that he had risen up in the bed and flown, hands clasped, out of the window, like a soul escaping from the body, leaving his inert physical envelope next to an undisturbed Tissy. He thought of this on the following day and found it exaggerated. He could not have said that he was unhappy, but equally he could not have said that he was happy. He supposed, mildly, that he would go on as he was, living in the same house, with the same wife, writing his book (which he could not abandon, although he knew it to be finished), but once he had registered this sameness he felt almost faint. He dismissed his reaction as excessive, for his life was comfortable, safe, even pleasant. He arrived at a state of indifference: no harsh words, no protest, no criticism. With this armour he was able to confront and to endure the daily routines of his existence. He sometimes felt in relation to his wife as if he were some honourable but sexless connection – an uncle, a father-in-law – rather than a husband. They made love willingly, but she remained polite, formal. He said nothing, for this was the attitude she preferred. What he preferred he hardly knew any more, so dulled and hazed was he with his self-imposed withdrawal from himself.

Therefore his fury with the smoking student was an unwelcome reminder of the strength of his residual feelings. At that moment he would have defended the library to the death and been glad to do so. Such passion he could not remember, and it unsettled him. It went with boldness, carelessness, rashness, all of which were absent from the life he was called on to live. He told himself that the books were, and always had been, his only companions, that his deepest, in fact his only loyalty was towards the content of the books. As he returned to his desk he shook slightly with the after-effects of his anger. All of this was unwelcome, had no place in his moderate existence. It was not merely the student's insolence, his flouting of the rules, that had enraged him: it was his sudden vision of a world in which no attention

126

was paid to the wisdom of books – a world in which he would die of heartbreak – that had impelled his arm and his despairing grasp. Despairing, certainly, he thought, breathing hard. Yes, certainly despairing. He felt shocked, uneasy, and was only able to dismiss the incident after prolonged attention to a collection of essays on neo-classicism and the eighteenth-century theatre.

The sort of Pooterish character he strove so hard to become gradually returned, and he began to think about lunch. There was no sign of Pen, which was unusual; the rows of empty chairs and unoccupied tables indicated effervescence in another part of the building. These days he sometimes had the library almost to himself, for Goldsborough's place was with the multitude, and Stephens and Tracy, the other two assistants, thought it politic to join him. Old Arthur Tooth, a long-retired librarian and actual retainer, ranged with crab-like slowness round the stacks, shelving the books: there was no getting rid of him. Two student helpers, Alan and Bridget, sorted the books into piles and put them on a table to which he made creaking return journeys throughout the day. The work could have been done in an hour by a person of normal vigour, but Arthur, who had decided, on the strength of his long experience, to undertake the task, remained entrenched, and was a warning to those in office to regard volunteers like gift-bearing Greeks. At twelve noon Arthur would haul his watch out of his waistcoat pocket, tuck it back again, disappear into the general office, reappear in top coat and bowler hat, and go off to his club for lunch. At two-thirty he would return, wheezing slightly, and surrounded by a fine bouquet of claret, and set to work again, though more slowly. The job had no beginning and no end and could therefore never be judged to have been completed. Whatever remained undone at the end of the day, before the next influx of returned books, would fall to Lewis, who found it mindless but satisfying. Plodding round the silent library with an armful of texts made him feel like an honest labourer, in touch with his materials, one who would deserve a respite after a day of toil.

The mild atmosphere of his working life both suited and maddened him, making him long to run, laugh, sing, burn his boats, fracture for ever that solemn silence in such a way that they would never allow him back. Sometimes his eyes would actually dull and mist over as a result of peering into the even gloom and the shaded lights. Then he would remind himself of Pen's observation that his tasks were innocent, even honourable, causing no harm or injury. He supposed that this was how the world's work was done, that men in offices throughout the land, across the globe, sighed in frustration or felt the small sad protest of the bored child sent out to play. Is this all? If the end of life were to be the same as the beginning, how was he to endure the middle years? And yet he had all the things a man was supposed to have, had attained man's estate, had married . . . Cold recognition stole unbidden through the barriers he had erected against it. Yet he determined to be a man of good will, would not become crabbed or sour, blushed at the very thought of expressing dissatisfaction. He saw virtue in a certain *naïveté* and fought to keep the hopeful smile on his face. He was determined to value his life, as it was, for not to do so seemed to him a cardinal sin. Making an effort, he stayed resolutely within the terms of the given. And when he thought of old Arthur Tooth, who lived in an hotel in Queen's Gate, and for whom the library was his very life, he felt ashamed of his discontent, and thought with gratitude of his home and of his wife. I must strive for simplicity, he thought; otherwise I shall fail to do justice to what I already have.

When Pen arrived, unusually late, he had Emmy in tow. Lewis had not seen her since the dinner party of the previous week. She had, surprisingly, not telephoned Tissy to thank her: Pen had done that. 'I'm sorry,' Emmy had announced. 'I thought she was a crashing bore, and I can't think of anything to say to her. Anyway, she didn't like me. She likes you. You do it.'

'How rude,' Tissy had said. 'It was the least she could have done.'

Lewis had felt a little hurt on his wife's behalf, although Tissy had cheered up as she recounted the evening to her mother. Mrs Harper, as might have been expected, was unrelenting in her condemnation. 'The least she could have done,' she said accusingly to Lewis. 'Well, you won't want her here again.' Yet he had wanted her. He had hoped for a friend for his wife, someone of her own, to whom she could talk freely. He supposed that she would talk freely to someone, if that ideal person could be found. And yet there had been an antagonism between the two women which he had tried hard to ignore. He could understand how someone as fragile as Tissy would arm herself against the obviously anarchic Emmy, but why should Emmy, who had nothing to fear, waste her time and feelings on Tissy, whom she might never see again? He shook his head in disappointment. He knew nothing of antipathy between women, although he could recognize jealousy. He supposed the antipathy to be almost chemical, an affair of the humours, the lymphatic coldly repulsing the sanguine, the sanguine exasperated by the slow-moving lymphatic's lack of response. There was no possibility of friendship there, Lewis saw, and this was another small disappointment to add to those he already sought to ignore. It also worried him that he should have such a friend in Pen, but that the friendship should be limited by Tissy's reluctance. He hoped that this would make no difference to either of them. He hoped against hope that he would not be forced, through loyalty to his wife, to have to distance himself from Pen.

But Pen's face was as open as ever as he approached Lewis's desk. Emmy, dressed in a brown suit with a long skirt, and boots, her hair loose, followed him. Lewis could see clearly the resemblance between them, in their brown eyes and their confident smiles. They were privileged children, he thought; they would always expect to be greeted with smiles. They had never been frustrated or gagged. Even Pen's friendship with George Cheveley, irregular though it undoubtedly was, had received a sort of sanction through Pen's upright and excellent character, but also through his position, his status, his gentlemanliness. Lewis reflected that with Pen's advantages a man need never explain himself. The same, of course, would apply to Emmy. She had tacit permission to do whatever she wanted: no one would oppose her. She might have her critics (he thought of Mrs Harper) but she would be immune to such criticism. He could imagine her incredulous smile should anyone ever disagree with her on a point of conduct. She would feel pity for any antagonist, not rage. Lewis saw that she probably felt pity for Tissy, and the thought made him uncomfortable. Yet he had to admire her fine clear face and her flushed cheeks. She looked as if she had come in from a long country walk.

'Lewis,' said Pen. 'You wouldn't like to do me a favour, would you? Could you possibly take Emmy out to lunch? The thing is, I must get my hair cut before this evening; it's *Don Giovanni* and George only got the tickets at the last moment. You may have noticed that I'm a trifle late.'

'Yes, I had noticed,' said Lewis, smiling.

'Blame Emmy. She kept me up talking half the night and then collared my alarm. I didn't wake up till nine. I really don't know why I came in at all. But one does, doesn't one?' He nodded in the direction of Goldsborough's door. 'Keeping himself busy, is he?'

'Oh, yes. He's away most of the time. The place is half empty, anyway.'

In the stacks Arthur Tooth groaned his way through the works of Bergson, on whom someone was writing a dissertation. Lewis realized that soon he and Arthur would be the only ones who took this particular library seriously, and he wished that he too might have an apanage of allowable distractions. In academic life fortune favours those who have their eccentricities to speak for them. But Lewis supposed himself to be too dull ever to give eccentricity a foothold. He was doomed to a sobering consciousness of life's unrelenting inconsistency.

'I'll take Emmy to lunch with pleasure,' he said, again with a smile. They brought good humour with them, these two, and he was grateful.

Her own smile broadened to meet his.

'Could we have a picnic?' she asked. 'It's such a lovely day. We could take a cab to Selfridges, pick up something to eat, and sit in the park.'

This relieved Lewis, who had not known where to take her; he rarely ate in fashionable restaurants, where he supposed she would want to go. It never occurred to him that she might have taken care of herself for an hour or two, or if it did only fleetingly; the idea made him ashamed. People like Emmy, and probably Pen too, were not forced to find their entertainment, or their sustenance on their own. They were the natural recipients of the solicitude of others. Besides, the adventure appealed to him. It was a fine day, sunny, though a little windy; the inhibitions of winter cried out to be cast aside. And there was something innocent in the prospect of a picnic, although he doubted if he would tell Tissy about it. This thought constituted his first infidelity.

'What will you want to do afterwards?' he asked her. 'Will you want to come back here and wait for Pen?'

'Oh, no,' she said, looking at him. 'I'll go home afterwards.'

'Only I shall have to be back by about two-thirty.'

'Oh, don't let her be a nuisance,' said Pen. 'Just put her in a cab. I'm off. Terribly good of you, Lewis. Behave yourself,' he said to Emmy, and kissed her. Briefly, the library took on a broader, more permissive aura, a place where plans could be discussed and meetings arranged. Lewis had never thought of it in this light before. He liked the thought; it enlarged the dimension of the day's activities. The work too might benefit, although he could see that far less would get done. But he was tired of his labours, and even of the honourable spirit in which they were conceived.

131

All was effort in his life. And it was such a beautiful spring day. Surely even he, Lewis Percy, was entitled to enjoy the spring?

In the taxi he was aware of the smell of her mimosa scent. They said very little, merely watching the hectic sun flashing on the glass fronts of shops, aware of the growing green of the trees. He turned to her with a feeling of ease, a new feeling.

'Will you go back to Wales?' he asked. 'Or have you moved into the flat already?'

'Oh, I'll go back and collect some furniture,' she said, running her hand through her hair, which the sun had turned to a reddish brown. 'About the end of the month, I suppose. The flat is an absolute tip. I dare say I'll stay with Pen while I get it cleaned up.'

'Will you want any help?' he was surprised to hear himself say. He half hoped that she had not heard him. There was no way in which he could explain anything of this kind to Tissy, although it might have amused him to watch Emmy in her native habitat. In fact any excuse to get out would have been welcome. Life at home was so restrained that their habits had settled round them like grave clothes. Tissy hardly noticed if he went out for a walk in the evenings, although she would be sure to notice if he went anywhere specific. Very occasionally, she would accompany him as far as her mother's, this being the only location she could accept. Even here, few words were exchanged, for they found Mrs Harper in front of her own television, and, as far as Lewis could see, more or less happy with her own taciturn company. This exercise was known as 'looking in on Mother'. 'You see her every day,' Lewis would point out. 'Yes, but she gets lonely in the evenings.' It amazed him that women could be content with so little.

'Are you very hungry?' he asked.

'I'm always hungry,' said Emmy.

'So am I,' he said.

At Selfridges she took charge, bought rolls, butter, cheese, fruit, and a bottle of Muscadet. He followed her with a carrier bag. 'We'll need knives,' he warned her. 'And glasses.'

'Downstairs,' she said. She surveyed the contents of the bag. 'You go,' she urged. 'Give me the bag. I'll wait here.' By the time he got back she had added a box of doughnuts, half a pound of bacon, and a dozen eggs. 'I hope you don't mind,' she smiled. 'I got some stuff for this evening.' Lewis surrendered a large note. 'Hang on,' said Emmy, darting away. She came back with two bars of chocolate and a pineapple. Her attitude to food seemed to be temporary, festive, far removed from the rendering of raw materials that engaged so much of Tissy's time. The results of his wife's cooking were acceptable, but not particularly gratifying. This lunch was more in the nature of a children's party. He knew he would be hungry later, for he could not concentrate on eating when there was so much of Emmy to engage his attention. Together they carried the bag out into the lunchtime crowds.

'Pen tells me you're writing a book,' she said. 'What's it about?'

'Actually, it's finished,' he said, with some surprise. He had not registered the fact until now. 'I've only got a couple of pages of notes to type up. I can do that tomorrow and send it off by the weekend. I know it by heart.' He wondered briefly what he would do with himself once he no longer had his book to keep him company. He supposed he would simply have to start another one.

'I expect you'll start another one,' she said, echoing his thoughts. He quailed as he thought of the unpopularity this would cause at home. Yet Emmy did not seem to think that writing a book was a bad idea, and he warmed to her, on this slight pretext, for her acceptance. The fact that the pretext was so slight, so infinitesimal, should have alerted him. That it did not – that the remark probably reflected only indifference – was nothing to him; he still accepted it gratefully.

They settled themselves in deck chairs, ate hastily and ravenously. He noticed her onyx pendant and ear-rings, and the shape of her breast as she leaned forward to return the bottle to the bag. She was too big, he told himself; too untidy. Yet her hands were long and fine; a ring gleamed gold on her little finger. He hoped that she was not easily bored, for he doubted that he had the resources to entertain her as she expected to be entertained; perhaps she was naturally restless. As he lifted his face to the sun, she brushed crumbs from her skirt and stood up. 'Let's walk,' she said. 'You're not in a hurry, are you?'

'Well, I should be getting back soon . . . '

'Oh, come on. It's far too nice a day for mouldering indoors, and I'm sure you're entitled to a few hours off. Everyone else seems to be. Who was that incredibly old man creeping around? You don't want to end up like him, do you?'

'Ah,' said Lewis. 'That was Arthur Tooth. And I may very well end up like him. Bound to, I should say.'

'Then I reckon you ought to strike out while you can. As far as the Serpentine, at any rate.'

The wind had dropped, and the air seemed milder. The sun had died down, leaving a white even calm. With this calm came a curious silence, an absence of volatility. They wandered away from the little groups of people, already dispersing to do the afternoon's work, down to the water's edge. Here the silence was almost palpable. Only the feet of an occasional duck, fluttering the surface as it came in to land, disturbed the peace. Light lay flatly on the water. The wide empty scene was touched by a very slight melancholy; the still sunless sky promised a wet evening. The unvarying grey, opaque, without brilliance, yet harsh to the eyes, oppressed Lewis, making him long for some gorgeous manifestation of the new season, some generosity, some expansiveness. He was conscious of something withheld. He found himself without the resources necessary to break the curious spell cast by the white light, the mild air, and the silence. They walked on, not speaking, past the Serpentine, into the secret depths of the park, towards the Long Water. Conscious now of his failure to be amusing, conscious of a child-like distress, he felt the onset of an immense disappointment.

They stopped finally by the Italian Garden and kissed. He had thought her vivid, disruptive, but now she looked at him sternly. The need for a statement of intention was present in his mind, although he delayed it as long as possible. When they finally broke free, he smoothed the hair from her forehead, and said,

'What is all this about, do you suppose?'

'This is how it starts, Lewis. Don't you know that by now?'

'But nothing can start, we both know that. I'm a married man, and you, well, you're Pen's sister.'

'What an ass you are,' she said. 'You can't leave me now.' She was flushed and nervous; her insistence impressed him, for it was no less than his own. He brushed aside his reasons in the surprise occasioned by her forwardness. He was not shocked, but he felt immeasurably older. As he took her hand and led her to the balustrade he knew that he was probably ruining his life, or, rather, some part of it.

'Emmy,' he said gently, as if to someone very young. 'You don't want me. I'm not really your type, am I? I'm dull, loyal, pedestrian – all the things you despise. I'm not even good-looking. I'm suburban man. I go to work every day and I read myself silly, and I watch Arthur Tooth and think I'll be like that when I'm old. And then I walk home in the evening. To my wife. And we eat dinner, and perhaps watch television, and then we go to bed.'

'You don't love her, do you?'

'I can't decide,' he said. This constituted his second infidelity. 'Perhaps I do. I feel for her, I want to protect her, I can't bear for her to be hurt.'

'That's not love, Lewis. That's responsibility.'

'Yes, but you see, I *am* responsible. And I shall go on being responsible. There's no way out of responsibility once it has become your lot.'

'Couldn't you look on me as a sort of good conduct prize? An award for your constancy?'

'Do you think I could take you as lightly as that?'

She shrugged. 'Most men do. Men with wives. Most of them are so famously married that they think they deserve a treat. Men who have everything. The day comes when they reckon they've done such a splendid job that they can take on a mistress as well. The difference being that the men have someone to go home to and the mistress is left alone.'

'How do you know all this?'

'I've had lovers since I was sixteen.' She smiled sadly. 'I'm supposed to be immoral, aren't I? Even if things are changing. And I'm involved with somebody now, although he's only involved to the extent of once a fortnight. I never wanted this, do you know that? I wanted to be married, like you. I wanted children, roses round the door, the whole thing. The trouble is, I don't look the part, so I never got the offers. And now I'm typecast, I suppose.'

She burst into tears of frustration, like a child. He kissed her again, put his arm round her waist, held her while she wept. Presently she wiped her eyes.

'I hated your wife,' she said. 'I hated her resistance, her unpreparedness. I imagined all the wives banding together, ready to turn me out of their houses. And making no effort to please. That disgusted me. Only mistresses make that sort of effort, and they get called all sorts of names for doing so. Why don't you come home with me, Lewis? No one will ever know. I won't ruin your marriage. I've never ruined anybody's. I'm too accommodating.'

'You don't want me, Emmy. One afternoon with me isn't going to solve anything for either of us. And I can't marry you, you know. That's what you really want, isn't it? To be married. My dear girl, you couldn't stand me on that basis. I'd bore you to tears.'

She said stubbornly, her tears now dry, her cheeks still flushed, 'Come home with me now.'

'Ah,' he said sadly. 'But, you see, you don't love me. And

I would certainly love you. And you would soon get tired of me. You don't love me – you just hate my wife, all wives. I understand, I truly do understand. You are a marvellous girl, but I can't come home with you. I might just be the sort of unfaithful husband whose marriage you really did break up. And you wouldn't like that half as much as you think you would. And then you'd be stuck with me.'

They walked in silence to the Bayswater entrance.

'In fact, I have to say, I can't be sorry for you without being sorry for myself. But it has to stop there. I should like to behave well, I really should. And if that makes me a prig, I can't help it. Priggishness may yet make a comeback, who knows?'

'It already has,' she said.

They both laughed, and then he kissed her goodbye, leaning into her soft strong body, which was everything he wanted a woman's body to be. He watched her as she marched off towards Notting Hill Gate. He was immensely proud of her.

'This is unlike you, Lewis,' said Goldsborough, looking quite normal without his cap. 'Arthur was quite concerned when you failed to return after lunch.' One of Arthur's less ingratiating habits was his overwhelming punctuality. 'Nothing wrong, I hope? Not trouble at home?'

'I'm sorry, Arnold,' said Lewis. 'I had a very pressing commitment in town.' He could not think why he had said 'in town', when the image of that flat light-deflecting water would stay with him forever. 'I'll come in on Saturday morning to make up for it.'

'Very good, Lewis. But let me know in advance if you're going to do this sort of thing, won't you? Dentist, was it?'

In that moment Lewis saw Goldsborough as simple, harmless, and greedy, the sort of man who has been a lonely fat boy at school. Suddenly he felt extremely well disposed towards Goldsborough, and even towards Arthur Tooth. He felt the onset of an unfamiliar exuberance.

'I'll do the late night tonight,' he said to Goldsborough.

137

'You go off. You're more in demand than I am.' He longed to be alone, to examine the complexities that had been revealed to him, to wonder if Emmy were thinking of him, as he was thinking of her. He wanted time to himself, before he could decently go home.

He sat in the library until nine o'clock, having even remembered to telephone Tissy to warn her. He felt no embarrassment, no division of loyalties, in speaking affectionately, reassuringly, to his wife. As the evening darkened, his euphoria, his feeling of having done the right thing, gradually waned, and he reviewed his behaviour with appalled misgivings. An episode, he tried telling himself; not even worth thinking about. Yet he did think about it, insistently, and the more he thought about it the more he blamed himself. He had rejected her, and nobody forgives a rejection, just as no one forgets a humiliation. But what could he have done? She was inconstant, she had told him so herself; for all he knew she did this all the time. He tried to feel sorry that any of this had happened, yet what he really felt was an awakening, a slow mobilization of all his dormant energies.

He put his head in his hands. What I said to her was in effect true, truer than I meant it to be, he thought. Why should she care for me? Why should anyone? Even Tissy does not love me, although she assures me that she is happy. But how can I go on like this? I never wanted moderation. He nodded to the last student, checked out the last book, then wandered round, turning off the lights. He cursed the reasonable words he had spoken to her, yet could not call them back. A figure of fun, he reflected, virtuous and vacillating. And her role in all this? She was there to make trouble, and to think nothing of it. He disapproved violently, and yet he adored her boldness. The difficulty – the supreme difficulty – was that he might have loved her. If things had been different, he thought, if he had been free. But he was not free. As he locked the door behind him, he reflected that at home he would find his dinner in the oven and an unflustered Tissy watching television. The thought did not comfort him. But at least nobody got hurt, he thought, as he took the enormous burden of his disordered feelings and his cancelled expectations out with him, into the dark and now rainy street.

10

In the weeks that followed Lewis was extremely attentive to his wife, who suddenly appeared to him as she had done when he had first been attracted to her. He saw only her fragility, her docility, her virginal lack of independence. This gave her a legendary quality, rather as if she had stepped out of the Unicorn tapestry, or wore a metaphorical wimple. Above all, she carried about her an aura of chastity, which was, he saw, never to be entirely confounded. These qualities still moved him, mixed though they were in his mind with his own impatience, exasperation, and a degree of bewilderment that began to reach epic proportions. He strove heroically to maintain in himself the requisite family piety. When he saw Tissy moving about the quiet rooms of his house, or caught her carrying, hieratically, a dish for his supper, or watched her bent head as she read her book, his heart smote him, and there was nothing in the world he would not have done to shield and protect her. He felt a very real sadness when her large unclouded eyes ranged over his face and then beyond it, when her hesitant steps told him that she needed his arm to lean on. Sometimes, walking slowly with her in the quiet streets of early summer, he would detect within himself the seeds of a quite serious longing. He could say nothing of this to her, although she was the subject of his most pitiful speculations. Silently he addressed her in his mind, willing her to be alive to his confusion. Dearest little wife, he thought, when will you be strong enough to do without me? What will quieten your fears? And on these wordless evening promenades, so staid, so undemanding, do you think of me at all? How will it be for you in the years ahead, when, contrary to expectation, life becomes more difficult? How will you age, or, rather, when will your eternal innocence yield to experience? When will you begin to learn those lessons – of concealment, of imitation, of duplicity – of which even I now have an inkling? This peaceful, even silent life came about as a result of your hesitations, the limits that had been imposed on you and which you now impose on me, for I begin to think that you are very strong, or rather that you possess a force of will that I never suspected. But that force is negative, dedicated to the preservation of a status quo that will not, cannot threaten you. As I walk with you, slowly, prudently, our eyes cast down, I feel that we have been married since the beginning of time, as if my own youth – which was as hesitant as yours – were bound to end in this becalmed state, as if old age will not surprise us, or, if it does, will be found not to differ very greatly from this strange condition. For if we still look young, it is a youth of which most young people would feel ashamed. Yet your white arm, in its short sleeve, is passed so naturally through mine that I could not now bear it to be absent. And although we are going, as usual, to visit your mother, the sun is mild, the air is kindly, the lime tree is full of scent, and there is nothing really wrong with either of us. Is there?

At other times, when he was away from her, he felt, more maturely, a disgust at his own virtue, in itself not entirely sincere or voluntary, a disgust for the whole idea of virtue in its diminished Christian interpretation: continence. Great deeds were not always undertaken virtuously, nor were great loves blamelessly consummated. It seemed to him that since his marriage he had become debilitated, passive, that his essential self had deteriorated, and his simplicity been compromised. When he thought of Emmy he felt sour, rancorous, as if she had no right to provoke him by existing,

141

as if she summoned up from hidden depths a furious dissatisfaction with the life he had been called on to live, and which
might, if he exerted the requisite vigilance, pass for normal.
Indifference faded away, leaving a new scrutiny in its wake.
He was surprised by destructive impulses, which he always
suppressed, ravenous yet sickly appetites, and restless nights
which demoralized him. Sometimes he longed for the peace
of those ruminant years before he had ever seen her. He
knew that she had the power to lift him into a more heroic
future, a life fit for a man, but that this would cause damage,
abandonment, injury, and also loss. Beneath his half-hearted
and sorrowful obedience – an obedience that brought with it
a certain peace – he detected a deep unreadiness for adventure, and this was a source of dismay to him, and of mature
disappointment.

When Pen and Emmy issued an invitation to dinner it
was more or less easy to decline, pleading an indisposition
of Tissy's. In any event Tissy refused to go, so his excuse
was more or less honourable. How much more, how much
less preoccupied him for several days.

He began to leave home earlier in the mornings and
to return home later at the end of the day, although it
would never have occurred to him to go anywhere else, or
even to break his journey. Filled with an unforgiving energy
he walked both to and from work, hoping to exhaust himself. But his energies simply redoubled, and he slept badly,
sometimes hardly at all. Tissy accepted this without criticism,
ascribing it to the fact that he had finished his book and was
uneasy without its physical presence in the house. Oddly
enough, she was not unhelpful to him: her calm, even her
silence, assured him that nothing was really amiss.

On one such day he received a rather nasty shock. Shopping in Selfridges in his lunch hour – for he had a sentimental
attachment to the place – he heard himself greeted loudly,
delightedly, by a stout woman in a brilliant blue dress, with
whom, as far as he knew, he had no connection.

'Lewis! Lewis Percy!'

He turned, amazed to be discovered here, and looked into the still handsome but now ageing face of someone whom he could not call to mind.

'Don't you remember me? I recognized you at once. You haven't changed at all. It's Roberta! You remember me now, don't you? Roberta, from Paris! From that funny flat we all lived in.'

'Roberta! Of course!'

He took her in his arms and kissed her. But in fact he would not have known her. She had put on a great deal of weight and looked quite old. But she must be in her early fifties, he calculated, and then came the thought: it was nearly twelve years since Paris, and if the years had dealt so harshly with her what had they done to him?

'So you left Paris?' he said. 'I didn't think you ever would.'

'Well, I got homesick for a place of my own. I've got a lovely little flat in St John's Wood now. Of course, I paid the penalty financially, but I'm quite happy. I'm working for a printing firm – a bit of a comedown, but what can you expect? I reckon I'm very lucky. But I often think of those days. We had some laughs, didn't we?'

She surveyed him fondly. He wanted to bury his face in her neck and tell her all his troubles, but merely planted another kiss on her cheek and smiled.

'And what about you? What about your work?'

'I made it into a book,' he said. He did not think he could tell her about the stunning monotony of his everyday life, for she would simply look at him with the rounded eyes of incomprehension. As it was she smiled at him fondly.

'You always were a clever boy. And you're quite handsome now, quite distinguished. You've filled out, grown even taller. Yet I knew you at once, didn't I?' She laughed delightedly.

'I'm married,' he said.

'So that accounts for it. Well, dear, I'm so glad you've done well. Perhaps you'll bring your wife to see me one of these days. Ring me any time: I'm in the book. Try some of this salami,' she went on. 'Have you still got your appetite? That's one of the things I remember about you.'

'You were always good to me, Roberta.'

'Me?' Her eyes widened. 'We all liked you, Lewis. You were our pet. Well, I mustn't keep you. Take care of yourself, dear. And give me a call sometime.'

He felt inadequate to deal with such generosity of spirit, and merely watched her as she took up her position at the bread counter, still trim, still bold, despite her weight and her greying hair, still uninhibited, He loved her bright colours, so totally in character. He pictured her in her little flat, cooking exquisite meals, bossing her guests around. A contented woman, avid for the good things in life, and, no doubt, just as unnervingly direct. If he took Tissy to visit her she would sum up their marriage in a trice. He remembered how she had upbraided the virginal Cynthia. *'Faites de la gymnastique ou faites-vous baiser!'* He smiled as he remembered, and then sighed. Much gained, much lost. Would it always be like this? Yet throughout the afternoon, in the silent library, the smile returned when he thought of Roberta, now stout, now kindly, with an innocence of goodwill that surpassed anything he had to offer. He pondered the mystery of kindliness, not very evenly distributed, appearances deceiving more in this area than in any other. Curious, he looked her up in the telephone directory and saw that she lived in Hall Road. On his way home he sent her a large bunch of roses.

For he was still seduced and beguiled by the company of women, and more by their company than by their unsettling challenges. He longed to relax, if that were possible, in their benign presence, and to begin his sentimental education all over again. He pictured a kind of seminar, where women would do the teaching, for was that not their business? Without them he had started off in different directions, possibly the wrong ones; nothing worked as he had expected it to work; even conversation had broken down. This must account for Tissy's muteness, and for the unspoken questions that separated them. He did not in all honesty see how her present life could satisfy her, although it was clearly an improvement on the one she had known with her mother. Her very silences bespoke withdrawal, a private judgement, although he never heard her voice a single criticism. She was, in many ways, a stranger to him, a stranger whom he was duty bound to accommodate. He sometimes imagined that she felt the same way about him. Yet this marriage was by now so established that he had no choice but to continue it. There was no good reason not to do so. In comparison with Tissy, in her official role, Emmy appeared almost insubstantial, with no more authority than an outlaw. Faced with the problems they both presented he longed to be young again, immature, hopeful, comfortable, yes, comfortable, as he had not been for many years.

But if Emmy appeared insubstantial, she was also extremely persistent. In his mind's eye he conjured her up before him: she wore her long brown skirt, and her expression was severe, her eyes sorrowful. He could not mistake the fact that even in dreams and fantasies she appeared to be condemning him. So anxious did this make him that he was determined never to court such condemnation again. In the light of her contempt his chivalrous behaviour withered, and he realized that what he had thought of as a certain dull decency, a candidature for honest citizenship, would, by worldly standards, pass for impotence. He wanted to do the right thing, whatever that was: he was no longer sure. This thought raised certain fascinating speculations about what constituted heroic behaviour in those who lived in the real world and were not bound – or protected – by the conventions of literature. Dimly he began to perceive a second volume, an updating of his first: the hero enters the twentieth century. Or does he? As the mechanism of his mind began to function once more he felt a sensation of pure relief. This persisted in spite of his love for women in general and his wife and his putative mistress in particular. In fact the function of his work, as opposed to his imagination, was to safeguard him from such dangers as the unwary might fall into. In a new notebook he began to

145

sketch out a plan, rejoicing as the titles of books to re-read began to multiply, and as tentative chapter headings began to take shape. It was time, he reckoned, to champion the cause of men in literature. The sympathy of the feminists was beginning to elevate women to impossibly heroic status. In realizing that both he and his subjects were bound by male conventions he felt distinctly refreshed. For the first time in many days he was able to lunch with Pen without thinking of him as Emmy's brother. Pen's fine ruddy face, with its agreeable air of amiability, evoked no other face in his tender memory but remained attached to Pen himself. He suspected that Pen knew something of what had passed between Emmy and himself but was too courteous to mention it. This evidence of masculine good manners cheered Lewis, making him feel less alone. Women, he reflected, would have been all over each other in similar circumstances. The idea of being invited to confide his troubles raised in him an instinctive shudder. The *urge* to confide was one thing: he had felt the urge to confide in Roberta. But this had been almost theoretical. The *invitation* to confide seemed to him to be situated on the line that divided friendship from conspiracy; women crossed it habitually, men never. So much did he admire his friend's reticence that he wondered how he might convey this to him, then realized that to do so would have caused them both profound embarrassment.

Although the library habitually had the shaded air of winter, Lewis realized, on his journeys to and from work, that the long summer days were now established. The sky continued white until past nine o'clock, sometimes until nearly ten. Lewis and Tissy were drawn by the beautiful calm evenings to take their walks under trees in full leaf, and past front gardens full of roses. On such evening walks, which by tacit consent did not always coincide with a visit to Mrs Harper (the air being too solemn, too healthful for so short a journey) Lewis admired, as he had never done before, the tact of his natural setting. He had described himself to Emmy as suburban man, hoping thus to discourage her, for her background was markedly more aristocratic than his own. Yet now he felt that to be suburban was almost a calling in itself, involving steadiness, a certain humility in the face of temptation, social or otherwise, and a loving, almost painful attachment to home. The stamp of a suburban childhood, he reflected, probably marked one for life. It was more difficult to move either up or down if one were born and bred in a quiet street, in a large but unpretentious house whose wide windows looked across to others of the same pattern, and behind whose curtains one could, very occasionally, discern the vague pale shape of a woman, moving about her innocuous business, waiting for the breadwinner to come home. There was for him a sweetness in the absence of excitement that such a condition implied, or perhaps imposed. Arm in arm with his wife, sauntering wordlessly, almost becalmed, he knew himself to be in his natural setting, in the place where he belonged. Sometimes this saddened him, but then sadness was also inherent in those silent streets, those tranced hot afternoons. He thought of a hundred Madame Bovarys waiting for a lover, while their husbands were away plying some harmless trade. Perhaps even Tissy entertained seditious thoughts. That was the trouble with women, he told himself: on balance they were so much bolder than men. Then he realized that he would abhor in his wife behaviour that he considered natural in himself, although it might intrigue him in others. He shook his head: there was no answer to any of it.

One evening, as they were drinking a last cup of tea, the telephone rang. Tissy answered it.

'It's for you,' she said, her lips pursed. 'It's that woman, Emmy. She wants to speak to you. Says it's important.'

Surely she would not, could not be so bold as to pursue him here? Lewis felt almost righteously shocked as he took the receiver from Tissy. Nevertheless, he allowed her to retreat into the kitchen before clearing his throat and speaking.

'Emmy?'

'Lewis? Could you come over to Pen's house?' Her voice sounded distant and tearful.

'Why? Is anything wrong?'

'It's Pen,' she went on. 'There's been a bit of an upset. He's all right, but we've had the most tremendous row. I think he's rather drunk. Could you possibly come over? I think he'd like you to.'

'Well, of course,' he said, his mouth suddenly dry. 'I'll be with you in half an hour.

'Something's happened to Pen,' he told Tissy. 'I'm going there now. Don't wait up for me – I may have to stay.'

His after-image of her was of a pale form slowly backing away from the kitchen door, gathering the cups from the table and lowering them equally slowly into the sink. She seemed ghostly, marginal, insubstantial, in comparison with the prospect of seeing Emmy again, but he was too agitated to examine the implications of this. He was also aware that she was displeased, but he postponed consideration of this too until later. He was in no sense, despite his anxiety, conscious that anything untoward was afoot.

He flew down to the main road and picked up a providential taxi. Pen's house, a cottage by London standards, yet with the desirable chic that his own house lacked, was in Pitt Street. The sky was now dark; crowds were leaving the cinema. He had always liked this district, from whose animation his own house seemed too far removed, seemed, when seen across this distance, countrified, somnolent, provincial. Instinctively he straighted his tie before ringing the bell.

Emmy stood there, in a long purplish skirt and a cream silk shirt half obscured by rows of tortoiseshell and amber beads. She looked at him without interest, her expression every bit as severe as he had imagined it. This, if anything, made her more attractive. He found himself longing for her indulgence.

'What's happened?' he asked.

She shrugged and indicated the drawing room, where Pen sat foursquare in an armchair, looking flushed but curiously abstracted, as if practising some form of higher thought. He was nursing a glass of whisky. He smiled wearily when he saw Lewis, as if Lewis's presence merely reminded him of a circumstance which he was prepared to overlook or even forget. Lewis immediately had a sense of something suppressed, unexplained, one of those family affairs to which no outsider should be admitted.

'She really shouldn't have telephoned you,' said Pen, unable to keep a note of irritation out of his voice. Without his normal manner and his confident smile, he had lost some of his authority. Naturally charming, by virtue of his certainties, he was at a loss, Lewis saw, when faced with certain types of confusion, which deprived him of his dignity and left him bereft of an appropriate attitude.

'Are you all right, Pen?'

'Of course I'm all right. A minor disagreement. Too silly, the whole thing.'

'George lost his temper,' pronounced Emmy, leaning against the jamb of the door. 'He can't stand me, that's the trouble. He doesn't like my having a key. I'm supposed to stay out of his way. I ask you!' Her eyes rounded with indignation as she contemplated this assault on her priorities.

'Emmy,' said Pen tightly. 'I love you dearly, but I really don't appreciate your interfering in my affairs. If it comes to that, I really don't want you dropping in all the time. Not without warning, that is. My domestic arrangements are no concern of yours. I'm sorry, Lewis. She had no business to telephone you. Do help yourself to a drink. Not that we're much in the way of entertainment. But then we weren't expecting company. At least, I wasn't. Emmy apparently was.' He finished what was in his glass and began to hum the overture to *La Traviata*.

Lewis felt sorrow for Emmy, whose eyes had filled with tears. How quickly and easily her tears fell! Yet here was a genuine cause: the rebuke was cruel. In that moment he could see how the two of them must have been when much younger: the importunate adoring sister and the controlled and controlling older brother. At the same time he became aware of a discrepancy in their accounts: Pen did not need him, did not even want him. Why then was he here? Something regrettable had happened, that was quite clear; what was equally clear was that it was none of his business. He felt the slight impatience of one who has been called in as a witness to a matter in which he is not involved. At the same time he was anxious to justify his presence.

'Will George be coming back tonight?' he asked.

In reply Pen poured himself more whisky. This action alerted Lewis to the irregularity of the circumstances. Pen, who had never before allowed himself to be seen in this undignified light, with the details of his life on show, had temporarily deserted his normally adult self. Yet over and above this desertion, there was, to Lewis, something questionable about the whole affair; it was not in character for Pen to have allowed it. In this he was unlike his sister, who was single-minded and demonstrative; if there were some kind of trouble in which she were involved she would require supporters, to whom she could hotly complain. Perhaps that was unfair, he thought, yet he was uneasy. He was being petitioned as a friend, although he was a friend on a wholly different basis, mild, discreet, undemanding, modest. The rules of the genre had been breached, and here he was, on a lurid pretext, which everyone would soon deplore, not knowing exactly what was required of him. This sort of incident had no precedent in his world. He felt acutely conscious of his own narrow horizons, felt ashamed of his reluctance, and castigated himself for his prudishness.

'Well, George can't expect to have everything his own way,' said Emmy, unwilling to let the matter rest. 'And you're not to apologize. It's none of his business whether I have a key or not.'

'Emmy,' said Pen, with enormous distaste. 'Will you please shut up?'

But she would not. Lewis saw her as excitable and

damaging, as she strode up and down the little room, her cheeks flushing with her mounting indignation. She was also very desirable. As a spectacle she was in a class of her own: she was not an actress for nothing, he noted. He began to perceive her strange and easily mobilized anger, which settled on and clung to every pretext, as a protest against those who had so monstrously let her down. She was, he supposed, fairly monstrous herself, and yet he understood her. He understood that she would always be looking for that ideal court of appeal to which she might present her case, and that her inability to find it would simply increase her desperation. She wanted to be compensated for what he could only intuit as the disappointments that life had meted out to her. In the absence of total, immediate, and permanent gratification, or at least justification, she would react with amazed tears, incomprehension, and further bad behaviour. Lewis respected her grief, although it seemed to him trivial, much as his own did, but shook his head over her inability to see how inconvenient she was. That, of course, was what had occasioned her enormous tactlessness in dislodging him from his virtuous wife and bringing him across London to take sides in a private quarrel. He saw that Pen's status, too, had very slightly shifted as a result of his presence. There must, he thought, have been many occasions when Emmy had made the sort of undignified intervention that she was making now. She spread about her an air of folly, to which even Pen was not immune. If he had been he would have stopped her.

Lewis cleared his throat. 'It's getting late,' he said. 'I must be getting back. Why don't you go to bed, Pen?'

'Lewis,' said Pen, with application. 'Good of you to come. All nonsense, of course. Emmy . . . Well, never mind. I have the feeling,' he went on, 'that I might not be in tomorrow. Tell Goldsborough, would you?'

'Of course,' said Lewis, hoisting Pen to his feet. He noticed the reality of Pen's condition, which gave a certain validity to Emmy's appeal. This was something of a relief to him. 'I'll see you upstairs, shall I? Then I'll put Emmy in a cab. Don't worry about tomorrow.'

He shepherded Pen up the stairs to his bedroom, picked up a book and read it while Pen was in the bathroom, and then waited until he could safely put out the light.

'Goodnight,' he said. There was no reply. He closed the door quietly behind him.

'What was that about?' he asked Emmy in the kitchen.

She shrugged. 'George has a nasty temper. They had a row, obviously about me – I don't know the details. Pen is going to be furious that I sent for you: he's terribly secretive as a rule. It's difficult for him, you see. Our parents don't know. I've always known, of course. Unfortunately, I can't stand George. It's mutual, I may say.'

'Why exactly did you send for me?' asked Lewis. 'You could have managed on your own.'

'Of course I could,' she retorted angrily. 'I sent for you because I wanted to see you again, and because I could see you wouldn't have the guts to do anything about it. It's been two months, Lewis. *Two months.* Why didn't you get in touch? It was the least you could have done.'

'Emmy,' said Lewis. 'Don't let's go through this again. You seem determined to put me in a false position. I see you find it laughable – so do I, as a matter of fact. And I dare say you hate husbands as much as you hate wives, but I am one, whether you like it or not.'

'So what? I'm talking about you and me. I don't care about your other feelings. You can have those on your own. When I've gone.'

'Gone?'

'Yes. I'm going abroad to make a film, and even if I weren't I wouldn't see you again. Anyway,' she added, 'I doubt if you're all that important. After all, it's not as if I were in love with you.'

'No,' he agreed. 'One certainly couldn't say that. And please don't start crying again. If you don't love me why are you crying? Because you can't have what you want? That is what small children do.'

'There's no need to be angry with me,' she said, bursting into tears. 'Everybody's angry with me, Lewis,' she sobbed. 'Nobody wants me. Why don't you stay? I need you to stay. You can't go home now, it's too late.'

'If I leave now,' he said, stroking her hair, feeling her warmth against him, 'there's no real harm done. And anyway, we're in Pen's house.'

'There's masses of bedrooms,' she assured him. 'Pen won't know anything. I never discuss these matters.'

He smiled, in spite of himself. She urged him deftly up the stairs, along the corridor. 'Nobody will know. Your wife will think you're with Pen.' She unclipped her ear-rings, took off her many necklaces. He sat on a strange bed and watched her, aware that she was dangerous and that he was endangered. When he kissed her it was with the knowledge that the timing of this affair, if affair it was to be, was drastically wrong. Unprepared himself, he was disconcerted by the speediness of her behaviour. There was, to his mind, something a little too decisive about her actions. They were not consistent with the hesitations of a nascent attachment. He felt discomforted, almost angry. She was treating him, he thought, like one of those unsatisfactory lovers of whom she complained, but he could see that in fact she insulted her lovers by her very truculence, delivering her insults well in advance of their intentions. In effect, where she saw villainy, they saw only prudence, their own overtures being met with such practicality that they backed out, much as hotel guests entering the wrong room might excuse their mistake. For surely one was entitled to envisage an answering vulnerability? Desire left him, to be replaced by a curious concern, as if she were entirely his responsibility. He remembered her expression of desolation, almost of fear, when Pen had rebuked her. As if she thought there were no place for her anywhere! But what was her place? More to the point, what was his? And how could he restore some dignity to them both, caught as they were in this nearly farcical trap? How could he expect her to love him, as he now knew he loved her, when they were both so unsure of being acceptable? In love, he knew, humiliation could easily turn to hatred. And Emmy had been humiliated before he arrived on the scene. Whatever his actions, he would be blamed for them.

'Wait a moment,' he said. 'There are things that ought to be discussed.'

'What things?' she said incredulously. 'Are you serious?'

'Things that don't matter to you but matter to me. What is right in the circumstances. How to proceed. Whether to proceed at all. What follows from this. What you want. What I want. My wife is not to blame for this, whatever you might think. I can't leave her,' he said, with a sinking heart, aware that he had failed them both, had done a fatal thing.

'So you're going home now, are you?' Her voice was hard now, unforgiving, but she turned her face momentarily away, unwilling for him to see her disappointment.

'You don't love me, do you?' he asked her, taking her face in his hands.

'How do I know?' She shrugged his hands away.

'I know.'

She studied him curiously, hesitated, and then made up her mind, not, he could see, in his favour.

'What a husband you are,' she said. 'And from my point of view, what a shit.'

'Both, inevitably.'

She rebuttoned her shirt. 'Are you sure you can get home on your own?' she asked, in a light acid tone. 'Or would you like me to telephone your wife to come and collect you?'

'Please, Emmy, don't do this. I do love you. I want to be with you, but not here, like this. I want a better life,' he said desperately. 'Not just this. This is not good enough. Do you understand?'

'Good enough?' she said, with the faintest suggestion of

a sneer, which he heard with dread. 'Nothing is ever good enough, don't you know that? At least, it never has been for me. And now you're making it worse. You could have made me happy, but you chose not to – that's all I understand. I'm not happy either. Did you think of that?'

'You see,' he said. 'My feelings are quite different. I doubt if I can get you to understand that – there isn't time – but what you propose is not the answer. Most men would jump at it. But these are the men you complain about, with their little arrangements. One is damned either way with you, isn't one?'

'Perhaps,' she said, in a bored tone, her back to him. 'But then, you see, you didn't offer much, did you? You say you love me, and yet you stayed away. That was wrong, Lewis. We could have met, gone for another walk, talked. I don't care for your feelings if you insist on keeping them to yourself. I consider that paltry, puny. If you loved me, what were you prepared to do about it? Think of me when you were in bed with your wife? I rather think my way is better. Cleaner, more honest.'

'Neither way would have been the right one,' he said, now feeling very cold.

'I'm rather tired,' she said. 'Would you mind leaving now? You can find your way out, can't you?'

Neither of them moved. 'I want you to have so much more,' he said. 'I want to give it to you. Not like this.'

'And what do you think I want?' she said. They looked at each other, stricken with knowledge.

'I despise men who make promises they can't keep,' he said. 'So I can't promise anything. I've got to go home – that seems to be my place, whether I like it or not. I wish it were otherwise, but I can't make it so. I can't offer you anything, you see. I can't offer you anything in the way of continuation. I don't even know if that's what you have in mind. You say you're going away. But I'm bound to stay here. How do you suppose that would feel?'

She appeared not to hear him, but sat on the bed,

frowning, not in anger, he thought, but in bewilderment.

'Isn't it curious how everybody turns me out?' she said. He looked at her, but she was lost in some thought that antedated him. 'I only want the same as other women. To be taken care of, like you take care of your wife. That's what I want, really. To come first. And I thought I could with you.'

'Is that all you want?' he asked, appalled by the nakedness of her reasoning.

'Oh, I don't know, I don't know,' she said, with a return to her normal manner. 'Why don't you go home if you're going?'

'I don't know how to leave you,' he said.

'Oh, men always say that. Then they push off, never to be seen again, Go, just go.'

But he took her in his arms, and held her for a time, until he felt the anger leave her, and something like his own sorrow take its place. Then he kissed her and left.

It was very late and the streets were deserted. Not a car passed. He walked down Pembridge Crescent, the large houses ghostly in the moonlight. In Kensington High Street he thought he might pick up a taxi, but there was nothing to be seen. He walked down Earl's Court Road into Old Brompton Road, then down Redcliffe Gardens and Edith Grove into the King's Road. From there it was his usual walk home. He glanced at his watch almost indifferently. It was three o'clock. The entire adventure had been concluded in under four hours, exactly as if he were guilty. He felt clandestine, ignoble, sick at heart. The very irregularity of the evening disturbed him; the fact that he should be out on the streets at this hour seemed to him so unsettling, so much against the natural order, that guilt for this was added to his already heavy burden. Matters being equal, he might have regarded this night-time excursion as intriguing, even stimulating, but when the very reason for it was grounded in shame he doubted whether he could even bear to remember it, always supposing that it might be concluded without incident, which was by no means certain. There would have to be explanations, reassurances. His heart smote him as he thought of his home life, put in danger because of Emmy, yet unbearable without the thought of her. And Pen: how would Pen behave towards him when they next met? Was he to lose Pen as well as Emmy? If so, his life would be a desert, a penitential round of work and home, without a refuge from all that he was beginning to feel was most alien to him.

He preoccupied himself with thoughts of Pen. When he thought of Emmy, he felt a quaking, an inner desolation, as if his physical foundations had literally shifted. And with the thought of Emmy came the unwelcome memory of his own behaviour. He felt utterly reduced, as if he could not bear to look at himself again. Perhaps she had been right: no harm would have been done. Yet he knew, with a melancholy knowledge, that he was not a good enough actor for adultery, was not sufficiently self-serving. In any event it was not what he wanted. And Tissy was still innocent, there was no getting round that. What he had told Emmy was true: he wanted a better life. His face burned steadily as he thought of what had taken place. In addition to his shame and regret, he felt guilty of a grave fault merely by being involved in behaviour that was henceforth to be entered on his record. He felt himself to be in a serious state of error, and that no one who claimed to be above board should be in the streets at three o'clock in the morning, and finally, furtively, entering his own house like a burglar, intent on making no noise.

Tissy was awake. He knew she was awake, although she insisted on pretending to be asleep. He spoke her name experimentally, whispered it into her ear, but her body remained still, her eyes closed. Only her rigidity gave her away. He knew that it would be worse than useless to try out some sort of an explanation: the thought was not even to be entertained. The truth was out of the question and any falsehood would be immediately detected. He knew that her suspicions of Emmy had been aroused at their first meeting. The situation was unendurable but would have to be endured; he did not see how he could face the following day. For his wife he felt a reluctant pity, not because she had been injured by his own defeat – he had, he hoped, saved her from that – but because the events of this horrible evening might have injured her in ways she could not even contemplate. For now he loved Emmy, whom he had renounced, and there was no hope for him.

Yet at some level he seemed to be unalterably married, and thus it was from his wife that he sought absolution, or at least as much as would provide a safe passage back to whatever normality could be salvaged from the ruins. Once or twice during the course of his sleepless night he made as if to wake her, shaking her gently, and murmuring, 'Tissy? Tissy?' But she remained adamant, and when the first light of a beautiful day pierced the gap in the curtains he knew that she had condemned him, without his having to say a word.

11

From her expression, Lewis could see that it was all up with Mrs Harper. Consideration of this distracted him momentarily from the situation in which he found himself. Mrs Harper's habitual grimness of feature, from which the original petulance and coquetry had long departed, was now overlaid with an air of desperation, and also of incredulity, as if she could not believe that she had once again been clobbered by fate. Whatever wordless plans she had made for her own future – at the bridge table, perhaps, in sunnier climes, or merely baking cakes for the doctor – had been swept away by this throw of the dice, of which she knew nothing beyond the fact that Tissy had returned to her, evidently with the intention of staying. Opening the door of her house on to its crimson interior, now a little darker, a little shabbier than when Lewis had first seen it, she welcomed him almost as an ally. He came, of course, as a suppliant, knowing himself to be deeply in the wrong, but not as wrong as all that, simply wrong in the way that men have always felt themselves to be in the light of a woman's accusatory disapproval.

Tissy's accusations were silent and therefore menacing, hinting at a limitless number held in reserve. They had lived together uneasily after his night of – what had it been? Love? Infidelity? Or rather fidelity? He no longer knew – unwilling to sever the ties that still held them together, but frighteningly, separately, angry. Was it for this? This was the question in Lewis's mind as Tissy sat tight-lipped and unbelieving throughout his explanations. To her the insult was mortal. Her status as a married woman had been deprived of its dignity, and she found that righteousness, which in her case had always been authentic, no longer served her as well when it was assumed for other purposes. In the guise of outrage her innocence no longer pleased, became ugly, middle-aged. Lewis came home nervously in the evenings: weekends were torture. And yet nothing had happened. He repeated this until it began to sound false even to himself. After all, something had happened, and Tissy was not stupid enough to think otherwise. What had really happened soon dwindled in his mind into a wistfulness, not fully remembered, and certainly not weighty enough to measure up to what was being enacted here: his estrangement from his wife and her growing resentment at his presence.

When he thought about it later he wondered whether this resentment had not always been there, but disguised as tolerance, a tolerance for which he had always been grateful since it was slightly ostentatious and therefore made him feel humble. There was something non-negotiable about this tolerance of Tissy's: he could not always expect it. He was grateful to be forgiven, yet again, for faults so native to men that their existence could be assumed, taken for granted even, by women who might, but then again might not, extend the hand of mercy. Nothing less than total incorruptibility, he thought, would satisfy her, and yet he had tried to be incorruptible. But he could no longer ignore the fact that in her eyes he was damned, whatever he might or might not have done. And he could see no way in which he might undo this. His inability to defend himself grew in proportion to her refusal to believe him. There is something contemptible about a man who says, 'But nothing happened!' Her mouth tightened when she looked at him; she became an expert at leaving the room in a manner which established her innocence and his guilt. He became exasperated but still felt helpless. Since they continued to sleep in the same bed he very occasionally made love to her. But this was in the dark, when they were both half asleep, and in any event wordless. He never knew what she felt, since the morning restored her to her tight-lipped self-sufficiency. She probably added these incidents to the weight of the evidence already piled up against him. That she should become pregnant as a result of one of these half-conscious encounters demonstrated, finally, how base her husband had turned out to be.

She was older than he was and had always been frail, or so she said: Lewis was accustomed to treating her as if this was in fact the case, although she seemed to have as much stamina as the next person when she wanted to use it. It was simply that she had fallen, early in her life, into a series of attitudes that ensured the protection of others. In this way she had never had to learn the skills appropriate to maturity. She had remained young, *jeune fille*, as if the years had no purchase on her. Others were there to serve her; their company was necessary if she wanted to go out. She never betrayed any interest in the character of anyone but her mother, whom she pitied for her hard life, yet this pity held something unexamined, a mixture of incuriosity and rivalry, all disguised as a need for her mother's company, as if her mother could not properly exist without her, whereas, as far as Lewis could see, Mrs Harper still had ambitions for herself. She was still a good-looking woman, although Lewis was now forced to add 'for her age'. Not a lot more would happen to Mrs Harper; he supposed that that was why she clung to the doctor. That Tissy should want to go back to this pair seemed to him quite simply unbelievable: that she should deliver her pregnant self to her mother, to the extent of moving back into her old room, was, to Lewis, something so awful that he could hardly bear to contemplate it. That she should want to do this instead of staying with him, as surely even nature intended, simply marked the width and depth of the gulf that now existed between them.

He did not for a moment believe that she had left him. The suspicion began later, as the weeks passed. He thought at first that for a person of Tissy's susceptibilities pregnancy, and a late pregnancy at that, was bound to be upsetting. What he was unprepared for was the muteness of her rage and grief, her fury at him and his kind, her hatred for his very helplessness. Guilty and helpless: that was precisely how they both knew him to be, in his very essence, his blameless appearance, his attempts to pacify her. One day she was gone, a note on the kitchen table merely stating, 'I am at Mother's'. At first he supposed her simply to be there for the evening: this was unusual but within the bounds of possibility. He even enjoyed the peace and silence of the house, although he was surprised to see that no food had been prepared. He wondered if Mrs Harper had been taken ill, but surely she would have telephoned him in that case. 'I am at Mother's' probably meant just what it said. Yet Mrs Harper could not be expected to bring her home at the end of the evening. Lewis had sighed and got to his feet, yet a nebulous anxiety had made the sigh a mere formality. In any event he felt at a loss without her. Even if she disliked him, as he feared she really did, he had no wish to see her go.

He loved her, in a hurt damaged way. He loved her as a child might love a broken doll, half frightened at having caused the breakage. He loved her with all the dark mournful memories of a child's loneliness, that loneliness which age almost though never entirely obscures. His love seemed to him a pitiful thing, literally filled with pity, not only for his wife but for himself. When Emmy had appeared in his life it was as if she had come to him as an adult and thus called to him to be an adult as well, leaving behind the shameful needs of childhood. This was the virtue of Emmy, that she had thought him to be as bold as she was herself. And he had disappointed her. He no longer pondered the rights and wrongs of the case, but merely knew that he had disappointed her. For this reason he was ignoble. Yet his wife presumed him to be ignoble in quite another way, and for quite another reason. In this he knew that she too reasoned as a child does, for she refused to listen to him, turned her head obstinately away when he held her by the arms and tried to speak to her. He wondered whether either of them had ever been worth all this trouble. Yet of the two his wife moved him more, precisely because of that smarting childishness that he had recognized in himself when Emmy's scorn had fallen on his undefended head, when he had awkwardly picked up his jacket and put it on. The gesture had made him feel as Adam must have felt in the Garden, his accusation dying on his lips. Lewis felt the tears rise to his eyes when he thought of either woman. He ached for both of them, and only incidentally for himself.

Mrs Harper seemed unsure of her attitude towards him. She had flung wide the door, as was her custom, but she had not invited him into the crimson interior. Lewis considered the possibility that she too hated him: nothing would have seemed more natural. That he should be despised by all women seemed to be his destiny, whether or not they had the measure of his crimes. But Mrs Harper had been forced to make terms with him, when it became apparent that she was unwilling to shoulder once again the burden of her daughter. And if there were to be a baby Mrs Harper would prefer the baby to live in Lewis's house rather than her own. She had discovered the delights of living alone, the early nights, the leisurely sauntering days, the absence of all encumbrances save that of her lover, the light delicate meals, the stupor of television. When, these days, she said, 'I'm getting old,' no one contradicted her, although she still dressed carefully and prepared her appearance before going out. She continued to strike a variety of false notes, too dressed up for the local parade of shops, too compromised, too discontented for the centre of town, where, like many idle women, she might have spent pleasant harmless days, as women of her generation were accustomed to do. She had never worked. What she lived on Lewis never knew, but money did not appear to be a problem. Lewis supposed her to be something of a remittance woman, turned out of the family home for some early misdemeanour and paid an allowance in lieu of her expectations of an inheritance. The family was, apparently, a good one, highly thought of in Jersey, although Lewis imagined that exaggerations of grandeur were called for in her situation. Jersey was always spoken of as the place where all right-thinking people lived, yet no explanation was offered for her long exile. It was assumed, by her and by everyone else, that she would eventually make her home there, presumably when she judged it appropriate to do so. Had she not married, Tissy would have accompanied her, met various cousins whom she did not know, and begun her career as a *jeune fille* all over again. Without Tissy Mrs Harper's projected exile had taken on a bolder outline, more colourful lineaments. Might she not marry the doctor, himself, to judge from his appearance, a remittance man of sorts? Might they not, together, make a late bid for respectability? And might it not become them, as it occasionally does, after a lifetime of inglorious freedom?

But Mrs Harper's expression, as she stood in the doorway of her red house, was uncertain. She was too proud, too case-hardened, to exhibit helplessness, although it was quite apparent that that was what she felt.

'She says she's not coming back.' She delivered the message expressionlessly, as if her own competence to deal with the matter were not in play.

'Not coming back?' Lewis laughed slightly, as if to demonstrate that this could not be serious. 'Not coming back? Look, do you think I could come in for a minute? I don't quite understand what's happened.'

Reluctantly she had let him in, although she made no move towards the drawing-room. Lewis had found it quite reassuring that she should remain in character, to the extent of letting him stand in the hall. So far he was not really worried, believing vaguely that all women ran to their mothers when they were upset.

'She says she's not coming back to you, Lewis. It's no good your looking at me like that. None of this is my doing. Far from it.'

'Where is she?' he asked. 'Is she all right?'

164

'Perfectly all right. She always is when she gets her own way. She's up in her room, her old room, I mean. And as far as I can see she intends to stay there.'

Mrs Harper breathed hard, as her ordinary life, the life she had lived between Tissy's marriage and the events of this evening, receded in an aura of distant happiness.

'I don't know what you did,' she went on. 'And I don't want to know. All I know is that she's decided to leave you.'

'Did she walk here by herself?' asked Lewis stupidly.

'No. She telephoned me to come and get her. Oh, I know her in this mood. But what could I do? She is my daughter after all. She has no one else.'

'She has me,' said Lewis.

'Oh, men,' Mrs Harper retorted, with something of her old asperity. 'Take it from me, Lewis, a woman can't rely on a man. I should know. Not that I've anything against you: you've been good to her. But I wonder if these feminists aren't right. Only women really understand women.'

As she talked, Lewis was aware that the two of them, mother and daughter, would soon work their way back into a type of female collusion that he had disrupted but not obliterated. By intemperately marrying Tissy he had taken her from her rightful place, from the ranks of all those women who would presumably understand what she was doing. Yet they all wanted to get married, didn't they? They were not above the odd sly move in this direction, the odd ploy, the odd plan. What more could he have done to please her, once he knew that this was her intention?

In Mrs Harper's face there began to dawn the first signs of a look of dangerous disappointment, which would soon, Lewis knew, be directed against himself. In no time at all she would be blaming him for what had happened. He marvelled at the irrational faultlessness with which their minds worked: so swift to reach the correct conclusion, yet getting there by means which he would consider irregular, almost gangsterish. His shoulders slumped in weariness: he would never find mercy at this tribunal. He saw himself condemned to repeat his defence throughout eternity, without ever a hope of swaying the jury. 'But nothing happened!' he said to himself, miserably aware of how paltry a man sounds when he utters this particular excuse. If nothing happened, then this was the final blow to his masculinity, no matter how ardently he might proclaim his virtue. And to a man there was something unseemly in this raking over the ashes, this jealous watchfulness, when what had taken place should have been an affair of the utmost privacy, of secrecy. He did not know the rules, he concluded, had merely thought in terms of admiring, longing, loving, when what apparently counted was a calculation of the sexual score, as if everyone were keeping a tally. Did you or didn't you? Tissy had humiliatingly asked him. Either you did or you didn't. But she had left the room without waiting for an answer. Either answer would have counted against him. And, will you or won't you? Emmy had demanded. And all that he had wanted was to examine, quite delicately, this feeling that had brought them together, to experience its novelty, to dream of its possibility. But a passage of arms was what had been in mind, so that she too could add him to her list of unsatisfactory or impossible men.

It still did not occur to him that Tissy had left him for good. He thought this retreat to her old room was part of an elaborate ritual, and that once he had played his part, confessed that he was penitent, remorseful, and helpless without her, she would return.

'Can I see her?' he asked Mrs Harper.

'I shouldn't advise it. I've put her to bed with some hot milk and an aspirin. I'll give her a sleeping pill later.'

'Well, what would you advise?' he had said, exasperated by this show of invalidism. If this was where they were heading the outlook was poor.

'You could call round tomorrow, I suppose. Or better still, leave it for a couple of days. It won't do you any harm to look after yourself for a bit, show you what women have to do.'

166

'I do work, you know.'

'Oh, work,' she said, with a look of disgust. 'I know all about men's work.'

'As a matter of fact, Thea, it would have done Tissy no harm to have had a job of sorts. Part-time. Nor you either.' He knew he was on dangerous ground but a wave of anger had made him bold. 'You've both got too much time to think about yourselves. About what pleases *you*. And you're both competent women. Tissy is much too young just to sit at home. She had more energy when she was working in the library. Why couldn't she go back there?'

'You don't know what you're talking about, Lewis. You forget how handicapped she is.'

'But the point is she was getting so much better. She could have overcome it altogether if you'd let her. You kept treating her as if she were a little girl. You colluded with her. And don't tell me your life couldn't have been different if you'd met more people. You might have married again. You're still a good-looking woman.'

The 'still' was perhaps unfortunate. But now that he was speaking the truth he thought there was no point in pretending that things were other than they were.

'That'll do, Lewis. You've no business criticizing me.'

'No, you're right, I haven't. But Tissy is a married woman now. My wife. It's time she stopped behaving like a baby. She's going to *have* a baby, for God's sake. What kind of a mother is she going to be?'

He thought of a daughter, undergoing the same claustration, the same reclusion as Tissy had done, with all her childishness preserved intact. Yet a daughter would be better than a son. A son would be denatured by such a mother. Or would he? He himself had been brought up by his mother, and he did not truly think that he was any the worse for it, although the women in his present life – or out of it – would no doubt accuse him of nameless faults in this connection. But his mother had been all sweetness, and her only fault had been to lead him to overvalue sweetness in others. He himself half hoped for a boy. But when he thought of Tissy he knew it was unrealistic to calculate in terms of a son or a daughter. He saw the child in terms of infinite babyhood, a babyhood enduring throughout its adult life. Sexless loyalty was Tissy's requirement, and if she could not get it from her husband she would exact it from her child.

'Whether I call round or not,' he said, 'I expect Tissy to get in touch with me tomorrow.'

'I can't answer for her,' said her mother.

'Surely you can see how unsatisfactory this is? It's in nobody's interest . . . And anyway, she's my *wife*.'

'Yes, well, you should have thought of that.'

But her voice was weary and her eyes seemed tearful, as the prospect of the rest of her life unrolled before her. She doubted whether the doctor would come to heel now, although he might have done if Jersey and its delights had been on the horizon. Instead of that she was to have a grandchild in the house, for there was a distinct possibility that Tissy might stay indefinitely. Tissy's revenge would be extended to everyone she had ever known, beginning with her mother. Forgiveness was beyond her; forgetting out of the question. Her sole pleasure, in the future, would consist of being an uncomfortable reminder of how they had all wronged her. And no doubt the baby would come in for some of that as well.

The fact that throughout this interview he had not been asked, let alone invited, to sit down, seemed to Lewis emblematic of the whole affair. His status, he saw, was henceforth to be that of an intruder. As he was already classed as the guilty party, this new attitude, which had formed remarkably quickly, simply edged him further towards marginality. Steps would soon be taken to remove him altogether. He would be redundant, irrelevant in a household of women. For although there were only two of them he saw them as the centre of a grievance that would inevitably bring others to their side. They would benefit from their situation, however precarious, however unenviable it might seem to be, and

168

the longer they persisted in it the more incapable it would become of any resolution. Pride, reputation, honour were in the balance, and all would fall if the masculine will were to prevail. This contest, in which love had no part – had indeed not been mentioned throughout the proceedings – seemed to Lewis the height of insanity. He had hardly time to consider his own situation, since he still could not calculate the time-scale of Tissy's absence. But at last he began to perceive his predicament, if Tissy chose to stay away. He could see that just as it was a matter of honour for her to leave him, it was a matter of *his* honour that she should return. There was simply no point at which they could compromise. And the poor little baby, torn between the two of them! But he did not really believe that they would still be in this mess in seven months' time, when the baby was due to be born. If they were he would simply have to abandon the child to his or her mother and grandmother. He would be too heartbroken to bring it up on his own. He thought of Silas Marner, and felt the beginning of tears again as he saw himself, a grey-haired old man, devoting his life to a pretty and unsuspecting little girl. Yet tears were not to be shed, it seemed, neither his nor Mrs Harper's. Tissy's tears would, of course, have preceded her arrival.

Above his overriding and immediate dilemma there hovered a more abstract speculation. Something about this mother and daughter repelled him. Their behaviour towards each other, towards the world, was not as it should be. He had never, except at the wedding ceremony, seen them embrace. His reading had led him to expect more, much, much more, perhaps an outpouring of love and anguish such as he himself felt ready to bestow. He imagined an ideal mother and daughter, whom he might have devised himself, greeting each other. The picture was vivid: he could see it quite clearly, over and beyond Mrs Harper's discomposed features. Such kisses, such sighs, such patting of cheeks! There was none of that here, nor, to his knowledge, had there ever been. Emotion was something they did without; at least, their

constricted view of emotion was translated into silent dem-
onstrations of attachment, of loyalty, certainly, of fidelity of
an unquestioning kind, but also of an inability to go further,
into pleasurable feeling. If Tissy loved him – if she had ever
loved him – it was in the same way that Mrs Harper loved the
doctor, almost with a sort of reluctance, as if this were all that
could be expected of them. It pained him to discover within
himself a sympathy with the doctor, whom he unreservedly
disliked, but he could see that both of them must often have
retreated into resignation. It was Emmy who had opened
this new perspective in his thinking. She was outrageous,
but she was also spontaneous, instinctive: the surge of the
id was there, however disastrous the consequences. She was
at the other extreme from Tissy. Then he remembered that
they both appeared to hate him, and that whatever he had
done, or not done, had apparently removed them both. A
coldness settled on him, and he began to face the fact that he
had somehow, simultaneously, let them both down. It would
have been better if he had been unfaithful: what comfort
could there be in inadequacy? Yet the idea that he had failed
his marriage was his predominant anxiety: this was a crime,
and, like the shooting of the Duc d'Enghien, worse than a
crime, an error. Who would have thought Tissy capable of
the action that now confronted him? And how was he to
live, if not as a married man, the fate that he felt had been
bestowed on him almost since birth?

Marriage to him meant order, infidelity disorder, even
chaos. And behind this simple fact came the subdivisions of
order: a quiet and regulated life, predictable but manageable
longings, an old age that could be anticipated without fear.
And children: he longed for children. Apart from Andrew,
whom he saw perhaps once a year, he had no family. He
came from a short line of dead people. Surely, even with
her restricted imagination, Tissy could see that his was the
natural path? He was in no sense exceptional, and never
would be. Perhaps his disappointment in finding his wife to
be as unexceptional as himself was unworthy. He knew now

170

that together they might have had a peaceable life, but that it would have been a life without growth. Yet he dreaded to see the possibility of such a life taken away by this ugly hackneyed return to the red house, with its over-large, over-important furniture, and its smell of caramel. That reminded him: he had not eaten since breakfast. He had missed lunch, had wandered round Lincoln's Inn Fields, thinking of Emmy. Even that had been wrong. Disorder was already apparent in everything he did. Miserably, he longed for his wife, and the restitution of their life together before this unimaginable, this ludicrous disaster had overtaken him. That he must appear apologetic, importunate, a figure of fun, did nothing to reassure him.

At last, heavy-hearted, he had turned to go. He was obliged to open the front door himself, since Mrs Harper's brand of hospitality had reverted to the peculiar unfriendliness that had been his impression on first meeting her. She stood and watched him, not hostile, not really indifferent, merely incurious as to the state of his own feelings. That, of course, was the quality which both mother and daughter shared: incuriosity. Faced with this he felt suddenly frightened. Who would care for him now? How long would he have to go home to an empty house? Pure panic seized him when he thought of his inevitable descent into illness and squalor, or, if not these, then certainly eccentricity, of which he had previously given no sign. He had seen elderly scholars in the library, locked for years inside someone else's biography, and now recognizable by their dull ties, their unpolished shoes, the hair straggling down their necks. He would probably become like one of them. His heart broke with loneliness, and because he could not trust his voice to speak he had merely lifted his arm in farewell to Mrs Harper and gone out into the night.

This, then, was what he had to face, and he knew he must be very vigilant. He knew that he must lose neither his feelings nor his manners in the days to come. Dignity would go as soon as he would be forced to explain himself and his situation to a third party, but sensibility, with a bit of luck, could be retained. No heroic attitude would be available to him, and he now began to doubt the reality of such attitudes. Heroic behaviour was a contributory factor to the madness of art: it had little to do with the untidiness, the shabbiness, the sheer randomness of life itself.

At home he noted that Tissy had apparently disposed of everything in the larder, and had disdained further shopping as being beneath her wounded dignity. This was as much as he had expected; in that sense he was adapting to the situation. He poured himself a glass of milk and went into the bedroom. Oddly enough, he did not miss her here. In bed with her, he had always felt uncomforted, and sometimes his dreams had shown himself as longing to be free. What he felt now was a coldness, as if he were, or had become, a much older man. It even seemed to him that there was a new stiffness in his movements, but the hour was late, and he was uneasy on so many levels that he sought the solace of his bed without any further nod towards the implications of his condition. He slept the black sleep of grief, or of bereavement.

In the morning he went to the library as usual. He did not think he looked any different, met no surprised glances as he walked past the porter's lodge and up the stairs. At some point during the morning Goldsborough, now adorned with several CND badges, loomed into view.

'A word with you, Lewis, if you would be so kind. In my office.'

Lewis wondered if he were to be dismissed. On grounds of moral cowardice, no doubt, word having got round. He was to be indicted as a poltroon, unworthy, among other things, of the office of librarian. He was sure that there was nothing wrong with his work, so it could only be his utter failure as a human being that was giving rise to Goldsborough's concern. For Goldsborough was undoubtedly concerned; his face was uncharacteristically grave. Goldsborough too must be getting on, Lewis thought, although disguised by a protracted boyishness, a very real *naïveté*. Yet his girth was increasing; there was no mistaking his figure for that of a younger man. He had appeared twice on a television panel discussion, but despite his grasp of events had been judged too old to appeal to the young and had been replaced by a pop singer who had found Jesus. The elements of a dawning maturity, never fully to be realized, had sent him back to his former work. Deconstruction, when all was said and done, offered more dignity and better career prospects. He had begun to feel left out of it when Lewis's book had been accepted for publication, but had handsomely said nothing. In this way he was able not to offer congratulations, but that, he thought, was by the by. He did not believe in encouraging vanity in others.

Lewis was aware of a portentous clearing of the throat that augured no good for his situation.

'I think you ought to know, Lewis, that your wife telephoned, very early, before you arrived, in fact. Hilary took the call; I'd only just got here myself. She said to tell you not to go round this evening. She said she was staying at her mother's until further notice.' He paused significantly. 'Nothing *wrong*, is there, Lewis?'

'Not at all,' he said. He was burning with humiliation. 'My wife hasn't been too well lately. She's gone to her mother's for a rest.'

'Of course, of course. These things happen. Not to worry. Take time off, if you like. Not too long, mind you.'

He managed to smile. 'I shan't need time off, Arnold. Thanks all the same. I've got rather a lot to do. If you'll excuse me . . . '

He reached the haven of his desk, which was now to be his only haven, having just managed to fight back the wave of scarlet that threatened to engulf him, and which, even now, he could feel draining away, leaving a deadly pallor behind. It was only by telling himself that he would never, in the whole of his life, be so utterly miserable again that he was still able to function. So this is it, he thought, journey's end. What made it infinitely worse was the way in which Tissy had told the world of his plight. Everybody knew, of course. It was no use pretending that nothing was wrong. At this point he accepted that he was alone again. He looked humbly round him at the library, and applied himself with infinite care to his index cards. In the middle of the morning Pen came to his desk, laid a hand briefly on his shoulder, and said, 'Usual place? Half-past twelve?' Some little while later Arthur Tooth came creaking alongside and deposited a barley sugar on one of the piles of off-prints that he was cataloguing. 'Thanks, Arthur,' said Lewis, clearing his throat.

He found that he had very little to say to Pen, who, in turn, had very little to say for himself. By mutual consent they avoided the subjects of Tissy and Emmy, and Lewis would not mention George unless Pen brought his name into the conversation. But having reached some sort of parity of exposure both knew that their friendship was intact, and that only a little delicacy was needed to keep it in good repair. At the end of a largely silent hour they turned to each other and smiled.

'Well,' said Lewis, with an attempt at cheerfulness. 'I suppose we're grown up now. Not that I ever entertained serious hopes of any real wisdom.'

'I suppose you could say that. Although it doesn't feel right, somehow, does it?'

They walked thoughtfully back to the college.

'One last word, Lewis,' said Pen. 'Don't get drunk. It doesn't help. We could have a meal this evening, if you like?'

'I'd better go home,' said Lewis. 'In case I'm needed, or there's a message, or something. I'd better stay in, if you don't mind.'

He knew, in a curious way, that he had to begin a new apprenticeship, and that the sooner he applied himself the better it would be for him. If, as he supposed, solitariness was again to be his portion, he would embrace it, and do his best to see what it would teach him. For he did not doubt that there was still much to be learnt. With this new resolution he managed the afternoon quite well, although he found himself nervous as the hands of the big clock advanced towards six. He had offered to stay late, but everyone seemed to think that he should be offered the treat of a leisurely evening.

He walked home, through drizzling rain, making the uncomfortable journey last as long as possible. He ate a vile pie and drank a half of bitter in a pub. As he approached his house his steps quickened, and he told himself that he could see a light in an upstairs window. But it was only the reflection of a street lamp, as he really knew, and he let himself into an empty house. There was truly no one there. He looked for a letter or a message, but all he found was a parcel, which must have been taken in by Mrs Joliffe. It contained six copies of *The Hero as Archetype*, sent by the publisher. He glanced at them indifferently, stowed them at the back of a cupboard, and went to bed.

12

His daughter, Jessica, was born early one evening after a cold day in March. Lewis was surprised by Mrs Harper's telephone call: he thought all babies were born in the small hours. Instead of settling down with a book he put his coat back on and went to the hospital. He was by no means confident that he would be allowed in. Relations between Tissy and himself were non-existent: she might never have been his wife. He tried to calculate when he had last had a serious conversation with her. He had called round repeatedly in the early days of their estrangement, but Tissy was nowhere to be seen. Standing in the hall with Mrs Harper, who was now completely won over to Tissy's cause, Lewis found his assurance draining away: quite simply, he was aware that he had been phased out of their lives, which had, he supposed, reverted to what they had been when Tissy was growing up. He remembered how hard he had had to strive for their attention even in the promising early days of his courtship. He had felt then as if he were violently interposing himself between Mrs Harper and her native preoccupations, whatever they were. He had never been made privy to anything she thought or felt, although he knew that somewhere, in the obscure depths of her personality, there was a story waiting to be unlocked. He had not exactly felt this about Tissy, although he was aware that there were certain hidden areas, certain matters not explained, to which he had no access. But she had been so docile, so obedient, that he had not thought to look beyond these qualities. He had thought her happy, or rather contented, and had not criticized the use she made of her time, although he privately thought her too passive. He wondered why she did not attempt some sort of work instead of sitting still, so still, and eating chocolates. Nothing had moved her in this direction, and eventually he had dropped the subject. Yet the last time he had submitted himself to an interview with Mrs Harper, it was to be told, with an air of finality, that Tissy was out.

'Out? She's never out. Out by herself? But this is unheard of. Where is she?'

'She's gone to her women's group,' said Mrs Harper. 'A friend calls for her and brings her back.'

'Really,' said Lewis. 'And what does she do there?'

'Well, last week they got to know their bodies. This week they're getting in touch with the pain.'

'What pain?' He was alarmed. 'Is anything wrong with her? Is the baby all right?'

Mrs Harper gave him a look of scorn.

'The pain of being a woman, Lewis. I dare say you wouldn't understand that.'

'Well, no,' he said. 'You don't mind if I sit down, do you? This has come as a bit of a surprise. Is this what they call liberation? If so, and if I understand you correctly,' he said weightily, speaking with enormous deliberation, 'my wife has liberated herself right out of her marriage. What about me? What about my pain?'

'All right. But it's your turn to suffer, isn't it? Women have been oppressed for far too long.'

'Oh, really? Who's been oppressing them?'

'The system, Lewis. The patriarchy.'

'You make them sound like the victims of persecution. Don't you think that's rather insulting to people unjustly imprisoned, people with no rights, no freedom? As I understand it, I have been oppressing my wife by keeping her in relative comfort, by not wilfully infringing her liberty to do as she pleases, and by deferring to her on every important matter. And for that she decamps, taking my baby with her. What about my pain?'

'Haven't you forgotten something?'

'No, I don't think so.'

'That woman.'

'That woman's name is Emmy Douglas. Was. I dare say it still is. I haven't seen her from that day to this. She disappeared from my life about three months before Tissy walked out. And I miss her very much. I never see her, not even to bump into. Did you think I did? Is that what this ridiculous exile of Tissy's is all about?'

'She would have left you anyway. She said she saw signs that you were interested in that woman when she came to dinner that evening.'

'Oh, God, Thea, this is ridiculous. Surely you understand a bit more about men than that? They may be curious about other women – they usually are – but that doesn't make them monsters of infidelity. Real infidelity means leaving your wife altogether for another woman. Rather difficult to do, even supposing one wanted to. And quite rare; more often than not out of the question, simply not possible. And I didn't do that, did I?'

'Well, if that's all you've got to say for yourself . . . '

'No. It isn't. I'd like to know why I'm kept standing here like a salesman. I'd like to know why no enquiry is made about my feelings, or how I'm living, or what I intend to do. I'd like to know how my wife has the nerve to hide from me and to go out on the evenings when she knows I'll be coming round. I'd like to know how my child is going to be brought up. I'd like to be treated with a certain amount of respect, instead of this unbelievable rudeness. You've always been a rude woman, Thea. I put it down to your hard life, although I doubt if your life has been harder than anybody else's. You haven't improved, have you? I detect no change. And it looks as if your daughter is following in your footsteps. Does she want a divorce, by the way? If so, she can have one, and I'll marry Emmy. That might be a good idea all round.'

'She'll never divorce you, Lewis.'

'In that case she'll have to put up with my visits. At least until the child is old enough to look after itself and make its own choices. Rational choices, I hope. In the meantime I have some rights, you know. For instance, I demand to see my baby and I shall do so. If you don't tell me the minute it's born, Thea, and if I'm not allowed full access, I shall divorce Tissy. For desertion. And she can blame that on the system if she likes. And I shall have custody of the child.'

Mrs Harper snorted. 'You? You couldn't bring up a child. What do you know about children?'

'Oh, but I'd marry again, I told you. And at least if the child lived with me I'd teach it some manners.'

But the thought immediately saddened him and put paid to his fighting spirit. Mrs Harper, it seemed, had been shamed into some sort of acquiescence, if nothing more. Was there even a hint of admiration in her eye? If her standard of masculinity had been formed by the stained and supine doctor, might she not welcome this little demonstration of energy? In any event the expression on her face changed to something less challenging – one could hardly call it deference, Lewis thought – as she came to the main motif of the conversation.

'Of course, you'll want to continue her allowance.'

'There's no of course about it. I'm a man, aren't I? Anything can be expected of me, any violation of the rules. The rules, of course, have to be set by you. I'll continue her allowance because I don't want my wife's comfort to suffer, that's all.'

'The child will have the best, I can assure you of that.'

'No, it won't. It will start with an enormous handicap: parents who are separated, and who don't even talk to each other. I'll make a deal with you, Thea. You can look after the baby as long as I have the growing child. There are things I can teach it that Tissy can't. There are places to see . . .'

His throat thickened, as longing for those places grew

in him, suddenly became intolerable. What was he doing here? He was as free as he ever would be. Why not leave it all, the whole mess, disappear, and come back in ten years' time? No-one would miss him, that was clear. And if home were no longer home, what was to be lost by seeking another? In his mind's eye, the street that led to his house, and which he always thought of as bathed in sunshine, became suffused with a darkish mist, drained of colour: a spiteful wind drove dismembered newspapers round his ankles, and dogs barked. The truth of the matter was that he hated now to go home. Every evening his heart sank as the hour approached when he would have to switch off his desk lamp, pick up his briefcase, and begin the long trudge back to Stokenchurch Street. He would have wanted the journey to be even longer. He invented detours, stopped in pubs, although he hated the smell, the noise, and even the beer. He knew he should make an effort, and felt quite pleased with himself on the evenings when he went into a supermarket and bought a bottle of wine and some bread, cheese and fruit. But this pleasure turned into disappointment as soon as he entered his kitchen, and he could no longer be bothered to lay the table. The same plate, the same glass, the same knife, washed the night before and left to drain, were used again and again. One evening, as he sat at the kitchen table, a crust of bread and a rind of cheese on his plate, the plate itself resting on the *Evening Standard*, the visible parts of which he was reading, the doorbell rang. It was Pen: they had had a vague arrangement to see a film which Lewis had forgotten.

'Don't worry,' said Pen, following Lewis into the kitchen and taking in the frugal fare and the workman's place setting. 'Any evening will do.' And then, looking quite stern, 'This has got to stop, Lewis. You can't go on living like this.'

Lewis's shame was compounded by the fact that for the first time in his life he had drunk most of the bottle of wine. He could not even offer a glass to Pen. He felt disarmed, defenceless, and also confused: he knew he was in no fit state to answer any more accusations. Nor did he want to be told to pull himself together, to make a fresh start, to take decisive action. He did not even want to be told to do what he secretly wanted to do anyway, which was to divorce his wife and marry Emmy. This pressing desire, which was kept at bay when he was not drunk by exercise of the higher mind, by all the weight of his responsibilities, had to be treated with caution. For he was a sentimental bourgeois: nothing less than marriage would do, and it would be months – years, perhaps – before he was free. What he firmly did not want was a brief liaison with the volatile Emmy who, he knew, was incapable of fidelity. He had thought about this a great deal. He forgave her everything, her childishness, her neediness, her disappointment, her desire to punish. She had wanted marriage, and complained that all she got was married men. He would give her marriage: that would be a gauge of his love. But in return he would expect her to behave like a wife. He almost struck his head at his own folly at this point in his reasoning. She would never be faithful to him, that was clear. And why should she be? Faithfulness seemed to have gone out of fashion, replaced by more aggressive, more affirmative modes. Women now had duties towards their own bodies, or so he was told; even Tissy was studying the problem. So that a union with Emmy would be flawed, fatally compromised, for he believed that she would not change. After the first few months she would find somebody new, and then she would tell him that she did not see why she should not have both a husband and a lover. Or lovers. It would not mean that she loved him any the less. He could see her crumpled forehead, her rosy cheeks, her growing puzzlement as she came up against his quaint old-fashioned prejudices. He could see it all because this was the state in which she appeared to him when he had first kissed her, in the park. She was involved with someone then, she told him. And yet she had wanted him, had, in fact, been determined to have him. He wondered if a new lover was always selected to punish the current one, whether she ever rested between them. This, to him, was the difficulty. He had to face the possibility that she was a genuinely amoral woman, although he understood that they were not called that any more. There was another possibility – and one supremely embarrassing to him – that she belonged to a superior class in which these habits were rife, and that he revealed his genuine lack of sophistication – his essential suburbanity – in failing to come up to her standards.

And he himself was sinking socially all the time, using the newspaper as a tablecloth, finishing the bottle of wine in an effort to procure a decent night's sleep. He was deeply, mortally ashamed, and sufficiently frightened to vow that things should be different.

'Don't worry about it,' said Pen, whom nothing escaped. 'This doesn't matter. What matters is the future. You'll have to get a divorce, Lewis. This business with Tissy is putting you in a false position. It's ruining your life.'

'It's the child, you see,' said Lewis, looking down at his hands. 'If it weren't for the child I'd, well, cut loose in some way. But I don't even know whether she's coming back or not. She's left some of her clothes behind. She hasn't gone altogether.'

'And do you want her back?'

'Yes,' he said, disturbed by the emotion he felt. 'Yes, I want her back.' For who does not want the wanderer, the prodigal, to return? Lewis felt, in that instant, that nothing could be worse than to be abandoned, and to feel this dereliction which had so rapidly been translated into physical shabbiness. He saw his glass on the table, surrounded by crumbs. And it was not even a proper wine glass; it had previously held Dijon mustard. He felt like an elderly alcoholic. And Pen had seen him like this, when he had thought himself without a witness . . .

'I could do with some coffee, if you're making it, Lewis,' said Pen agreeably, and thus signalling that the awkward moment was over. 'We ought to talk about holidays. Easter's early this year, you know. I wondered whether you'd like to come down to us in Wales? The family will be there. Emmy, of course, you know.'

'My dear old thing,' said Lewis. 'I know what you're saying. But I'll be a father by then. I can't just turn my back on that, can I? Perhaps I can come to you some other time. I'd love to meet your parents. And Emmy, of course, I know.' He smiled sadly.

'Then you ought to get away, after the baby's born. Look here, Lewis, they don't want you. I don't know why but they don't. You can lose nothing by going away for a week or two, or even a month. After all, it's not as if they'll be going anywhere. And it might give them a bit of a jolt, surprise them a bit. Let them do the worrying for a change. Just disappear for a while.'

'I might do that,' said Lewis, who privately did not think he would. Then he put on a new recording of Mahler's Sixth that Pen wanted to hear and they gave themselves over to the pure pleasure of listening. They were both quite calm by the end of the evening.

Showing Pen to the door Lewis said, 'It's all so unnecessary. I mean, I wasn't unfaithful to Tissy, you know.' He found he could not mention Emmy's name in this connection, particularly to Emmy's brother.

'I know you too well to think you were,' said Pen, and then, 'I think I'll walk part of the way home. I don't walk half enough, not like you. And I like to saunter a bit after listening to music. George and I often walk home from the Garden.' On the step he said, 'She's a strange girl, my sister. Always upsetting someone or other. No harm in her really, but she causes a certain amount of trouble. See you tomorrow. Sleep well.'

In the midst of this sadness – for it was a real sadness, as if everything were over for him, as if middle age had closed down on him without warning, and for ever – it was a relief to receive Mrs Harper's telephone call, and to put on his coat again and hurry to the hospital. It was a relief to receive the call at all, for he had not been in touch for some weeks, unable to bring himself to face Mrs Harper's curious obduracy. It occurred to him that she might have taken

Tissy away to have the baby somewhere else, possibly to a hospital in Jersey. He had stayed away because he could not bear his own tired arguments and the helpless anger they inevitably aroused in him, an anger he would not have been able to control had he encountered the doctor, whose part in this miserable history he particularly loathed. Although he mourned his abandoned condition he longed for a clean slate. He would have to relinquish the baby: that he knew without a doubt. He could not work and look after a small child, and if he were out all day who would care for it? Remembering the colonization of his house by Mrs Joliffe, who threatened to sweep back unopposed, now that Tissy was no longer there to keep her in check, he doubted his ability to find a suitable nurse or housekeeper. No, the child would have to stay with its mother, and its grandmother, and, no doubt, the doctor. The idea made him sick at heart. Yet he still promised himself that he would reclaim it in later life, when they could live intelligently together. If he could wait ten years he would get his son or daughter back. But ten years! How was he to live in that time? It was impossible to think of himself carrying on as he was. He seriously wondered if it would not be better if he were to disappear in some way, remove himself from the various embarrassments he seemed to have brought on himself. But how to do this? What money he had must go to the child. And where would he go? For a dark moment he thought of just going to bed and staying there until he wasted away. They could call it a nervous breakdown if they liked, whoever they were, and always supposing that they were sufficiently interested to enquire. But he was too healthy, too stalwart: he could not ever remember being ill. With a sigh he resigned himself to carrying on.

He was not much interested in babies, but the various reversals he had undergone filled him with both longing and pity for his own child, whom he found asleep in a crib at the foot of Tissy's bed. A perfectly ordinary baby, as far as he could see, although he was alarmed at the sight of its fragile head, in which a pulse seemed to be beating. He touched a tiny hand, which obligingly retracted. He would have liked to pick her up, but did not trust himself not to display too much sadness in doing so, and therefore resisted the temptation. Tissy, blank-faced with fatigue, and also with astonishment at what she had undergone, lay back on several pillows and held her mother's hand. The doctor, his hat and coat piled untidily on the radiator, sat in the only other chair, eating grapes. For once they seemed faintly uneasy in Lewis's presence. He did not intend to embarrass them for long. He only wanted to see his child, his daughter, and, no doubt, to say goodbye to her until she was ten years old.

'Lovely, isn't she?' said a nurse, who had come in to settle Tissy for the night. 'What are you going to call her?'

Lewis wanted to call her Grace, after his mother, but thought, on reflection, that his mother had no place in this alliance. He tried to think of a heroine in literature, under whose protection he could place her, so to speak. Dorothea Brooke, perhaps?

'I thought Jessica,' said Tissy, speaking for the first time.

He was surprised. Yes, why not? The name pleased him.

'And mother's name as a second name.'

'Thea? he asked.

'Dorothea,' said Mrs Harper, wiping her normally wintry eyes.

So it was meant, then. And she was Jessica Dorothea Percy, and he registered her name the following day.

He could not, of course, resist going back to see her. He told himself that he would have been the same with a kitten, a puppy, or simply anyone else's baby. It was their smallness that was so beguiling, he would have said, but he knew it was more than that. At least, that may have been a part of it, but at the heart there was a helpless love, a love that was truly helpless, for he did not see how he could impose himself on this baby, when his role was to be largely absent, a visitor rather than a guide. He hardened his heart against the little hands, the limp legs, and he was glad to find the baby asleep, so that he did not have to meet its

185

large incurious blue eyes. He doubted whether he could have sustained the encounter. Tissy, in all this time, said as little as possible. He found her unchanged. She looked totally at home in her hospital bed, seemed indifferent to his comings and goings, but kept a fierce maternal eye on him when he hovered too closely over the crib. The following evening he found her with the baby in her arms, held awkwardly, as a child holds a new doll. It appeared that she loved her. Whatever misgivings she may have had about her role as a wife had left her when she became a mother. For was this not the ultimate proof that she was a woman, grown up, free from tutelage at last? With this act, Lewis thought, she had accomplished something that had always been in doubt: her own late entry into maturity. He was forced to admire her, while at the same time realizing that she would never come back to him. For all the awkwardness of her gestures, the timidity of her utterances, she was now someone to be reckoned with. If she did not always answer him when he spoke to her it was because she did not want to. Even her mother deferred to her now. She had put on a considerable amount of weight, and her face had coarsened; she no longer paid much attention to her hair, which had grown longer and looked slightly neglected. He hardly recognized her as the shy girl whom he had followed from the library so long ago.

They had been married for nearly ten years, he realized. He was too married to be anything else now. Like an education in a foreign language, this would never leave him. He could be either married or divorced, but nothing else. He could not, in the appalling euphemism of the day, have 'relationships'. He was doomed, obsolete, a relic of a forgotten species. Whatever sad fate was to be his lot, he could do nothing to change his condition.

What had befallen him now took on the dimensions of a tragedy. When Tissy left the hospital – and she seemed reluctant to do so, as if she too were unwilling to face the rest of her life – he felt as if his baby were being taken away from him. He knew that he could not be a frequent visitor to the house in Britannia Road, for he was not wanted there, nor did he want to be there, a suppliant faced with a barrier of indifference. At the same time he knew that he was sinking into an indifference of his own, one of vast dimensions, almost life-threatening in its totality. Once again his evening meal was eaten on a tablecloth of newsprint. The windows of his house needed cleaning, and his shirts, reluctantly washed by Mrs Joliffe and ironed by her for an extra consideration, were not as he would have wished them to be. Her trace was noticeable in the house, now that she was no longer supervised by Tissy: a plate broken, a vase chipped, polish stickily applied to a table and leaving traces – all attested a further lack of care. And even Mrs Joliffe threatened to leave him. The newsagent's which had belonged to her brother-in-law had been taken over by an Indian lady in a sari and turned into a flourishing business: Barry, now a schoolboy, delivered the morning papers. If Lewis were bold enough to request Mrs Joliffe to clean the cooker or wash the bathroom floor, matters to which she was no longer willing to turn her attention, she would let drop, 'Shamila's after me to work in the shop. I'm thinking it over. After all, there's not much to do here, is there? Now that you're on your own.' So far she had made no decision, nor did he think she would. But it added an irritation, an anxiety to his homecoming, which was already unpleasant enough, and he was careful to leave early in the mornings, before she arrived.

He found himself with an enormous amount of time on his hands, for he woke at four or five, and frequently got up and had his bath before six. It seemed to him that he had to wait a long time before the newspaper arrived at seven, and then he would have the leisure to read most of it before setting off to work at eight. He felt apologetic about this, as if he had not managed the calculation correctly, knowing that others did better, to the extent of complaining of too much to do, of not enough time to relax. He never relaxed now. He was in a state of permanent vigilance. When not thinking about himself he thought of his daughter. He dared not see her for fear that she would utterly unman him. He merely telephoned every day at lunchtime, to ask how she was. Sometimes he spoke to Tissy, sometimes to Mrs Harper. To his surprise Tissy seemed quite amiable. Amiable but distant. Such solicitude as she demonstrated was that of a social worker.

'Getting on all right, are you?' she might ask, in a light tone that precluded any response, let alone the register of hopelessness that he would have felt bound to offer, but never did. Because her lack of interest was so apparent he did not tell her that he was falling apart, that buttons had come off his shirts, that he could not find the laundry list, that there were too many empty bottles in the dustbin. If he mentioned any domestic matter, she would simply say, 'Well, now you know what a woman has to do each day.' So he would change the subject and ask about the baby. 'She's fine,' Tissy would say, as if mildly surprised by his interest. From which he deduced that she either hated him implacably or had forgotten her connection with him altogether. Probably the latter, he thought.

He noticed that the warmer weather had arrived, found the laundry list, and took all his shirts to the cleaner's, asking for them to be repaired. They seemed not to find this request excessive, which cheered him slightly. On his way to the library he breathed the scents of hawthorn and early lilac. His demeanour was that of an invalid, false confidence, enormous goodwill fading without warning to an intimate knowledge of mortal weakness. He knew, and strove against the knowledge, that some fundamental damage had been done. Yet he did not quite go under. However much he foundered in the evenings he regulated himself the following day. This took care, allowing no time for distractions. He had not gone away at Easter, as Pen had advised him to. He had stayed in the house, thinking of the baby. It had done him no good, no good at all. And now there was a Bank Holiday to cope with, and suddenly he could not face it. On an impulse, and because he was ashamed of what he was becoming, he booked a ticket for Paris.

What he had intended was a sentimental pilgrimage, although the thought of the past, his past, did not cheer him. The ardent studies of those early days had led to nothing. His book had received one complimentary notice, in the *Times Literary Supplement,* and that was all. His own copies, still swathed in their original brown wrapping paper, remained at the back of a cupboard. As far as he could see, his ideas, once so eagerly charted, were utterly ignored. And all the frugality that had gone into the writing of the book: how could he bear to remember it? Or to realize that now, on the verge of middle age, and with the addition of undoubted material comforts, he was living in a manner so restricted that he might still be that boy with his briefcase and his notes, his inconvenient appetite, and his love of female company? He repressed a sigh as he thought of the itinerary before him, already vowed to disillusionment. He would retrace his steps, he supposed, try to pick up old habits. This, he already knew, was an infallible recipe for disappointment, but he did not see how else he could fill his days. If time were a problem in London, where he had work to do, how much more taxing it would be in Paris, where he had no obligations and few friends.

Yet when he reached his hotel, in the rue Jacob, and looked round his room, which was muted and hazy, with faded blue paper on the walls, his anguish fell away from him, and he knew that he had made the right decision. In that moment of recognition he also knew that he could outwit time by ignoring its demands. Instinctively, although it was early afternoon, and a mild sun was trying to emerge, he removed the blue coverlet from the bed, lay down, and slept. He awoke some two hours later, with a sensation of refreshment that was new to him. He bathed, dressed carefully, and went out into the street. He found a café that was neither smart nor popular, ordered a glass of wine, and sat peaceably until a short walk took him to a small restaurant, with few customers, where he ate a simple meal. When he saw the sky darkening to a deeper blue he paid his bill and left. The rue Jacob was silent as he made his way back to the hotel. That night, despite the rest he had taken in the afternoon, he slipped easily into unconsciousness, and woke, just as easily, on the morning of the following day.

He set out without a single plan or direction in mind, merely registering the fact that the weather was mild, milky, damp, and the streets newly washed. He was anonymous: Paris did not know him, nor, he discovered, did he know Paris. In that instant, walking down the rue Jacob, he decided to jettison his past and to abandon whatever dreams of continuity he might have had. In the soft air he felt himself becoming invisible, accountable to no one. This, for some reason, failed to frighten him, although he was aware that the irresponsibility towards which he was tending might, at more secure moments in his life, have been perceived as a danger. He felt weightless, impalpable, and suddenly free. This curious condition filled him with a momentary rapture: he would not even let the memory of recent months come to the surface, and if he thought of his life at all it was with distaste, an objective distaste in strict contrast to the oceans of morbidity in which he had recently almost drowned. With an expression of cautious wonder on his face he began to walk, not caring much where his steps led him as long as his progress was unplanned, without the known palliatives of library and notebook. He would, he decided, stay here for a while and try to discover whether this blessed state, which had awaited him on his first morning in Paris, was an aberration, the first sign of a breakdown, or, as he felt it to be, an announcement, a preview, of a state of perfect health.

He walked. As if he had been delivered from a serious illness he noticed every detail of the passing scene, cherishing above all those that pertained to ordinary living: a shopkeeper arranging apples on a stall, or an elderly woman buying bread. Even the sight of small children emerging from a kindergarten at midday did not upset him. He drifted, without any feeling of fatigue, until he felt that it was time to eat, and then stopped wherever he happened to be and ordered a meal. He was not really conscious of time passing, but was aware that his state of remission must be consolidated before real life reclaimed him. Beyond this he did not care to think. He felt that all he could do, in this new dry marvellous state in which he found himself, was to reject all forms of sentimentality, and merely confine himself to conjuring systems out of the air, systems which made provision for the future while leaving him almost untouched, his emotions restored to him for other purposes, other uses. He was marvellously aware that he was not being taken to task, for any crimes committed or not committed. Unknown to him, the expression on his face conveyed thankfulness, even contentment.

He explored different districts, the 4th, the 13th, the 20th, sat in obscure churches, not all of them of architectural interest or importance, examined the Music Room in the Bibliothèque de l'Arsenal, and stood happily at counters with paint-splashed workmen in the rue Quincampoix and the Boulevard de l'Hôpital. He spent an afternoon in the Conservatoire des Arts et Métiers, with its orreries, its pendulums, and its solemn whirring clocks. He took the bus to Ville d'Avray and walked to Sèvres. He walked lightly, his hands free. Only towards the end of his stay did he glance at newspapers, but with a certain absent-mindedness. By the end of ten days, having not uttered more than a few words since his arrival, he felt completely at peace. As he took his leave of the blue room he felt a stab of the old melancholy, as if he knew the world would soon be with him again. Yet some act of repossession had taken place, some essential work of repair. When the plane landed at Heathrow he said good-bye to the pretty woman who had sat next to him and made his way to the taxi rank. He was aware that he had undergone some sort of cure, and the knowledge that this was within his grasp cheered him immeasurably.

13

His daughter: a pale, silent, delicate child, much as her mother must have been, a child with an unreasonable desire to be good. Dressed elaborately in smocks and white stockings, hair ribbons and patent leather shoes, she seemed conscious of the burden of being her grandmother's pride and joy. For she was Mrs Harper's child rather than Tissy's. When Lewis rang the bell of the house in Britannia Road, and Mrs Harper – never Tissy – opened the door, the child would hide behind her, fearful of this stranger, not, Lewis thought, because he was a stranger, but because he was a man. A natural prejudice against men was in the air she breathed. She seemed to know, even at two years old, that a man might spoil her dress, ruffle her hair, insist on disturbing exercise. When Lewis eventually succeeded in coaxing her out from behind the bulk of Mrs Harper, she looked uncertain, kept a hand on her grandmother's skirt. He hated to bribe her with toys, but could not resist bringing her a doll now and again, telling himself that when she was old enough he would furnish her with an entire library. The doll called Mildred never left her: she held it in both arms, much as Tissy had once held her, but without an expression of excitement or pleasure. Holding the doll carefully, she seemed weighed down with responsibility and maternal anxiety.

Lewis's heart ached for her. He could see loneliness there,

sadness, fear. He tried to draw her to him: she came, reluctantly. He took her out on Sunday mornings, to the park, to feed the ducks and the geese, but she hated their noise, their squabbling and flapping, and he could see that after half an hour she was anxious to get home. She was only happy sitting in her little chair in the red drawing-room, or walking with Mrs Harper to the shops. She seemed to prefer the company of her grandmother, or, more surprisingly, of the doctor, whose deteriorating bloodshot face she allowed to nestle her own. She was well looked after, Lewis could see, although the atmosphere around her was elderly. The doctor, in particular, was now in poor health and relying more and more on the comforts Mrs Harper could provide, without, however, doing so in any way that would endanger his independence.

Lewis knew that it was bad for the child to be brought up by these defeated people, but he could see that his daughter had something innately pitiful about her. This he ascribed to some melancholy native gene emanating from himself, for he had forgotten the days when he was happy. He could not in all conscience indict Tissy, although he was surprised at the off-handedness of her mothering. Once Jessica had outgrown her status as a baby, Tissy had more or less relinquished her, and had pursued other, rather less tangible, but presumably more rewarding, interests. When he caught a fleeting glimpse of her these days he found her extremely disconcerting, almost a stranger. Compared with the assiduity she had shown in her early days as a wife, the limits of her concern were very soon reached. Lewis put this down to her recent indoctrination, which had freed her from the restrictions under which she had previously laboured. When she was not at her job with Lancelot Antiques, she was at her group, or with her new friends, Kate and Fran. He rarely saw her for more than a few minutes at a time.

When he did, however, when he happened to be at the door as she was going out, she was breezily nice to him, as she might have been to a stranger. Yet there was a distance in the niceness which proclaimed: I have made my decision, I shall never go back on it. The other life that I lived with you was so benighted that you cannot expect me to admit it to my newly raised consciousness except to laugh at my folly. Of course, I serve as an example to the group. Remember how I couldn't go out alone? Shackled, you see, by false expectations. And look at me now. I earn my living, I've got friends, I'm *involved*. And I don't have to bother with men any more. That's what's so wonderful. We have a very good social life, the three of us; we go to exhibitions, see the new films, have plenty to talk about. Mother looks after Jess. It's given her a new lease of life; she was getting so low before. Now that she's got something to occupy her mind she's a different person. The baby's fine. She doesn't miss me. And later on, when she's older, she'll have me as a role model. That's extremely important for a girl. When I think how backward I used to be I don't know whether to laugh or cry. Fortunately, that's all behind me now.

She did not, of course, say any of this. He marvelled at her but was forced to come to terms with the fact that he hardly knew her in this radiant new guise. To begin with she looked different. She had never lost the weight she had put on when the baby was born, but what had previously been flaccid was now tough, hard-packed into a pair of jeans and a sweatshirt. These garments were clean but not noticeably attractive. Nevertheless, they gave her an air of being ready for action, ready to get her hands dirty in the course of some honest job: dismantling a car, for example, or working a petrol pump. Her colour was high, higher than it had ever been, and she laughed frequently, revealing her rather large teeth. Her hair was the same, though, limp, and held back by a velvet band.

Lewis could now define what had originally attracted him to her in the very absence of those qualities of delicacy, hesitancy, timidity, which had been laid aside for ever. These same qualities were now vested in his little girl. He would have preferred the child to be bold, even wicked, but it seemed as if she would have to go through the whole evolutionary process on her own, although, to judge by Tissy's present state, this was now redundant. Every time he saw her his determination to rescue her increased. But she must grow up first: he could not uproot a child with such a pronounced leaning towards what he could only assume was introspection. She must mature and harden a little before she was ready for him, just as he must be firm and decisive if he were ever to be a reasonable father to so fragile a creature. Yet, thinking of her mother, who had turned out to be unexpectedly resourceful, he wondered if she might not eventually be just as determined. For this reason he cherished her childishness, and was not anxious for her to grow up. He would have liked, merely, to figure a little in her world, without interfering or creating conflicts in her infant mind. He brought her books, which he was sometimes allowed to read to her.

She was his whole life. When he was not with her he was thinking about her. He called round most evenings on his way home, and if he were lucky he would see her before she went to sleep. The Sunday morning excursions were not a success: there was always the little reaction of retreat when she first saw him, and she tired easily. He thought that she would never get used to him, and despaired of making her love him, but decided to be tactful, self-effacing, as he was now, without knowing it, most of the time. The idea of demanding love sickened him, particularly of one so easily frightened. Besides, love . . . He had been twice defeated. He no longer expected anyone to love him, although he himself had not grown cynical. In many ways he was still ready to love, was, in certain moments, abounding in love, but no longer to a painful or even a nervous extent. Everyone now seemed to him to be worthy of love, even the stranger he passed in the street. The highest good, he perceived, was to love and be loved. But somehow, unconsciously, he dealt himself out of the whole affair. He could love but not be loved. He was only one half of the equation.

So, delicately, fearfully – with a fear and a delicacy to match her own – he loved his daughter, forcing himself to be content to care for her at a distance, never bringing a note of disagreement into Mrs Harper's house, even when he saw or heard something that pained him, always calm with the child, never letting his disappointment show when she failed to run into his arms as he held them out to her.

Because of her he was valiant. Living alone, which had initially caused him such despair, became a daily battle against inertia, lethargy, carelessness. Without knowing it he assumed the steady hopeful smile that had characterized him as a very young man as he got out of bed, had his bath, prepared his breakfast, always determined to put a good face on things, to create a discipline for himself, to maintain decent standards, so that his daughter need never be ashamed of him. For her susceptibility, he knew, was extreme, and would increase rather than diminish as she grew older and began to take the world's measure. Still smiling, he would leave for the library, breathing the morning air conscientiously, greeting the postman, the milkman, noticing the passers-by, all of whom seemed to him worthy of love. He knew a brief, very brief, failure of energy after accomplishing this exercise and before beginning the day's work, but a cup of coffee in the sandwich bar near the college gave him a moment's respite from his determination to win his victory over the day, and after that he was able to resume the smile, the mask, the endeavour. The day passed smoothly and in silence. Sometimes he would look up from his desk in a panic. Supposing this were to be taken away from him! How would he exist with a whole day to fill? How did other people manage? For there must be other people like him, virtually alone in the world? But this did not bear thinking about, and with only a very little reluctance he was able to turn his attention once more to his eternal index cards, thankful that the engine of the day was now fully engaged, and that it could run on to its close without further efforts on his part.

The end of the afternoon was more difficult, as indeed

it is for most people. Melancholy overcame him for a while at the approach of six o'clock; his movements slowed down as he bent to pick up his briefcase and straightened up to say goodnight. At this point fear dictated his thoughts. These people, these other people, of whom he was so anxious to think well, were no doubt going home to wives, to children, to comfort, to reassurance, to life! And these young secretaries and their boyfriends, busy selecting a film to see, and these ladies joining their husbands in town for a visit to the theatre: how enviable they all seemed! In the early days of his solitary new life he had gone with Pen to the opera, but had had to give it up: it upset him too much. The nobility of the gestures and the sentiments filled him with despair, and when anybody died he could not bear it. He had to concede that Pen and even George Cheveley had behaved impeccably when he had broken down in the middle of *Manon*. They had thought it would appeal to him, since he loved the novel, but instead it had brought forth tears which he was unable to suppress. '*Adieu, notre petite table,*' Manon had sung, and he was done for. They had taken him home like an invalid at the end of the evening, had insisted that he drink a little whisky, and had only left when he pronounced himself ready for bed.

'Funny how that should have set him off,' said George to Pen on the way home.

'Oh, well, any kind of loss, you know. It doesn't really matter who feels it. Or for whom.'

So he no longer went to the opera, but saw Pen, and occasionally George, on a Sunday afternoon, after his run in the park. He was forced to acknowledge that he had misjudged George, whose taciturn presence he now found unexpectedly soothing.

His evenings consisted, in essence, of his long walk home and his visit to his daughter. In time he managed to think the others out of the way: they were servants, handmaidens, liegemen, surrounding the child and guaranteeing her safety. The discordant personalities of Mrs Harper and the doctor, the new-found insolence of his wife, failed to move him. Their importance was reduced to the sole function of looking after his daughter. He would find her in her nightdress and slippers, ready for bed. She always ran to the door when she heard his ring, but looked doubtful as soon as she saw him. He wondered whether she felt the same fear of everyone. Unlike most children she enjoyed going to bed. He had always done so himself, and was gratified to see evidence of this inherited trait. If she were not too sleepy he would read to her from one of the books he had brought with him. 'When I was one, I was just begun,' he read. 'When I was two, I was nearly new.' She would gaze at him with eyes as serious but as abstracted as her mother's had been. He read on, cherishing every moment; therefore he was doubly disappointed when he called and found that she had been put to bed early and was already asleep. On these evenings he barely stopped to exchange a few words with Mrs Harper, who was no longer reluctant to talk to him, and had on more than one occasion invited him to stay and share their meal. But he never did. He would have nothing to do with a false domesticity, a pretence at normality, acceptance of the status quo. Besides, only his daughter interested him. He accepted the others as inevitable, but did not choose to remain in their company.

Then began his ordeal, repeated every evening, when he returned to his empty house and became aware of his loneliness. But he was still determined to sustain the effort of the day. He laid his table, ate carefully, even elaborately, and washed up after himself. What he ate was not interesting to him; it was only the ceremony that counted. And then that frightening hour before he could go thankfully to bed. Music was dangerous. Sometimes television could be relied on, although his attention wandered. More often than not he switched on the radio and took it from room to room with him as he tidied up. He had become meticulous in the upkeep of his house. Mrs Joliffe came only intermittently now. He left the same money for her, but she put in only a

brief half-hour now and then, on various days of the week
– sometimes twice, sometimes not at all – as if she too knew
that he was no longer a real householder. Her obligations to
him were dwindling away. She no longer saw any reason to
take him seriously.

Sleep, therefore, was not only a valuable commodity but
an essential one, the consolation after the effort of the day,
with its endless exercise of goodwill. Once safely in bed, it
was easy to feel generous again. The smile returned as he
thought, quite prayerfully, of his good friends, his pleasant
house, his interesting work, and above all his daughter. This
was what people meant by counting one's blessings, he supposed, and it was easy to do so in these moments of respite,
when all was quiet and easeful, and the darkness was kind.
After all, he reminded himself, he was in good health. That
was what counted, wasn't it? And he had a little money put
aside: his daughter would want for nothing. The only thing
that wearied him was that it seemed such a long time to wait
for her to come and join him. Sometimes the waiting seemed
intolerable. Sleep usually delivered him from thoughts like
these, and in the morning, with just that little necessary
effort, he was ready, once more, to face another day. Of
good and evil he thought little. He apportioned no blame, not
to Tissy, not to himself. Or, rather, no longer to himself. All
that mattered was to think of life as an experience which he,
like everyone else, was in the process of undergoing. There
were to be no excuses, no heavenly alibis. One day he would
be old. And it would be important then to have no unfinished
business with which to torment himself. He did not want to
be a burden to anyone. To whom, in any case, could he be a
burden? Certainly not to his daughter, who would be as free
as she wanted to be. He saw that freedom might be difficult
for her, but he also saw that she must learn the discipline for
herself. He knew, somehow, that when she was grown up
he would be far away. He would leave the house for her,
and leave her in it, perhaps to work, perhaps to marry. This
part of her future was unclear to him. He only knew that he

himself would not be on hand to witness it. For he would have gone, although he did not yet know where he would have gone, or why, or even how. All he could look forward to, before this happened, was a few years alone with her, teaching her, guiding her, endowing her, before he left her, perhaps for ever.

Of course there were bad days, days when he noticed the grey hairs coming through, when his daughter was already asleep on the evenings of his visits, when all his resources failed him. Then it was even more important to pretend that everything was all right, or at least going according to plan. But it was not easy. And without a woman to comfort him he found life very painful. Yet he knew that he could never again enter the great game. Once, when calling on Pen early one Sunday evening, he had found Emmy there. His heart had given a great knock. She had looked no different, unlike himself. She lay rather than sat in a chair, her full skirts looping down to her ankles, her hand idly fingering her long strings of beads. He saw that she was not as put out by the encounter as he was, having no doubt heard all about his situation from Pen, and from this he deduced that she too had discarded him. Conversation was derisory; she was much too sophisticated to start asking searching questions. Only her eyes were speculative. Pen's presence ensured that only the most general, the most anodyne of matters were discussed, but Lewis was conscious of all that was not being said. He found it a strain, and announced that he had to be getting back, although he was only going home to an empty evening. 'I'll walk with you a little way,' said Emmy, and he was not as pleased as he might have been a year, two years ago.

'What are you doing with yourself these days, Lewis?' she asked. The afternoon was mild, windless; people in the streets looked aimless, distracted by Sunday melancholy.

'Oh, much the same as usual,' he answered. 'You know how dull I am.'

'I know what I know,' she said. 'Although you may be right.'

'And you?' he ventured.

'Madly busy,' she replied promptly. 'And I may be getting married. Did Pen tell you?'

'No,' he said. 'No, he didn't.'

'Well, it's about time somebody made an honest woman of me. And I do rather like the idea of being a rich lady. I think I'd look rather good, don't you?'

'Very good,' he said. 'And do you love him, whoever he is?'

'Not particularly.' She sounded surprised. 'I like him all right – I've known him for ages. But after all, marriage is a job like any other, isn't it? I mean, you have to work at it. Or so they tell me. I'd rather let someone else do all the work, actually. You see,' she said lightly, 'I always wanted to be married. I told you, didn't I?'

His heart turned in him, but mostly with pity for her childish obstinacy.

'You *were* daft, Lewis.'

'You knew my situation,' he said, still patient. Somehow he could not be angry with her, although he felt tired out, almost old. 'I find it hard to believe that you wanted me as much as you said you did. I always wanted to believe you did. But now I don't want you to tell me. I've lost you anyway. I lost you a long time ago. Do you know that every day I look in *The Times*, on the weddings page, to see if your name's there? I've thought of you every day since I last saw you. And now I've seen you again, and soon I shall see the announcement, presumably. And that's the end, I suppose.'

'What a fool you were to go and spoil it, Lewis. You could have had me. Others did. I didn't hear them making such a fuss as you're making now.'

'Perhaps I didn't want to be like the others. You didn't seem to like them very much.'

'Oh, Lewis, nothing lasts. Don't you know that?'

They walked on in silence. She seemed suddenly to make up her mind about something.

'Well, take care of yourself,' she said, stopping abruptly. 'You can always find me through Pen. That's about all I can say, isn't it?' And she turned away. When he looked back at her, striding along in her long skirts, she raised her hand and waved, without turning round, as if she knew he was looking at her. Then she seemed to melt into the shadows of the fast growing dusk.

'Emmy,' he called after her. She turned. He moved slowly towards her, as if under water, while she stood still and watched him.

'I love you,' he said. 'I loved you that first evening, at my house. But what could I expect? From you, I mean. I didn't want you to go on having what you tell me you hate, another married lover. Is that what you want?'

'What a carry on,' she said lightly. She was still angry, he could tell, and still unrepentant. But not unfair. She was not – never had been – unfair. 'I simply wanted you to choose me. Does that sound frivolous? It isn't. I wanted that . . . enactment. Not promises, not consolations – I've had those. I wanted to start again, with somebody straightforward.' She hesitated. 'Did you ever consider me at all?'

'I've never stopped thinking about you.'

'No, I dare say you haven't. It didn't take you very far, did it?'

'Come home with me now.'

'Oh, no,' she said. 'Even if I wanted to I wouldn't.'

'Did you want me?'

'You know I did. I *liked* you. We're not talking about love, now. I doubt if I can love – that's my trouble. You're stupid, but you're kind. You're kind to women – too kind, perhaps. Anyone else would have buggered off long ago. And I can tell you the truth and not be blamed for it. That's almost enough in itself. It's what I've never had.'

'Would you marry me?' he asked.

'If you were free, you mean? I've had proposals like that before. I might, that's all I can say. It's become serious, you see. Maybe it always was. If you'd slept with me it might not have done. You could have saved yourself all this bother.'

'Emmy, you're relentless. You tell me what you don't want and ask for it at the same time.'

'I'm not asking for it now, am I? This time I want more. Goodbye.'

She turned on her heel and left him. He ran after her.

'You wanted a husband – I know that. Strange, when nobody else seems to. But would anyone have done? That's what I want to know. I must know that.'

'You shouldn't ask me that, not now. It's up to you to make a few decisions – it always was. Couldn't you just do what you wanted? People do, you know.'

'It doesn't always answer,' he said. 'Life becomes full of discards.'

'What of it?'

'I wanted something better, you see. Something different, new. I didn't see how I could bring it about.'

'You fantasize too much. You've probably read too much.'

'Yes, I have. I see that. I've had unrealistic ideas, antiquated notions. All wrong – I see that too. But were the ideas wrong? Or did I just misapply them?'

'You see how safe I should have been with you? Your standards would have taken care of me. I don't have any standards myself. I want that taken into account,' she said seriously.

'We didn't know each other too well, then, did we? I probably envisaged more talk than you did. Forgive me if I'm wrong, but I always thought that necessary.'

'Yes, shut up, why don't you? And grow up. Look at yourself. You're an attractive man.'

'Am I?' he said, startled.

She smiled unwillingly. 'I'm not here to complete your sentimental education, you know. You have to do that for yourself. When you grow up give me a call. Now I really am late. Goodbye. I mean it this time.'

'But do you . . .' he shouted after her. 'Love me,' he

added more quietly, although there was no one in the street but themselves.

'Who knows? But in these circumstances, frankly, my dear, I don't give a damn.'

Watching her departing figure, disappearing, melting into the dusk, he wondered whether he were any happier. Oh, go home, he thought tiredly. Read a book. Men have problems too, he wanted to tell her. Endless conflicts. Being this, being that, being damned for either. He thought of his daughter, and gave thanks that she was a girl. But for the rest of the day he thought of Emmy.

She would never concede defeat, any more than his wife would ever be magnanimous in victory, or what she would understand as victory. She would never simply love or console. Somehow a gigantic conflict of principle seemed to have been mounted; that was the trouble. Both of them were now stuck in their respective corners, each a challenge to the other. He was disgusted with himself, with his life. He was also confused. Why had it been his lot to become involved with such implacable women? He had looked to women for mercy, not for conflict. Since his earliest days he had thought of women as kindly creatures, benevolent, well-disposed. This had apparently been all wrong. What they wanted was precisely to engage you on a matter of principle, even if that principle were improvised or matured in secret. He no longer had the key to his wife, who seemed to have changed into a complete stranger, and who was not made in the least thoughtful by the direction her life was taking, away from him. She saw it as a golden opportunity to cancel the past, her past, and had, so she implied, no further interest in him. There was something unyielding about her now, as there was about Emmy, although he had once thought of them both as fallible, weak, unprotected. He had thought that it was up to him to safeguard their honour. That was, in essence, what he had tried to do. But they regarded his efforts as misguided. Emmy, in particular, would have preferred a defiant flouting of the rules. He began to see what an affair with her would have meant. The logistics would have been frightful, for she would not have cared for concealment; on the contrary, she would have challenged it. She would have telephoned him at home, at work: she would have demanded openness, cards on the table. She would have wanted to establish them as a couple, with the intention that they should marry. And whereas her status would not have been damaged by such a stratagem, his own would have been ruined for ever. He had wanted so much to behave well. And although she professed so flagrantly her wish to marry she had in fact none of the attributes of a wife. She was easily bored, became impatient with routine, was ever alert for a new beginning. With her charm, her power, her inventiveness, she was born to be a mistress. And, knowing this, had come to hate men, the men who would not marry her but preferred her as she was. Tissy probably hated men too, he now thought, but for a different reason. There was nothing of the mistress about Tissy. But she considered that she had been sold into slavery, and all her efforts now were in the direction of emancipation. In the group she had probably learnt to compare herself with ethnic minorities or the working class, on whom it was beholden to rise in revolt, to claim freedoms that had been denied to them. Apparently that was what they were both doing. Emmy would marry her rich man and revenge herself yet again by despising or deceiving him, probably both. And Tissy, presumably, would never look at a man again. In many ways they had a lot in common.

He tried to understand, failed, and gave up. He only knew that he wanted his daughter to be different. When she considered him dubiously, unsmilingly, he wondered if the process of rejection had already started. It was then that he was at his most gentle with her, although he never failed to demand a full accounting from Mrs Harper. Did she eat well? Did she get enough fresh air? No detail of her day's activities went unscrutinized. To the child, if she were aware of him at all, he was merely the man who came in the evenings and sometimes read her a story. He realized that she probably felt more comfortable with the doctor than she did with him, for the doctor was all sprawling acceptance, all mumbling affection. The doctor sat her on his knee and stroked her hair, gave her titbits from his plate, kissed her lavishly. Although it pained Lewis to know this, and sometimes to witness it, he understood that his reaction was unreasonable. There was no real harm in the man, after all: he simply offended one's preferences in the matter of good behaviour, or, to be fair, of ideal behaviour, the behaviour demanded of a child's guardian. And he looked so awful, with his waistcoat undone and his abundant hair untidy. What his patients must have thought of him Lewis could not imagine. Perhaps he had no patients left. Apparently he had given up his surgery some time ago, and now went out on call, privately, to a favoured few. Old people, despairing of other company, would no doubt be glad to see him.

They were all getting older, that was the trouble. There was a lack of expectation in the air they breathed; he himself, with his arduous daily discipline, could see the futility of it all. For nothing got better. The relentless upholding of standards merely reinforced the status quo: crowded and uneventful days leading to empty nights. And that house, with its curious inhabitants, all strangers to him. Even his daughter, whom he loved so dearly, knew it as her home. The thought of Mrs Harper's house, filled with discordant lives, each of them irregular, made Lewis's head ache when he thought of it. If he felt sympathy for anyone it was for Mrs Harper, landed with all these incumbents, when she had wanted so much to be free. He had thought her a beauty, a bold-looking woman, when he had first met her. Now she merely looked harassed, old, her fine hands spoiled by all the washing and cooking that had accrued to her. Different meals had to be prepared for everyone, since they all ate at different times. She herself, Lewis suspected, ate next to nothing, but sat down once in a while with a cup of weak tea and a cigarette. She had never been communicative and was now even less so, but he sometimes thought she would like to present her case to him, as if he were the only sane person she knew. Perhaps he was. But she said nothing, and although he gradually got into the habit of drinking a cup of tea with her after his daughter had been put to bed he resisted the pity that overcame him on these occasions. He noticed the increasing shabbiness of the red drawing-room, with the smell of cooking seeping in from the kitchen and the fine bloom of dust on the cherry-wood table. It was as if all conviction were leaving the house. The cushion on his daughter's little chair was torn and musty. He tried not to see this, but saw it anyway.

He was at work when Mrs Harper telephoned to say that the doctor had had a heart attack. An ambulance had taken him to St Stephen's Hospital and he was in Intensive Care, but they had told her not to worry, that this was merely routine. She was going to visit him that evening: would Lewis stay with Jessica until she got back? Tissy would be late home; she was going out straight from work and it seemed a pity to spoil her evening. From the offhand way in which this information was imparted Lewis got the impression that Tissy was going out with a man. This volte-face was so amazing that it occupied his thoughts for the rest of the morning. So much for principle when there was advantage at stake. He had heard Mrs Harper refer to a certain Gilbert Bradshaw, the owner of Lancelot Antiques, and his high opinion of Tissy. Tissy herself had mentioned that she was helping Gilbert with an inventory, or that Gilbert wanted her to accompany him to a sale, but he had thought nothing of it. His wife, in her new guise, had appeared to him so asexual that he had failed to register the connection. But he registered it now. He wondered if Gilbert Bradshaw had been given Mrs Harper's cake treatment, and also whether Tissy could be persuaded to jettison her new ideology for a second marriage. If so, he would be free. He would be free but he would also lose his daughter. Tissy would lose nothing. She might gain a reputation as a traitor with her group, but then she would give up the group anyway. He had begun cautiously to devise ways of drawing up some form of legal contract which would ensure him access to, and eventual guardianship of, his daughter, when Mrs Harper telephoned again to say that the doctor had had a second heart attack in the hospital and had died, in some distress, two hours after being admitted. She herself had not been there. She had telephoned the shop, but Tissy was out. Could Lewis call in on his way home, but as early as possible? Her voice was high, frightened. 'I can't let Baby see me crying,' she had said, when he asked her if she was all right. So he went straight away.

She was profoundly shocked; that was clear. He sat her down and made a cup of tea, taking the child on his lap and speaking to her softly. But after a while the child got down and ran to her grandmother, who picked her up and buried her face in the little girl's fly-away hair. There was not very much that he could say. Mrs Harper had always been silent on the matter of her liaison with the doctor. Lewis did not know whether or not she had loved him, although he supposed that she had. Maybe the doctor had loved her, in his own inglorious way. But why, then, had they not married? What peculiar secrecy, or respectability, had kept them in their detached state when Tissy was there to bring them together? He had never doubted that the doctor was a villain, although he now realized that even this was unfair. He may have been a sick man, defeated, disappointed, ashamed. Who could understand anyone else's life?

Mrs Harper gave a tremendous, tremulous sigh.

'Are you all right?' he asked.

'I'm all right, I'm always all right. But that's half my life gone, Lewis.'

'You've been together a long time, I know.'

'You should have seen him as a young man,' she went on, turning the wet ball of her handkerchief in her hands and clenching and unclenching her thumbs. 'Handsome! All the girls were after him. But he married and then I married, and when we got back together again it all got complicated. Divorce wasn't easy in those days. I'll miss him,' she said, pressing the handkerchief to her mouth. Her face was red and exhausted. 'You never liked him, did you?'

'I should have liked to see you happier,' he said gently.

'Well, I'll never be happy now,' she said, but even as the tears came she suppressed them, and, taking the child by the hand, led her out into the kitchen.

'When will Tissy be home?' he asked.

'Oh, Tissy. Well, Tissy will have to be home a great deal more in future. Tissy can give up that job of hers and stay here with us. I'm not a young woman, Lewis. I want a bit of peace. I've done enough.' Her shoulders sagged under the weight of her grief, but her hands were steady as she buttered fingers of brown bread for the child. 'She'll have to have a boiled egg,' she said. 'I haven't done any shopping today.'

He stayed until Tissy came in. He could see from the way the excitement dropped from her face that she had had a good time and was now in for a bad one. It occurred to him that Mrs Harper might save her own life – and that of the child – by sacrificing Tissy's, and that Mr Bradshaw, or Gilbert, might soon be a thing of the past. The conversation, or argument, that would not take place until he had left hung heavily in the air. On the pretext of arranging the funeral, which Mrs Harper wanted to take place as soon as possible, he said goodbye, promising to look in on the following day. He just had time to notice Tissy's shoulders rounding into the docile posture that he recognized from the time when he had first known her. After so many shining possibilities it seemed that her resolve was not strong enough to withstand her mother's directives. Or was it? He wondered, with genuine curiosity, whether she would manage to get her own way this time. His sympathies for once were entirely with Mrs Harper, whose tired eyes were no longer beautiful and who saw the new determination in her daughter's face with the distaste she would have felt for a lewd display in her own drawing-room.

209

14

'You won't have to do that much longer, Lewis,' said
Goldsborough. 'Once we've installed the computers,' he
added.

'What will I be doing, then?' asked Lewis, who had learned
not to take Goldsborough's enthusiasms too seriously. He
noticed that Goldsborough had acquired a new persona since
taking up his latest career. He now appeared both brash
and deft, speedy, purposeful, unreliable, like a character in
a television commercial. This impression was assisted by
the serious grey suit, which was in turn enlivened by one
of the Brooks Brothers shirts in which Goldsborough had
invested on his recent trip to New York. The installation
of the computers had revealed a new world to his always
receptive mind: the world of the professional fund-raiser.
He had seized hold of, and welcomed, the fact that everyone was willing to put money into computers, particularly
in libraries, so that information could be beamed from one
institution to another. Goldsborough now thought in terms
of the global village. Whole bibliographies flashed before
his eyes, summoned up on screens to which scholars like
himself would soon have access. And he had always felt his
place to be among the lavish spenders: he was a profligate
at heart, with an innocent love of extravagance that referred
back to a meagre wartime childhood. He had learned to
incorporate early experience into objective study, had an

excellent degree in anthropology, but still yearned for a bit of a party. Conscientious though he was in his duties as librarian, Goldsborough had a hankering for the sort of activity that libraries do not normally accommodate. The grave impersonal friendliness of grant-giving bodies excited his eagerness to please, while the sums involved moved him almost to tears. He felt like Columbus, on one knee before Isabella the Catholic. Making his bid for this mysteriously available money Goldsborough saw the various strands of his life's work knitting themselves together. As an anthropologist he welcomed shift and change; as a librarian he simply welcomed funds. Besides, he was enjoying himself. To enjoy oneself in a good cause is a virtuous feeling quite unlike any other, and Goldsborough would have sacrificed many pleasures for this privilege. As it was, no sacrifice was involved; everything added up to immeasurable increase.

'We shall have to take on extra staff,' he said happily. 'I thought of giving you Morton and Quiney. Generally speaking I foresee quite a shake-up. Arthur will have to go, of course, and perhaps one or two others. The library is going to be a place for the young, Lewis. We'll be running courses in computer technology – all you have to do is familiarize yourself with the process. It's a little technical, but that's what's so exciting. The language, Lewis, is entirely new. Think of it as meta-language. I find it fascinating,' he went on unnecessarily. 'I'll let you know more about it when I come back from L.A. In the meantime just carry on as usual.'

'Just as a matter of interest, Arnold, what will happen to the index?'

'But my dear fellow!' exclaimed Goldsborough. 'This will be the index's finest hour! The index will henceforth be immortal. The index, Lewis, will be transformed into a permanent record. By you,' he added.

'You mean,' said Lewis slowly, 'that I transfer the index? That I key it in, or whatever one does, right from the beginning? In other words, that I start doing it all over again? This will create years of backlog, Arnold. Unless someone else does what I'm doing now. Is that how you see it?'

'This is unlike you, Lewis. Surely you can see the advantage of all this? Those index cards could have got damaged, burnt, even.'

'There is a microfilm, of course. What happened to microfilm, by the way? It was all the rage about ten years ago.'

'Superseded by the computer,' said Goldsborough triumphantly.

'This is all going to be very expensive, isn't it? With the extra staff and everything?'

'I can't go into that now, Lewis. Let me assure you that if you know where to look the money can be found. Several big companies are interested. We shall be competing with the major institutions, but I have the matter in hand. I shall rely on you to keep an eye on things here while I am in the States. I reckon to go over two or three times a year while our plans are being regularized. Cheer up, Lewis,' he urged robustly. 'Your job will be quite secure, you know. Unless, of course, you feel you'd like a change. I shan't want any dragging of the feet over this. Librarianship is about to become a whole new ball game. Younger people will be involved. We need new thinking at the interface, Lewis. Younger people will take to it like ducks to water: besides, they'll be easier to train. So let me know if you don't like the work. Think of it as an exciting new venture; that's what I'm doing. That's the attitude. I've been in touch with the psychology department. They run a very interesting course on meeting challenges. I've had one or two quite worthwhile sessions with them. Perhaps you ought to do the same, Lewis. I've noticed you're getting very set in your ways.'

'I believe he's right,' said Lewis to Pen over lunch. This now took place in a wine bar instead of a pub, as before; they ate slices of quiche and salad, and drank a couple of glasses of rosé. This seemed to be the approved diet of the contemporary man, although it left Lewis hungry. He was, however, so used to feeling hungry, that he was more or less resigned to the condition lasting out his lifetime, and possibly continuing beyond it. The one thing that put him off ideas of an after-life was its immateriality. This was a frivolous attitude, of which he was ashamed, but he was ashamed of so much these days, and there seemed to be no solution to any of it. Nevertheless, he hoped he was not going to develop one of those gourmet appetites that are simply an excuse for over-indulgence. He hoped he was never going to be found extolling a hill village in Provence for the quality of its mushrooms, or remembering a particularly amusing bottle of *Pinot noir* when he could remember practically nothing else.

'I believe I am set in my ways,' he said, spearing a slice of tomato. 'How does one avoid it? I mean, life catches up with you, takes you by surprise. Life, in fact, is not simply a series of exciting new ventures. The future is not always a whole new ball game. There tends to be unfinished business. One trails all sorts of things around with one, things that simply won't be got rid of.'

'I'm very much afraid that I'm now within shouting distance of forty,' said Pen, pushing aside his plate and lighting a cigarette. 'You're younger than me, of course, although I've never held it against you.'

'Not much,' said Lewis. 'Younger, I mean.'

'I'm about to make an announcement, Lewis. I'm too old to learn about computers. Goldsborough's right; it is a skill for the young. Basically I belong to the age of the quill pen. I doubt if I could fit in if the place changed radically, as it promises to do.'

'You don't mean you're thinking of leaving?' said Lewis, horrified.

'I'm afraid so. I'm going home to Wales, to help my father for a while. He has quite a substantial library, and he's always been a little hurt that I haven't offered to catalogue it. And I can help generally; there's no shortage of work around the place.'

The 'place', Lewis knew, was a fairly substantial estate,

farmed by Pen's older brother, Alexander, called Sandy.

'What about George?' he asked, swallowing his dismay.

'Well, that's what's good about the idea. George is thinking of establishing himself in Ludlow – he says the market's steadier in a country town. Less spectacular, but steadier. In time we'll buy a place together. I might even go into the business.'

'But Pen, this is quite a shock.'

'Yes, I know, and in many ways I hate to do it. I hate change as much as you do, Lewis; I'm a creature of habit too. It's just that the time has come to make other plans; I really don't want to have to learn about bytes and cursors. I couldn't have done this without George, of course.' Nevertheless he looked harassed and bemused at the prospect. 'Now, what about you? You'll stay on, will you? Or will you?'

'Until Jessica is older, yes, I suppose I will.'

Pen made a slight gesture of impatience. 'She's not exactly company for you, is she? I mean, she will be in time, but that's still a long way off. Later on is time to think of her as being real company. That gives you a few years to play with. Why not do something desperate, Lewis? My feeling is that you could always come back if you wanted to. The house is still in your name, isn't it?'

'Where could I go?' he said sadly. 'What could I do? I am what I am, a poor clerk. I'll never be anything different.'

'I can't stand that sort of talk, Lewis. If you feel like that then it's time to reinvent yourself. And what about the house, anyway? You haven't made it over to Tissy, have you?'

'The funny thing is, I've loved that house all my life, and now I hate to go back to it. I always thought of leaving it to Jessica, but these days I'm not so sure. Wouldn't it be better to sell it and leave her the money to buy something for herself?'

'Sell the house?' Pen in his turn was sincerely shocked.

'I dread the house, Pen. I feel like a curator, a caretaker. As long as I'm there nothing will change. I think of my mother a lot, something I haven't done for a long time. I think of how she lived in that house after my father died, of how lonely she must have been. I feel as if I'm turning into her. Does that sound mad? It's true, nevertheless. And right through everything that's happened to me I've gone on looking at the same view, out of the same windows; I've walked the same streets. I don't think I can bear to live there much longer. Yet where would I go?'

'Well, I suppose you could buy a small flat somewhere, closer to town.'

'It's all very unsettling,' Lewis said restlessly. 'I thought the computers were bad enough until I heard your news. Life will not be the same without you.' He spoke the words mockingly, but knew that they were serious.

'You won't lose sight of me entirely. We'll keep the house in London – can't do without the opera, you know. But we shan't see each other every day, that's true. That's why I think you ought to consider some sort of a change, Lewis. Don't give up like this. Don't give way to melancholy. You used not to be like this, you know.'

'When were you thinking of leaving?' he asked, as a dreadful sadness took hold of him.

'I thought I'd go home for Christmas and stay for a while. The end of the year seems to be a good time to make changes. So I'll be around for another six months. George is close to selling up, but he'll wait until he gets his price. And in the meantime I can start looking for a house for us. That way my parents can get used to the idea, and I'll be on hand if they ever need me. Oh, by the way, someone was asking for you. An American. You were in with Goldsborough. He said he'd look in again this afternoon.'

They walked back together in silence, each absorbed in what had passed between them. To Lewis the prospect was dispiriting. He did not doubt that he could master the computer, although the process would not be exhilarating; still, he was not enough of a Luddite to object to machines just because they were machines. What unsettled him was the thought of doing all this without the comfort of Pen in the background. I think like a boy, he said to himself. A boy who doesn't want to go to school without his friend. It was true, but it seemed to him that the friendships of men proceeded in this fashion. With Pen he had always been at his best, at his most reticent, his most natural, and Pen had responded in the same fashion. It was a mode that suited them both. In many ways they were strangers to each other's way of life, and although nothing was hidden between them in the matter of intimacies, love affairs, and, in one case, marriage, they found it easier to take knowledge of these for granted, as if discussion beyond the established facts were unnecessarily intrusive. Lewis knew that Pen was conversant with his affairs, just as he knew about Pen's, but neither had thought to have views on what the other had done or was doing. Moments of exceptional derangement, such as the night of Pen's argument with George, and Lewis's abortive seduction of Emmy, were passed over by mutual consent: the facts were known, even unhesitatingly accepted, but judgment was never passed.

This was very agreeable to both of them. All that each required of the other was a brief statistical acquaintance with the main points of reference. Lewis had regarded Pen as his safe and steady companion through many a difficult year, one from whom no harm would come. And now he was to lose him. There was no doubt of this, despite the projected visits to the opera. He would continue to see him from time to time, but he would lose what was essential to him, Pen's constant and tactful company. The idea that in years to come he would look up from his desk, or rather his keyboard, and not see Pen's elegant head across the room, not have his presence as a marker for the day, distressed him unutterably. What would be intolerable would be to continue down the same road in increasing solitude. At home there was no one. In Mrs Harper's establishment he sensed that the arrangement which had held good for a while – Tissy's new-found freedom, her mother's confinement to the house and the child – might soon undergo a major realignment. With the doctor gone he suspected that Mrs Harper might reclaim her daughter's company, or rather demand it, for it would not be lightly bestowed. She was a powerful character: he had always known that. And she was lonely. Maybe she always had been. Maybe behind that original basilisk stare there was a woman whom her lover had made lonely. Maybe for a woman of that generation, of that particular education in her Belgian convent, life with a lover instead of a husband would mean loneliness, inevitably; the irregularity would offend her. That was what had made her seem so unpleasant, so eager to marry off her daughter, to protect her from a similar fate. That the daughter might have been rendered impotent, insubstantial, by her mother's decisions, and above all by her peculiar reticence, her concealment of all information, no longer seemed to him surprising. He got on rather well with her these days, although he noticed that she was reverting to her earlier truculence. But if she were to annexe Tissy again, as she already had done once, there would be no further point in his presence. They would be inseparable, arm in arm, as he had first seen them, all those years ago, and if he wanted his wife back, always supposing that he still wanted his wife back, he would be as truly importunate as he had always felt, and had always been made to feel, by these very same people, whose family he had once thought, hopelessly, that he might join.

Tissy's attitude to all this was somehow not to be relied upon. While he had managed not to take her feminism seriously, nor the possibility of Gilbert Bradshaw, he knew very well how early habits, early routines, could clasp one in a deathly embrace, and could be similarly unrelenting, permitting of no negotiation. He sighed inwardly as he thought of the combat he would have to mount to win Tissy over a second time, if that were possible.

The truth of the matter was that he no longer entirely wanted to. Just as the prospect of going back to the beginning of the index and transcribing it all over again disheartened him he did not see how he could do the same thing with his ruin of a marriage. For it was a ruin; that was beyond all doubt. Whatever reservations he had about living alone, he recognized the fact that he would continue to do so. The sound of his feet on the summer pavements as he turned down the familiar street, the dying of the long light evenings that he so dreaded, were now, in a curious way, part of him, the authentic part. There was no ambiguity in them. That was his feeling now. To live alone was his destiny, and probably always had been. And it seemed natural to him, in later life, to be denied the exaltation of his early days. A coldness had grown on him, without in any way disturbing what he felt to be his innocence. Despite all his hopeful, even prayerful endeavours, he was now a colder man. He remained well-disposed. It was just that he no longer knew the world. If he had known it he would still have trusted it. But he was denied access; the world had grown away from him. His bright future, in which he so ardently believed, had disappeared, and had taken something of himself with it. He would still have liked to embrace the world, which he now perceived as flawed, but those to whom he would naturally have stretched out his arms had gone, subsumed into their own affairs or into ancient matters which he had merely disturbed, not resolved.

There was also the matter of the house. What he had said to Pen was true: he hated to go home. For all the comforts of custom and routine he hated to go home. Once he stepped inside his own front door he felt dread, and as the evening wore on he underwent an oppression from which only the prospect of sleep could deliver him. *Vite, soufflons la lampe* . . . He knew that it was irrational to displace his feelings on to the house, which stood there, blameless, in the late evening light, but he was becoming afraid of it. It reminded him that nothing had changed, that nothing ever would change, that he would grow old with the same wistfulness that he had known as a boy, as his mother's son, kept to her side by his care of her, and hers of him. And he was getting older all the while. He was only two years off forty, when they said that life began. But they said it, he reckoned, to cheer themselves up, knowing that by then the die was cast.

He was in charge of the library for most of the time, since Goldsborough was either in America or at one of his training sessions. Looking over the great room from his desk, Lewis regretted the long winter evenings, the dusky afternoons, the clicking on of the lights, the collective sigh as concentration was momentarily disturbed. The sunlight, streaming through dusty windows, seemed to him a vast aberration, making him feel out of place, out of time. Perhaps Goldsborough was right. Perhaps he was too old to adjust to new methods. He now saw a warning in Goldsborough's remarks which he had not noticed when he had first heard them, only that morning. A shift in all their destinies seemed to have taken place in the meantime. Pen's leaving he now accepted as something that had already happened. He saw himself as friendless, mute, confined to the library or to the house, a relic left by his lost youth. The important thing, he decided, was to come to terms with this, not to make too much of a fuss. He had had no more to bear than any other man. He still knew that in order to obtain grace he would have to play his part. Nevertheless, he did little work that afternoon. Heavy-heartedness set in and he began to fear the evening, although the sun was still high in the sky and would not set until late. He might have a meal out, he thought. Somehow he could not face his daughter when this sad mood was on him. Nor could he yet face the decisions that would be forced on him when he confronted his daughter's mother, as he was eventually bound to do. He went into the office and telephoned Mrs Harper.

'I shan't be round this evening, Thea,' he said. 'Pressure of work,' he added, unnecessarily, since no one ever asked him about his work.

'I see.'

He noticed that her voice had lapsed into the lustreless timbre he associated with the early days.

'Everything all right?'

'I suppose so.' There was resignation all round, it seemed. Then there was a brief gear change into a sharper mode. 'Tissy's allowance is about due, isn't it? There have been expenses.'

'I'll bring the cheque tomorrow,' he said. 'Although I thought it wasn't due until next week. In fact I know it isn't, Thea.'

'Yes, but there have been expenses, as I said. Children grow very fast, you know. I don't think you appreciate that. But then you wouldn't know anything about it, would you? I'm the one who does the worrying.'

'I'll see you tomorrow evening,' he said. 'We'll talk about it then.'

When he got back to his desk he found it occupied by a stranger. The stranger was young, slight, severe, finely fitted out in a lightweight summer suit of a muted but unmistakable transatlantic cut. Lewis remembered Pen saying something about an American: he assumed that this must be the man he meant. If he had thought about the matter at all in the general rush of events, it was to imagine some weighty representative of an international concern, one of Goldsborough's correspondents who had inadvertently come to the library on the wrong day, when Goldsborough was facing challenges in the psychology department. Yet this American, if this was the one in question, looked more like a minor Spanish grandee. Had he worn a ruff he might have been painted by El Greco, might have stood in as one of the mourners at the burial of Count Orgaz. He had the same precise face, the same narrow head, the same suffering nostrils. This man trailed clouds of an imprecise glory, vaguely connected with ancestors and money, though not the sort of money in which Goldsborough was interested. Goldsborough money was gross, impersonal, set off against tax. The visitor's money must be understood as delicate, fluent, understated. This impression went with the small ivory hand which was reaching out to touch the opaline goblet in which Lewis kept his pens and pencils. The hand was framed in precisely one inch of immaculate cuff. The nails, Lewis could see, were finely, perhaps professionally manicured. The stranger seemed entirely at home seated at Lewis's desk, and for one insane moment Lewis wondered if this were his replacement, smuggled in by Goldsborough while he, Lewis, had been making a telephone call. His panic was absurd, he knew, unreasonable. Nevertheless he reached his desk quite smartly, and waited for the man to express confusion, to, at least, struggle to his feet, overcome by embarrassment. When he did neither of these things it became clear that he had mistaken the desk for one that could be used by the general reader. Indeed, only the fact that it was set at right angles to the room distinguished it from the others. Lewis's appointments were modest: only the opaline goblet, at which the American was now staring in some puzzlement, proclaimed that the desk had an owner. But might not some fey academic, some exquisite, have brought this fetish along to assist him in contemplation, unable to work without the sight of this possession which would establish his identity, allay his anxiety? Might not the owner be in the grip of the true anxiety, the anxiety of leaving home, without having yet made the transition to this other home, where he would spend the rest of his life?

'Can I help you?' asked Lewis.

'I'm looking for a Dr Percy? Dr Lewis Percy?'

'I am Lewis Percy.' He felt his usual embarrassment in pronouncing his name.

The stranger extended his overbred hand.

'Howard Millinship.'

'Not the Howard Millinship who wrote that article on Mérimée? How very nice to meet you. I thought it was an impressive piece of work. That examination of the Spanish taste in nineteenth-century France, and the distinction between the true Spanish taste and Spanish kitsch. I thought it very well worked out, and very well written, if I may say so. But what can I do for you? Did you want to work in the library? Let me find you a place. This one is mine, I'm afraid.'

'I read your book,' said the American. 'That's why I'm here. Is there anywhere we can talk? Your office, for example?'

'I don't have one,' said Lewis apologetically. 'But we can go into Dr Goldsborough's office. I'm on duty here, actually; I mustn't be away too long. However, things seem to be quiet. If you'd like to come with me?'

He led the way to Goldsborough's office, gestured to the one armchair, and sat himself at Goldsborough's desk. Very quietly he moved Goldsborough's tin of blackcurrant pastilles behind a pile of papers, and then palmed it and put it into a drawer. If this man did turn out to be a potential benefactor it would not do to display these modest domestic appurtenances.

'What are you working on now?' he asked.

'Still Mérimée. But I wanted to discuss your book. I've been teaching from it this term. My students have been really appreciative of your ideas, Dr Percy. I was wondering if I could persuade you to come over and lecture to them?'

He taught, Lewis vaguely remembered, at a rather exclusive girls' college in Massachusetts. He was obviously younger than he looked, although he had the assurance of a mature, even a middle-aged, man. The decorum had purpose behind it. The 'Dr Percy', he imagined, was merely a tribute to his own rapidly greying hair. Even the thought of how shabby he must look to this polished creature could not dim his amusement, his surprise. He had not given any attention to his book since the day he had swept his free copies out of sight and into the back of a cupboard. It had aroused very little comment in England but had had a surprisingly kind reception in the States. This he had put down purely and simply to American generosity in these matters. He had thought of working on a second volume – had in fact made fairly full notes to that effect – but more pressing matters had intervened. Nothing had come of it, although it was not for want of time. He had all the time in the world.

But he was pleased to have his book remembered. Indeed, he was extraordinarily pleased. He felt as if he were looking at an old photograph of a smiling face. How kind Americans were, how charming! As to the strange proposition put to him, there was no hesitation: he instinctively and immediately rejected it.

'Mr Millinship . . . '

'Howard.'

'Howard. This is very nice of you. I count your invitation as the most enormous compliment. But I can't possibly accept. I've never given a lecture in my life, and I'm certainly too old to start now.' The minute he said this he realized how ridiculous it must sound. But it was true, he did feel too old to learn anything.

Howard Millinship looked pained, as if he had made a tactical error, framed his question badly, been deficient in courtesy. One vellum-coloured hand consulted his beard, his moustache. His mouth was childlike, Lewis saw, rosy and soft. How he must hate it for interfering with the seriousness of his demeanour! Yet he was impressive, for all his very real hesitations. He was impressive because he knew his place in the world, and had always known it, just as he had always known what to wear, what to eat, and whom to marry. Despite his youth he had a married, settled look, and even wore a wedding ring, an un-English custom. And he had the manners of another age; he was a young man from the pages of Henry James or Edith Wharton. In comparison Lewis felt immeasurably but not unpleasantly old, able to examine the stranger with curiosity, with indulgence, suddenly wanting to know all about him. He was so exactly like a character from a novel that Lewis could not bear to see him go.

But the American had no intention of going. Clearing his throat, as if to erase whatever he had erroneously done before, he started again.

'Perhaps not this year. I understand you have your commitments here. But if you could see your way to coming in a year's time? Or two years'? We would be most happy to welcome you.'

Lewis smiled at his earnestness, the earnestness of the young, with their infinite trust in the strength of their own intentions.

'You see, Howard, I really don't know that I can commit myself that far ahead. And I think you'd better not count on me, you know. I'm not really a teacher. Well, you must take my word for that,' he said kindly, as Howard Millinship showed signs of springing to the defence. 'You need a certain amount of conviction to be a teacher, or so it seems to me. I'm not sure that I have enough convictions. I'm really only good at things that require rumination, like reading and writing. I'm not what you're looking for, really.'

'We could offer you a house, of course,' Howard Millinship went on, exactly as if Lewis had not spoken. 'You could give one lecture or fifty. Or maybe just classes – our students, after all, might not be up to your standard. Literature, it seems, is on the wane. We're in a very beautiful part of the country,' he added. 'If you came in September you'd see the trees changing colour. I think you'd enjoy it.'

'I'll think about it,' said Lewis, amused and touched by such assiduity. He had little intention of doing what the American suggested. He had never wanted to teach, felt too humble to have opinions to order. And it was not his ideal, never had been. Transparency! What he wanted, what he needed, was some kind of interval in his life, away from the staleness of habits and obligations that bound him fast. Since everything was changing around him he began to crave change for himself. Yet it seemed impossible, for the simple reason that he had no idea of what he could change into. This was the central problem. With it, or preceding it, or at any rate intimately connected with it, was the fear of what would have to go if he did change. If his present self were to be sacrificed, was there not a tremendous risk that there might be nothing left? In what circumstances could this process – perhaps necessary, even overdue – take place? It must be tentative, experimental, cautious, and invisible. The forging of a new self could not be rushed. What he needed to do was to live somewhere, somehow, with none of the old props around him, no library to clock into, no house to return to, but also no simulacrum of a family, no distant wife, distant daughter, distant mother-in-law. He felt a surge of impatience as he thought of them, crammed into that house, uttering their constant lack-lustre demands, always on the verge of rancour. Stifling! If it were not for his daughter . . . But the little girl, who was growing to resemble her mother, would not be ready for him for many a long year. Suddenly he did not see why he should spend the intervening time alone, or waste it on people who did not, would never, love him. If he could make a home for them in America, might not his daughter want to live with him there? And would it not be an ideal solution, to welcome her to another country, a country which he imagined as a sort of paradise? Suddenly he felt a pang of pity for Tissy and for Mrs Harper, for their fatal lack of joy. It would be terrible if this inheritance were to be passed on to Jessica. His mission was to save her from everything that was prudent, watchful, careful, secretive, as she would indeed become if she stayed for ever in that house. If it had to be America, then so be it. However he did not think that he could face this on his own, in his present state. The self that he inhabited was so diminished, so nearly beaten, that it must be cast off before he could be the person that America demanded. He shook his head in amazement at the rapidity of the day's events.

'Howard, all I can give you is the vaguest of promises – I can't yet set a time. Does that sound ungracious? If it does, I'm sorry, truly sorry.'

He expected, after this, to be turned down flat, but Howard Millinship smiled and held out his hand. An agreement in principle was all that he seemed to require, but Lewis saw, too late, that this must at some time be implemented. The success of his mission brought about an almost visible relaxation in Howard Millinship's person. Oddly enough, this made him look older rather than younger. He now looked like a fairly well-worn thirty-year-old, with a not unattractive hardness about him. One day he will be formidable, thought Lewis. He is half-way there already.

'Where are you staying?' he asked.

'At the Stanhope Court Hotel. As a matter of fact my wife is waiting for me to call her. She said she wouldn't go out until I did. I expect she wants to do some shopping. She likes to go to the Scotch House.'

'Use this telephone,' said Lewis. 'And why don't you both have dinner with me? I'm free this evening, if you haven't anything planned.'

'I'm sure we'd be delighted,' said Howard Millinship. 'Jeannine would like to meet you. My wife is French,' he said. 'She read your book too. She loved it. I always tell her she's cleverer than I am.'

He made the call, was evidently pleased with what he heard, and issued the invitation for dinner. Then he turned to Lewis with a rather younger look on his face, domestic rather than professional.

'Where would you like to go?' asked Lewis. 'Do you know Meridiana? It was very popular a few years ago. I used to take my wife there before we were married.'

'Meridiana's fine. We were there last year. What time shall we meet you?'

'Eight o'clock? Not too late for you?'

'We'll see you then. Thanks a lot. Goodbye, Dr Percy.'

'You must call me Lewis,' said Lewis, to whom the American now appeared familiar, almost like a young relative. He felt like Howard Millinship's uncle. That was no bad thing, he reflected. A teacher is a sort of uncle to his students. And if he were to be a teacher, as it now seemed likely . . . He shook his head. He still did not see how it could be done.

He took the bus home. When he reached his street it was as though he had been away from it for a very long time. Curiously, he noted its charm, its strangeness, as if he were returning to it from abroad. In much the same way, and for much the same reason, it appeared smaller, humbler, even a little pathetic. Such innocence! White roses overhung the pavement from a bush that was almost a tree. Everywhere the gardens were luxuriant, proudly displaying flowers not normally praised for their beauty, purple rhododendrons, violet irises. Pansies in plastic boxes adorned every sill. Through the wide windows, each one backed with a sofa, he could see past French doors into further gardens. He remembered moving the sofa so that Tissy could sit there, where it caught the afternoon sun. He could almost smell the chocolate on her breath, could almost see her slight figure in its wide skirts as she glided out of the silent room. And if all this were to go? At first it seemed quite literally unthinkable. But he succumbed to what he felt was the pathos of the street, all unaware in the evening sunlight, as if it were the pathos of leave-taking. The street would remain, but he would go. Where he would go was as yet unclear to him, and he found himself unable to bring anything into focus. It was simply that matters would be painful for a while, for between leave-taking and arrival there is a vast area of doubt.

Tissy could have the house, he decided. She could bring up his daughter there. Mrs Harper could sell Britannia Road and move in with them. They would have enough to live on: he had heard that property in this area was now worth quite a lot. He had never touched the money his mother had left him, and now he regretted not having paid it more attention, investing it, or doing something clever with it. But in the division of the spoils that money could be his, at least for a while. He had no idea what he would do with it. He only knew, with infinite misgivings, that it was time to go. As he turned in at his own gate he pulled a flowering yellow rose – his own – towards him and inhaled deeply. Its honeyed sweetness spoke of pleasure, ardour, happiness. Not yet, he thought. But one day, perhaps.

15

The woman at the next table had brought her dog with her, a tiny animal that nestled timidly in her lap. This was not altogether pleasing to the waiters, who were nevertheless disarmed by the obvious wealth and glamour of its owner. She was dressed in black, with a glittering motif on her left breast; her hair was drawn severely back from her face and she smoked a long thin cigarillo, waving its smoke impatiently away, as if the cigarillo were being smoked by somebody else, an importunate companion perhaps. She appeared scornful, uninterested in the process of eating and drinking, only reluctantly present, conscious of the favour bestowed, and famously bored, or at least giving the impression of being so. Across the table a bulky man, in an expensive suit, seemed wary of her, although he appeared to be pouring out a rational yet pleading explanation of something Lewis could not catch. He was making no impression, Lewis reflected: the woman was not interested. He wondered what it would be like to be married to such a woman, to have to beg for her attention, to be relegated somewhere beyond the dog, whose quivering frame was being caressed by a firm red-nailed hand. It occurred to him that he might not marry again, an idea which he had been doing his best to avoid. The process seemed too arduous, and anyway he appeared to have been disqualified by his one, or one and a half, experiences. Even with Emmy, he thought, he would have failed, although he knew that the failure would have been Emmy's as much as his own. Women seemed more restless these days, less attracted by the prospect of settling down. In many ways his view of marriage still went hand in hand with the image of the silent sunny room he had just left, with a figure gliding out of the door to attend to something peaceable, domestic. He knew that he was fatally old-fashioned, and that this ideal did not appear to coincide with anybody else's. Besides, with his real wife living once more in his house, and himself in America, the image would remain unrealized in any future that would be left to him. Where would he live in the vacations? He supposed that he might take Pen's advice and look for a small flat somewhere. His wants were simple; he spent virtually nothing. He still had his mother's money, and a little that had been left him by his father; together they would cover the purchase of a flat and also Tissy's needs for the coming year if she chose to go on seeing him as a regular source of income. What he would do between now and his projected departure – still unreal in his mind – he had no idea. He supposed he would have to get down to the work he had neglected for so long and try to make it palatable to the young. He would have a lot to prepare.

His reluctance was occasioned not so much by the enormous prospect of leaving home and every kind of routine as by the incongruous thought that he could not face so vast an upheaval, was almost comically averse to making further efforts, without some sort of interval in which he might repossess himself, shed his disappointments, and begin again to be a person capable of directing his own life. That life had so far been so overshadowed with concerns that normal expectations had been banished as if by edict or decree. He felt elderly and at the same time unused. What he needed, quite urgently, was the faint stirring of pleasure, and, in addition, the increase of pleasurable occasions. The spring had been long and cold, perfectly matching his mood of disappointment, resignation. Only in the last two days had the sun shone and the temperature approached something that was normal for early June. And this evening was beautiful, voluptuous, bringing with it thoughts of happiness. How the change was to be achieved, if indeed it were ever to take place, was quite unclear to him, as was the whole idea of a future that would have no connection with the past. He was only thirty-eight, he thought. He was only half-way there, with the prospect of years ahead of him. However unfledged he still felt himself to be he had accumulated a certain amount of experience, although none of it had been particularly rewarding. His education would seem to have been faulty. At the same time he was no longer the idealistic creature whom he vaguely remembered as a boy, when he had truly believed that everybody meant what they said. The old Lewis Percy, the Lewis Percy who had wanted to be a character in a book and who had not managed to be one, had bowed out long ago. Something new would have to be fashioned from the ruins, something that would be just as authentic. He began, dimly, to perceive the need for new ideas, and for a rediscovery of some sense of self-esteem, without which, he knew, no one could survive. This last, he was sure, he would forgo at his peril.

Howard Millinship, in another immaculate suit, stood before him with an extravagantly beautiful woman by his side. Both smiling, they revealed identical sets of perfect teeth, which, in the woman's case, were emphasized by the oval of her face and a fall of long brown hair. She looked devastatingly self-possessed, with an assurance beyond her years. She wore a dark blue silk blouse, a white silk skirt, and white stockings and shoes. She was very impressive, thought Lewis, rising to his feet, fantastic by academic standards. Everything about her seemed devised in a spirit of luxury, from the gold chains round her neck to the small brown hand now extended towards him. Still smiling, she seemed perfectly at ease while Howard Millinship performed the introductions. Surely she could not be smiling at the prospect of a dull evening with a complete stranger? Surely her life was so arranged as to provide her with more adequate pastimes?

But perhaps her whole day was so filled with diversions that she could tolerate such an encounter with equanimity. It was only dinner, after all, and the restaurant was up to the standard she was entitled to expect.

'My wife, Jeannine,' said Howard Millinship, who did not seem to think it unlikely that he had won such a prize.

'How do you do?' said Lewis. 'It's very good of you to come at such short notice.' They appeared so exotic, so protected from the exigencies of real life as he knew it, so divorced from ideas of wear and change, that he felt their company to be something of an honour, as if they were minor deities from a world outside his own, just passing through on a tour of inspection. His hand, as he held it out, seemed to be made of a cruder material, more subject to the process of ageing, than the slim cool hands he clasped in greeting, releasing them reluctantly, as if they might have conferred on him the gift of everlasting youth, if only he had been able to retain them in his own.

'It had to be,' she said. 'We leave tomorrow.' And having performed her social duty, a duty condensed into merely meeting him and greeting him, she let her attention wander, and was soon distracted by the other diners, her amazing, perfectly regular face composed to receive appreciation. Even the woman with the dog was interested, a further shade of disdain added, in tribute, to features which Lewis had thought impressive enough before this impeccable creature had entered his sights.

Perhaps, but she was not as pleasant as she was beautiful. She made demands, she *had* demands, already in place: her attention was not to be wasted on him. She was too used to admiration to relinquish her autonomy. He saw that she would not notice him more than was absolutely necessary. He saw there an indifference which she regarded as her right: only the spectacular need apply. So it was to be him and Howard Millinship, he thought; and the decision still to be taken. The thought that he might have to rely on these people made him feel slightly faint, evidence that the former, unreconstructed Lewis Percy was still, however uncertainly, in place.

'You leave tomorrow?' he said. 'Then I'm very lucky that you were free this evening. Back to America?'

'No,' said Howard Millinship, neatly eating olives. 'We go to Paris. Jeannine's parents have a flat there. They've retired to the country now, so we take advantage. We usually spend the summers there, when everyone's away. Jeannine shops and I work. We go to the country at the weekends, of course, and we manage to have a month in the sun before flying home. Our semester begins in September,' he added. 'Earlier than yours. We break off in May. You'll get used to it. And it has the advantage of leaving you free to come to Europe before the tourists get there. Are you still terribly busy?' he asked. 'Grading papers, I suppose?'

'Well, I don't actually teach,' said Lewis. 'I just work in the library.'

'I admire you for that,' said Howard Millinship. 'It takes some courage to refuse a teaching post and devote yourself to research. I only hope you won't miss it too much when you come over to us.'

Lewis abandoned any attempt to confess the lowliness of his position, which had never struck him as abnormal, and which in many ways had suited him perfectly. In any event he was too fascinated by the neatness and dexterity with which Jeannine Millinship was wielding her fork and the thoughtful manner in which the smoked salmon was being inserted into her faultless mouth. This was a woman of high accomplishment, with exacting standards. He entirely understood her lack of interest in him. Women who looked so untouched by need or greed bore about them an invisible golden shower, like the one enjoyed by Danaë. Except that this woman would never be required to barter favours. The beauty had grown out of money, rather than the money out of the beauty. How did she fare, Lewis wondered, on a small campus in Massachusetts? Probably she was indolent enough to absorb whatever came her way, and supremely indifferent to Howard's colleagues, who might, for all he knew, be excellent men, handsome and hearty in the American fashion, pleasing to women. They would all be in love with her in any case, though their wives might not be so keen. But American women were better at fighting their corners, and she would wave away their dislike with a languid hand, attributing it to mere jealousy, and not feeling chilled by the absence of affection. In time she might become like the woman at the next table, he thought, starved out by the lack of her own desire, but still beautiful enough to attract overwhelming attention. And if she were a woman of conventional morality – he had no reason to think otherwise – she would see the admiration of other men as a just tribute, not only to herself but to her husband as well. Though she appeared quite cold, and beautiful, much as an idol or an icon is beautiful, Lewis hoped that there might be humanity hidden somewhere inside, as he hoped this of everyone, despite receiving information to the contrary. The friendship of these people might be problematic, he thought; he would prove too simple for them. And yet they appeared to find him acceptable. Howard Millinship, in particular, treated him as if he were older and more eminent than he could ever possibly be. Above all, they were gloriously diverting to look at, a fact on which he felt impelled to remark.

'Forgive me for staring,' he said. 'But you really are an amazing looking couple.'

At this they both smiled. Even Jeannine looked at him with something approaching warmth. Presumably they were so used to this kind of observation that they regarded it as an essential preliminary, and could not proceed until the formalities had taken place. But there was a perceptible relaxation in the atmosphere, and he no longer feared for the success of his evening.

He began to enjoy them simply as phenomena, who had raised the temperature of this unsettling day to something he recognized as detached aesthetic enjoyment. Modestly he hoped not to waste their time, and if that meant consenting to go to America then that was what he would have to do, if only to keep the agreeable expressions on their faces. In the meantime he would do his best to emulate their high standards. Even this he felt to be an innovation; in his mind certain constrictions were eased, leaving behind something precariously like appetite. He saw no reason why he should not dine out more often, even though he had few friends of the order of the Millinships. The benefit they bestowed was of a more metaphysical variety, something like the consciousness of a birthright. Life was not confined to what the rich and beautiful could command. The particular strength of such people – their function, in a sense – was an awareness of entitlements. That was their most valuable lesson. Not that I could stand this every night, he thought. And anyway I am not rich. But I am not all that poor either. I live below my means. That too is a metaphysical condition, and one that I must endeavour to correct. He ordered a bottle of wine and cautiously prepared to share a little pleasure. He reflected that it was a pity they were leaving so soon. He would have liked to have seen them again, just for the opportunity of being able to study them. Many intriguing lessons were there to be learnt. He felt like a man let out of prison, on probation. The world had moved on, was no longer as he remembered it.

Jeannine, after almost motionlessly conveying a considerable quantity of food to her mouth, accepted coffee and brandy and lit a cigarette. Lewis became aware that it would not do to discuss work or indeed anything of an abstract nature in this woman's presence: to do so would be to lose her always intermittent attention. To engage in a discourse of any profundity would be to court her displeasure, for although she was both intelligent and sophisticated she did not care to be ignored or overlooked. When her husband returned to the subject of Lewis's possible arrival in America, Jeannine took a lump of sugar and tried to tempt the little dog from the next table. It was a seduction, Lewis thought, and a rather cruel one; now she and the dog's owner were going to compete for the dog's favours. She was acting, he saw, out of the same sense of infallibility that was the consequence of her perfect appearance and which dictated all her actions, and it would not seem to her that she might be treading on others' toes; beauty had made her impermeable. As a stratagem for distracting her husband from his tedious preoccupations it worked perfectly. Soon all eyes were on this little contest, which had an underlying note of seriousness. Lewis's sympathies were with the dog, a poor nervous creature who started wildly after the sugar lump, only to be restrained by his mistress's iron hand. 'I don't think he likes to be teased,' said the luckless companion, leaning forward as if ready to separate the two women. 'He's very highly strung.' 'Oh, I understand dogs,' said Jeannine. 'I have had dogs all my life.' Nevertheless she dropped the sugar disdainfully and lit another cigarette. Her quest for her husband's attention was now so palpable that Lewis was forced to abandon any attempt to explain his present situation in the interest of changing the subject. 'Oh, absolutely,' he heard himself say rather hastily to Howard Millinship. 'If you'll leave me your address I'll write to you within the week. I just need a little more time to think.' At the back of his mind was the thought that he might somehow get out of it, but that it would not do to say so at this particular moment.

'Then you'll come? I can tell the Dean?'

'I'll let you know within a week, certainly. Some more coffee, Jeannine?'

He thought, rather hazily now, that a moment of decision might have been reached, might even have passed, but without his active participation. That would have to come later, or, on the other hand, it might not come at all. These people, charming though they might be, were, after all, strangers. The future was unreal, not to speak of the various social difficulties he might encounter if he were actually to leave. Resignation, moving house, possibly divorcing: how did one manage these matters? How did anyone? He had a vision of Mrs Harper and Goldsborough banding together to prevent him from leaving the country. Mrs Harper, he saw, was a massive obstacle on his route to freedom, if freedom was what it was. Even Tissy's future would have to be negotiated through Mrs Harper, who in all matters of importance acted as her daughter's broker. It seemed to him now as if his entire courtship had been conducted through Mrs Harper. She was better at being a grandmother than she had been as a mother, Lewis thought. She loved the child painfully, although her reticence was so entrenched that she could not say how much she loved her, did not in fact encourage anyone else to do so. She and the doctor had succumbed instead to the kind of untidy attention that Lewis associated with old age: damp kisses, the lowering of a heavy cheek onto the top of the small head, the fussing over collars and socks with spoiled reddish hands. Poor Mrs Harper. She had once been a beauty, no doubt proud, refined, with her Belgian accomplishments as her dowry. And she had squandered it all on a renegade husband and a reluctant lover. He supposed that there had been an awkward adultery at some stage, and the resulting pregnancy concealed until it was no longer possible. Was it then that the husband took off? If so, Mrs Harper had not been rewarded for her indiscretion. Instead she had found herself less loved than she had expected to be, and with a small child who insisted on her distracted attention. Lewis could now see the reason for those entwined figures, for Tissy's so voluntary incapacity, for the costive petulance with which Mrs Harper's disintegrating beauty had always been surrounded, like a miasma, so that it was difficult to know what one might have done to upset her.

And now that beauty had gone entirely. Now she was old, overweight, too discouraged to dye her hair. The doctor's death had hit her hard. Only the little girl retained her fierce loyalty, which might otherwise have been relinquished with gratitude. How difficult it was to be happy, Lewis thought, and yet it should be so easy. Even he knew it was easy, and in his not particularly interesting life (but unique, unique to him) had sensed transcendence at various unimportant

236

moments of the day, had felt it earlier this evening as he had pulled the yellow rose towards him and inhaled its scent. The future might yet yield happiness; it was poor-spirited to think otherwise. But for Mrs Harper it was no longer a possibility. For that reason he wanted to see her comfortable, dignified, in his house. She aroused a certain reluctant pity in his mind, and he felt she deserved a gesture of solidarity from someone, if only from himself. Without that, who could survive?

Tissy, who had so brilliantly managed to make herself weightless, imperceptible, would be more of a problem. Tissy was eternally unfinished business. He did not see what would or could happen to Tissy, for it was unlikely that her flush of liberation would last once family forces were brought to bear. Those friends of hers, Fran and Kate, still seemed to telephone her occasionally, but not to ask her to join them as they had formerly done. Possibly they viewed her association with Gilbert Bradshaw as a defection. Tissy had indeed assumed a manner of airy inconsequentiality when this man's name had been mentioned: it was the manner of a girl who wants to show off to her friends, and Lewis supposed that those friends, their roles reduced from participation to audience, had taken offence. In any event, all that was in abeyance. He had no way of knowing what Gilbert Bradshaw's intentions were, but he saw, with sudden penetrating clarity, that Tissy must marry him. She must marry Gilbert Bradshaw: in so doing she would be free, and so would her mother. And so would he. More and more it seemed to Lewis that all he had to do was to go away and stay out of sight until all these events had taken place.

And the little girl? He would have to trust her to remember him, he thought, and hope that she would eventually trust him to make her happy.

'I expect you'll be taking your vacation shortly,' said Howard Millinship, who now had his arm on the back of his wife's chair.

'Well, no,' said Lewis. 'My daughter is too little to be

taken from her mother, and I like to see her every day. She lives with her mother, not with me.'

'How old is she?' asked Jeannine.

'Nearly three. My wife and I are separated, you see.'

'You'd better divorce before you come to the States, then. You'll have a far better time if you're free. You'll probably marry again.'

'Well, I suppose my wife will divorce me, when she feels ready to.'

'Does she work?'

'I doubt if she earns much. She works for an antique dealer. I thought I might give her the house. I think – I hope – she was happy there.'

'Chic,' said Jeannine. 'And where will you live?'

'I must look for a flat,' he said, passing a rather anxious hand over his hair. 'I have a lot to do. How odd. This morning I had very little to do, or so it seemed. Suddenly everything has changed. I must start looking for a flat tomorrow. You know, I'm not sure that I can come to America this year – there's going to be so much work to do. I really ought to go back to Paris, for a start.'

'Why don't you?' she said negligently. 'You could have the flat.'

'The flat?'

'Yes, our flat. Nobody uses it except us. My mother might come up for a wedding or something, but that needn't interfere with you – there's plenty of room.'

'I should like that,' he said slowly. 'I could get on with some work again.' But it was with the ache of revived memory that he saw a vista of early mornings, and himself, with his briefcase, walking exultantly down great avenues: not much of an image for a man of thirty-eight, he thought, but for him it looked as if it might have to do.

'You really are most awfully kind,' he said. 'Could I take you up on that?'

'Of course. It's better for us to have someone staying there. I'll leave word with the concierge – she has a set of keys. Just let Howard know when you'll be going.'

'Where is the flat?' he asked.

She was carefully repairing her mouth, gazing intently into a small mirror. Finally, with a snap, she shut the little case.

'Place de l'Alma,' she said.

He remembered the market, and the buying of the cheese, as some men remember their childhood. It will all be changed, he thought. I am no longer twenty years old. This could all be a mistake. Had he not read somewhere, everywhere, in fact, that one should never go back? And now he would have to re-enter the time machine, and who knew how he would fare? He would leave the safety of his ordinary life and risk disillusion, even pain. And loneliness, of course. This would be a difficulty. No Pen, no Jessica. No more Tissy: Emmy gone for ever. But one way or another he had lost them anyway. If nothing awaited him, in this future from which all familiar landmarks had already disappeared, could this be more intolerable than to continue as he was? Recently he had noticed in himself a heaviness, a dullness, which he attributed to his way of life. It had affected him physically, making him weary. The weariness usually attacked him as he set out for Mrs Harper's house every evening. The unvarying nature of this excursion had turned his day into a series of utterly predictable events. And when he reached the house no attention was paid to him. Jessica, after greeting him – but still with that residual reluctance – would be absorbed in her supper. Mrs Harper would sit with her while she ate. And Tissy would not be at home, or, if she were, she would sit abstractedly to one side, like a visitor, but, unlike a visitor, clearly protective of her own independence, parading her absent-mindedness, her lack of attention, remote in a manner that he was supposed to decode, into which he was meant to read the fact that she no longer had anything to say to him. She would be called frequently to the telephone. Conversations, or what he could hear of them, were monosyllabic, from which he deduced, or was meant to deduce, that the caller was Gilbert Bradshaw. Of course! He now saw, and felt sure, that she had laid her plans; she was, he thought, remarkably consistent. What hindered her from bringing all this into the open was the kind of embarrassment that can only express itself as defiance. She might be consistent, but she was also consistently childish. She had never grown up, and yet she was capable of grown-up manoeuvres. She had left Mrs Harper no card to play except the happiness of the child.

For Tissy had never been a good mother. He had found this surprising, in view of the careful way in which she had hugged and rocked her baby, and had become anxiously solicitous in her place. No wonder that the child had not known what to make of him. He should have been able to make her laugh, but his love was so hedged about with his own vulnerability that he must have appeared almost tearful with anxiety. Indeed the tears had risen to his eyes on more than one occasion when he was playing with her. He had seen himself as one of those stricken fathers in Hans Andersen, roaming the friendless world with his child on his shoulders, and had been unable to bear it. Perhaps it would be better for Jessica if he disappeared. Gilbert Bradshaw, having no intimate ties with the child, could be jovial, reassuring. He and Tissy would be parents in the purely formal sense, producers of Christmas trees, holidays, bicycles, and that might arguably be better than a father with a broken heart. For when he was with her he truly felt his heart to be broken. Better then to concentrate on what he regarded as the direction of his wife's ambitions. Let her be happy, if that was what she wanted. Why should she not be? Happiness was not a matter of merit, after all, but of good fortune.

He signed to the waiter to bring the bill.

'I don't see why you should give up your house,' said Jeannine, who at last appeared to be taking an interest in him. 'Your wife might marry again. She ought to move out then.'

'Would that be fair?' he asked.

'Quite fair,' she said firmly.

'I can't thank you both enough,' he said, as they rose to go. 'You've helped me make a lot of decisions I didn't think I could make.'

'We can count on you, then?' said Howard.

'Yes, I think you can,' he said. 'I never thought this sort of thing could happen so quickly.'

'That's the way we do it,' said Howard with a smile. 'Why waste time?'

'Why indeed?' he said, as he shook their hands and got them a taxi. 'I'll be in touch,' he shouted, as the door slammed and the taxi moved off. Then he was alone on the pavement. A free man, he supposed.

None of this would be easy, he warned himself, as he strode off in the direction of Parsons Green. But when was leaving home ever easy? And who could make it easier? Certainly not anybody he knew. If anything his family, such as it was, would make it more onerous still. To feel like this at thirty-eight! He should be joyous, determined. But around his heart, which he had believed to be arid, he felt the sad blooming of regret, of longing. For certainty, he imagined. But there was no certainty: he had already found that out, and thus learned the most difficult of all lessons. As he walked along the Fulham Road his pace slackened and his euphoria, largely induced by the unexpected company, gradually ebbed away, leaving sadness and confusion in its wake. Surely none of this could be happening to him, he reasoned. No one had actually asked him if he wanted to go to America: the idea had never occurred to him. The intervening months between now and his departure, whether spent in Paris or in London, seemed irrelevant, and would, he knew, be filled with conflicting feelings; he would be torn between a desire to have everything stay the same and the sad knowledge that it never did. He began to feel appalled at the way his life had shifted into this uncomfortable dilemma. His reason told him that he must seize this opportunity to start again, yet what he felt, overwhelmingly, was distress at having to leave everything that meant safety to him. He knew that his life was shamefully dull by anybody's standards. He knew that he was too young to settle down into this dreamy troubled routine with which he had so easily – too easily – come to terms. Yet as he looked up into the whitish sky of a summer night he wondered under what skies he would soon find himself. It was for the furniture of his life rather than its inhabitants that he felt most longing, for he knew that his absence would make little difference to those he would leave behind. Would anyone even notice? Pen, possibly: the others not at all. His own love for his daughter would become a burden to her, while his wife had already indicated her forthcoming absence. She was more competent than he was, had brought her housewifely efficiency to bear on her plans in a way that had once amused him: he was forced to acknowledge in her the same gravity, the same concentration, the same lack of anything to say, now that her object was Gilbert Bradshaw rather than the maintenance of his, Lewis's, comfort and inheritance. Assiduous was the word he would have used to describe her. And notably unforthcoming. And still he went to her door, and still she eluded him. He wanted her attention, that notoriously scarce commodity, as he had always wanted it. He wanted to tell her of his woe, yet the idea of her wilfully evading this explanation, as she had evaded all the others, was unbearable to him. He knew that if she were to break off to answer the telephone in the middle of this hypothetical explanation he might feel the impulse to murder her.

Yet while longing to stay he knew that he would leave, leave the quiet house, the yellow roses in the garden, the allotted half-hour with his daughter, for a wasteland of unasked-for possibilities. And those intervening months in Paris, that probably misguided reprise of an earlier experience, would, he knew, be an error. For what had his youth yielded, apart from a modest ambition and a mistaken confidence in women? The ambition, which he supposed would now be satisfied, had all but disappeared: he had laid it aside without regret, leaving it at the back of the cupboard with the unwrapped copies of his book. And fate had seen to it that his naïf confidence had been wrongly invested. Fate would no doubt guarantee that he make the same mistake again, if ever he had the temerity to repeat the experiment. The worst of it was that he still could not see what else he could have done. And now he would leave home to make his mark, but all would be accomplished in desolation. Some essential hope had vanished, and he was about to be sent out to look for it again.

There was a light on in the downstairs window of Mrs Harper's house. Without thinking, he rang the bell. In her dressing-gown, now stout, but with the stand-offish air of a woman who habitually flings her head back at every encounter, she received him with the flared nostrils of old, and, as ever, he felt his vitality diminish as he contemplated the impossibility of winning her over to his point of view.

'Lewis!' she said, her hand to her breast as though he were an intruder. 'It's very late. I was just going to bed.'

'Is Tissy here, Thea? I want to speak to you both.'

'Tissy's not back yet. She went out for the evening.'

'I need to talk to her. In the meantime I want to tell you something, something that will affect you personally.'

'Oh?' She was prepared, he could see, to be affronted.

'Do you think we might sit down? This is rather important.'

Reluctantly she moved aside to allow him access to the drawing-room, following him as if he were some headlong and feckless stranger with whom she had to have dealings. He noted the thickening of her jaw, her weary eyelids, noted too the dust on the vase of dried flowers in the grate. The handsome jutting table, the overstuffed and swollen armchairs, the incongruity of the fragile cups and saucers in the corner cupboard, the heavy silver – no longer polished – his daughter's little chair, all affected him with a further desolation, further evidence of leave-taking.

'I want you to sell this house, Thea,' he said. 'I want

the three of you to move to my house. It can be yours if you live there, as I hope you will. I want Jessica to grow up there.'

'Tissy will never come back to you, Lewis. I told you that.'

'I'm going away, Thea. She won't have to come back to me. I'm going to America.' And then, at last, he knew that it was true.

She sank into a chair. 'You can't go away. You've got responsibilities.'

'They're also Tissy's responsibilities. I'm passing them over to her now. She can look after you both. And if she wants to make other plans she can do so without me as financial back-up. Where is she, by the way?'

'I don't think you're entitled to ask that, now that you're going away.'

'But you didn't know that before this evening, did you? I'm not blind, Thea, although I agree that it takes me an incredibly long time to see anything. Please ask her to stay in tomorrow. I must talk to her. But obviously I had to see you first.' There was no irony in this remark, merely a statement of fact.

'And when do you think you're going? To America?' She spoke sarcastically, as if America were some sort of illusion.

'I'm going next year. Until then I shall be in Paris. I shall leave for Paris' - here he consulted his watch - 'in a couple of months. In the next two months I shall have moved out of the house and into a flat somewhere. The flat can be for Jessica when she's grown up, if she wants it. Eventually,' he paused here, on delicate ground, 'I should hope to move back into the house. In the meantime I'm sure you'll all be more comfortable there.'

'Well, you'll have to make all the arrangements, Lewis. I can't say what Tissy will think.'

'I'll make the arrangements, of course. And perhaps Tissy would like to let me know what she thinks when I come round tomorrow evening. Cheer up, Thea. Tissy

244

always loved my house, and Jessica will have a proper garden to play in. And you'll be happy there, I'm sure.' He was saying all this very firmly, as if he believed it. Firmness was essential. There was no hope to be had from this particular quarter.

'I'll leave you now,' he said. 'You'll want to get to bed. I'll see you tomorrow.'

She followed him to the door, which, as usual, he had to open himself.

'I was thinking of going back to Jersey,' she said. 'I've still got a brother there. We could live with him.'

'Well, now you won't have to,' he said pleasantly. 'You won't have to live with anyone. The money you get from this place will see you through nicely for a few years. You can always get in touch with me if you need anything. But I'll have to have a divorce, Thea, you do see that, don't you? I've been alone too long now, and I can't go on. And I dare say Tissy has other plans. As I said, I'm not blind, although I am incredibly stupid.'

'I don't know, Lewis. You've always been good to her.'

'But she's not my wife any more, is she? I'm not leaving a wife, am I? She doesn't love me and I don't think she ever did. She just wanted to be married. As for my feelings . . . ' He stopped. He suddenly could not bear to discuss his feelings. He resolved to leave his feelings out of it, since they had so little influence on his wife: by this stage it seemed like an act of human economy, of rationalization, to leave them out altogether.

Through the open door the starless night beckoned, aloof and pure, no promise of human affection. The little hall was, as always, redolent of the smells of fine cooking, but now he noticed a staleness in the air. Part of the staleness emanated from Mrs Harper herself. Lewis felt for her his usual combination of dislike and compassion. On an impulse he bent down and kissed her, something he could not remember doing since the day of his wedding. She lowered her eyelids in acknowledgement. He waited outside on the step, until he heard her close the door, and then moved off into the night. A stranger might have remarked that he had acted like a man. Odd, therefore, how little he felt like one.

—— 16 ——

He awoke the following morning in a burst of anger. They would not be allowed to get away with this. Who 'they' were was quite unclear to him, nor did it matter; he was quite content to let their identity remain obscure. He simply felt entitled to a period – an intermission – of irrational and futile resentment, after which he would return to his mild-mannered and well-behaved ordinary self. In the meantime he enjoyed being angry. Energized and liberated, he tore through his breakfast and wrote a pungent note for Mrs Joliffe, asking her to pay more than usual attention to the cleaning of the bedrooms. He then became more angry when he realized that it was too early to go out and belabour estate agents. He would have liked to conclude his business within the space of a single morning, to have overseen the removals, to have bought the flat and installed the furniture, sent out the change of address cards, resigned from the library and packed his bags. He was ready to go. But this was anger speaking, and underneath the anger lurked something simpler, more tender, something unreasoning, something like the remnants of faith, hope, and charity, all three, in fact, something that looked forward, in the simplest sense, to his new life, while at the same time acknowledging his need for help. He felt newborn, unfledged. He remembered a picture he had once seen of the hand of God, conveniently cleaving a portion of the heavens to succour a martyr on the point of death. He remembered another, of a departing soul, hands joined for the upward flight, already dressed in other-worldly garments. He had thought of it as something reserved for believers, having no use for such things. But now he wondered. If help were to be needed, this particular resource must be borne in mind. For it became clear that help would come from no other direction. He had already received intimations of the future; now all that he required, but required in good measure, was the gift of acceptance. Perhaps this was not in the power of any human agency. Perhaps what he was feeling was forgivable, understandable, even justifiable – even better, perhaps it was natural to feel as he now felt. He had enjoyed the anger while it lasted, and had had the agreeable sensation that it was spontaneous, within his reach. And also that new vulnerability, quite unlike the old, the so familiar weakness. This new feeling was childlike, but without fear. He saw that while a certain amount of attack was needed to enjoy the world, this inwardness was required in order to make sense of it. He desired to make a bet with himself that he could go through with it. Already the emotions of the past hour had provided a brisk tutorial in possibilities. The only interference with these insights would come from the contingencies of ordinary living, which he saw as huge crudely fashioned roadblocks, barricades in his path, the day an endurance test of negotiations. He wished he had more cunning at his disposal. But there was no help for it: no-one would substitute for him. He must get through by himself.

From habit he scanned the social page of *The Times* for the announcement of Emmy's forthcoming marriage. As always there was nothing. He let the paper fall with his usual feelings of relief and dismay. What had happened to her, his poor girl? Why had she so singularly failed to do what other women, far less interesting, managed to do with such ease? There was something truly lost about her, as he had suspected long ago; he had not been mistaken. That infinite variety of moods which she possessed, that enormous aptitude for pleasure, those round brimming eyes, that brutal sophistication, all failed to disguise a desolate heart, a heart even more desolate than his own. Endlessly seeking without finding, she was in a more perilous condition than anyone he knew. In comparison Tissy, for whom he had sacrificed her, was a devious little girl. On an impulse, and despite the early hour, he dialled the number of Emmy's flat. It was, of course, a mistake, as he realized when a male voice answered the telephone.

'She's asleep,' said the voice austerely.

'Will you please tell her I called? It's Lewis Percy. She knows the number. I'd be very grateful if she got in touch.'

As he put the telephone down he realized how urgently he wanted to see her, not for his own sake but for hers. He wanted to tell her that he loved her, but in a different way, that he would always care for her, care what happened to her, that he would dry her tears. He foresaw a future in which she would return to him, half-ashamed, half-defiant, and he would take her in his arms and sit her down and comfort her, while she would recover her spirits and revert to being the Emmy he had loved and disappointed. There would be disappointment all round, he realized. His trustingness would be no match for her anarchy: he would suffer. And perhaps she would too, as if he had no right not to make her happy, which was what she wanted and thought she deserved. The worst of it was that she had a genuine disposition towards happiness which he was not in a position to satisfy. To her happiness meant diversion: parties, holidays, love affairs. She was a genuine woman of pleasure. And his own disposition towards happiness was entirely opposed to this. He wanted peace, silence, domesticity, the sunny room with the hieratic female figure, gliding, finger to her lips, out of the door. If they ever met again they would be alarmed, sorrowful, that they had failed to match, that they had failed to change. But this was perhaps the essence of a sentimental education, that nobody lived happily ever after, or that this condition was astonishingly rare, which was not what one had been led to believe. Perhaps one was eternally surprised at how endlessly renewing, and self-defeating, love affairs turned out to be. And the sheer impossibility of inhabiting another person's mind, of taking on their thoughts and fears – this must also be taken into account. It might be that there was sadness at the end of love, or, if not at the end, along the way. He only knew that his heart smote him when he thought of Emmy, as if he wished most painfully to find her again, to go to her rescue. He felt suddenly, scorchingly, ashamed that he had not got in touch with her. But this was simply an illustration of what he meant. His ideal had been marriage, or rather the married state, as hers had been, but while he had a wife and she had no husband they were bound to behave in different ways. He had considered himself disqualified, and viewed her freedom as dangerous to his condition. How she must have despised him! She had told him at the beginning that she hated marriage – for everyone but herself, he had understood her to mean. And he, with his facsimile of a marriage, still obeying the rules!

She would never come to him now, he thought, after so many disappointments. If they should be together again they would be like Adam and Eve, expelled from their respective Gardens of Eden, shamefaced with recognition. They would both know, having eaten of the apple, that they could not look forward to an uneventful and cloudless future but must face each other in the intimate knowledge of their own deficiencies. In each other's eyes their lineaments would be apparent: he would be dull and she would be disobedient. Yet what he wanted to say was that none of this mattered, or rather that it mattered but that it was not crucial. He wanted to care for her, and he wanted, more than anything in the world, that she should care for him. Without that he doubted his ability to live his own life as he would want it to be lived. He doubted his ability to do his work, his research, to go down once again to that sunless sea, without her warmth to return to. He felt as if he had been cold for months, for years, whereas in fact his discomfort had to do with her absence. He did not even care if she did not or would not love him. He accepted this as a possibility. He accepted the fact that his behaviour might have earned her contempt. He only knew that he must reach Pen as soon as possible, to get a message to her. He could not quite face another's voice at the end of the line, although such voices might become part of his future. For now he was determined to marry her.

With this realization came a crashing down of barriers in his mind, a cancellation of former loyalties. Even his daughter began to dwindle, remote, well-behaved, a little ghost. Wait for me, he thought, wait for me. I may have other children, but you belong to my real life, the life I was brought up to live, when men and women got married and had children and never even envisaged a second chance. How could they? They were too innocent, like my mother and father. Now I am older, wiser, sadder, and I know that innocence must be sacrificed, before it turns out merely to have been no better than ignorance. I may have other children, but they will have to grow up with this knowledge, for their parents will be filled with it: it will be the air they breathe. Whereas you, so solemn, so dubious, so full of *méfiance*, and, beneath it, a baffled need to trust, are the child I must have been, and your mother too, before it all went wrong, before devices, stratagems entered our lives. Our calculations were harmless; we married as children marry. I see the same simple assumptions in your eyes, because you will have nothing to hide. You will always be my best, my most loved child, not only because you are the first but because in a sense you are also the last. I say goodbye to myself in you. My other children will be wary, as I myself shall be.

Before getting to Pen, to whom it no longer seemed important to behave with strict honour, as he had once thought necessary, he must go through this ritual of organizing his departure, although he knew perfectly well that he would not go anywhere until he saw her. His anger was now gone, or rather it had been directed to another location: himself and his shameful reticence in the face of Emmy's desire. Worse, he had not even proved himself to be her friend; he was nothing more than Tissy's virtuous husband. Emmy would be justified in hating him, he thought. He had failed to give her that sign which would have brought her back to him. He remembered her saying, 'It's up to you,' crude, bleak words, and now for the first time he registered the full import of this. She had been waiting for him, whiling away the time with other lovers, towards whom she would act with varying degrees of resentment, but with whom she would continue the game. He saw great danger ahead, great obstacles to be overcome. He would have to convince her that he was a changed man. For surely he was changed? It was not a question of merit but of recognition. He had grown up, become a fully qualified member of the fallen world. All this must be conveyed to her. Yet before this essential work was done – and he still had a certain amount of trouble with it himself – he had to carry on as if everything were the same, as if he were the same patient, hopeful, faithful character, on whom everyone could rely. In many ways he regretted that character, mourned the death of the essential Lewis Percy. But in the light, the ferocious glare, rather, of his new destiny, he no longer had the time to pay his respects. After the death, the resurrection, or so he hoped. Who could say that there might not yet be some good in him?

The estate agent, whom he visited on his way to work, was enthusiastic. 'Britannia Road? No problem. I've got television producers queueing up for property in this area. You know how it is, once one moves in the others follow. If you wait here while I make a few calls I can probably set something up for the next few days. Viewing, and so forth. I take it there's somebody at home? Your wife?'

'There will be somebody there,' said Lewis. 'Although it would be better to make appointments for the evening, when I can be there myself.'

'No problem,' said the young man again.

'And I'm looking for a flat for myself. Somewhere a little closer to town.'

'Ah!' He tilted the chair back to a normal angle and applied himself to a card index. 'Flats are a bit short at the moment. The best I can do is put your name on the books and let you know if anything comes in.'

'The only thing is I'm in a bit of a hurry. I have to leave the country shortly, and I'm anxious to get something settled fairly soon.'

'No problem,' said the man for the third time. His attention span was limited, Lewis thought, as was his vocabulary. He was sorry he had not gone somewhere slightly more grandiose. 'Just leave it with me. I'm sure something will come in. Canning's the name. Hugh Canning.' Lewis felt pretty sure he would not be hearing from him again. As he turned to go Hugh Canning was greeting the next client with an expression of specious pleasure. He no doubt did this all day.

A delay might present difficulties. Lewis had had a vision of himself, removed to a perfectly bare, perfectly white, perfectly efficient flat, with only his books in place. The flat would of course be empty because he would not be in it, but it would be there, waiting for him, if he ever came back. He saw this failure to settle the matter out of hand as the first setback on a day which could not be other than problematic, but brushed it aside in his desire to get to the library to see Pen. But he found Pen busy with a student and was forced to content himself with leaving a note, suggesting, as they often did, lunch at the usual place, at the usual time. Then he marched to Goldsborough's office, only to realize that Goldsborough was still in America, and that he would not be able to make his resignation speech until the middle of the following week. Perhaps this was for the best, he thought. He had no desire to embarrass Goldsborough or cast a shadow over his happy tycoonery. He would have to manage somehow. There would be one of those discreet little occasions after the library had closed for the evening, with a couple of bottles of wine, and the secretaries in their best blouses. Goldsborough could say a few words and Lewis could tell them all how happy he had been. And he had been happy once, but that was in a past that now seemed distant, prelapsarian, infantile. He would leave without regrets.

The morning passed slowly, uneventfully, and with a beguiling normality. Lewis found it so soothing that he almost abandoned thoughts of departure and a new life. Like a man in a trance he raised his eyes every few minutes to the clock: every catalogue card took on the lustre of a reliquary. That this life would altogether come to an end was a fact which until now had not convinced him: somehow he had thought he would always return and that his place would be kept for him, his desk waiting, so that he, the prodigal son, could be painlessly reabsorbed into a routine which mere folly had led him to desert. The uncertain volatility that had greeted his earlier moments, when he had known so precisely what to do, gave way to an excruciating tenderness, so that he was moved by the most insignificant sights, a student's head bent over a book, a secretary placing a memo on Pen's desk, an assistant taking the slips out of the request box, hieratic motions and movements performed in an atmosphere of heavenly calm. Shafts of sun poured through dusty windows on to wood the colour of toffee. It was very quiet: examinations were in progress and there were few readers left. The library was a great wooden ship, manned by a skeleton crew. Overhead the timbers shivered as Arthur Tooth shelved books in the gallery. He would outlast them all, Lewis reflected, not for the first time. This was the sort of remark one heard several times a year: 'You'll outlast us all, Arthur,' spoken in hearty and slightly exasperated tones, usually at the end of a particularly irritating conversation with him. Although the weather was hot Arthur wore his usual three-piece suit. At lunchtime he would place his hat precisely on his head, take his umbrella and march off to his club. After lunch, when he had had a couple of peppermints to dispel the odour of claret he would sink into a doze at the back of the library, which lasted until Hilary brought him a cup of tea at four o'clock. This would restore him to normal spirits, and he would spend his remaining hour polishing the desks. Nobody seemed to find this strange, although he had frequently to displace the books requested by readers in his pursuit of ideal symmetry. The remarks addressed to him in the course of a day's work were of a ritual nature: 'Good morning, Arthur,' or 'Good evening, Arthur,' or, more usually, 'Not now, Arthur.' To Lewis he had once represented the shape of things to come, a prospect which now filled him with terror.

At lunch, pushing aside his untasted quiche, he came straight to the point.

'Pen,' he said. 'Can you get Emmy to ring me? You see, I want to marry her.'

Pen raised his eyes from a perfunctory salad. 'This place gets worse,' he said. 'I shan't be sorry to go. My dear old thing, you know there's nothing I'd like better. But I ought to tell you she's living with someone at the moment. Emmy's a problem to me,' he went on. 'I wouldn't normally talk about this sort of thing but she gives cause for concern. She's not always at home, for one thing: I don't know where she is half the time.'

'She was at home this morning,' said Lewis. 'But I couldn't speak to her. There was someone else there.'

'Well, that's Emmy. That's what she's like. I wish to God someone would take her in hand. I wish to God it could be you. But don't raise your hopes too high, Lewis. I'll tell her to get in touch with you – but that's by the by. You'll be doing that yourself. You're divorcing Tissy, then? And staying on here?'

'Well, no,' said Lewis. 'I'm going to America. And as for Tissy I'm seeing her this evening. I'll ask her to divorce me. She can have the house. I'm looking for a flat.'

'You could have George's flat,' said Pen. 'He's already moved half his stuff out. We can use my house when we come up to London. My God, what a lot of news. Brilliant, Lewis. I hated to think of you here for ever, though it didn't seem fair to say so. Was it that American, the one who was looking for you the other day? Bearing gifts?'

'Bearing the offer of a visiting professorship,' said Lewis. 'I'll be leaving at the end of the month. For Paris – the American has lent me his flat. I begin to feel the weight of the inevitable. Will we ever meet again, Pen? Where is George's flat, by the way?'

'St Petersburgh Place. Why don't you give him a ring? He'd be delighted to show it to you. Of course we'll meet again – you'll come down and stay with us. I'm really terribly glad, Lewis.'

'And if I marry Emmy . . .'

'Oh, well, Emmy. Don't bank on her, old thing. She's been a bad girl, I'm afraid. There's someone who wants to marry her now, as a matter of fact. Frankly, I'd rather not interfere. It would be a great relief to us all to see her settled.'

'There's always someone who wants to marry her, isn't there? There was the last time I saw her.'

'It's the same one. She's led him an awful dance, and of course it's made him that much keener. He's quite a bit older than she is; ideal, really. She says she doesn't love him, but in point of fact he'd do very well. He knows my parents, you see. Actually, we're all in favour.' Pen's smile, so well-known, was as agreeable as ever.

Lewis felt disheartened to have discovered a flaw in this friendship. When it came down to it, he reflected, like stuck to like: he was up against acres and privileges. It was the man who had to bring a dowry in such a suit and he had nothing to show for himself except his impeccable suburban background. He realized that he had been gently discouraged, and felt shocked and saddened. These emotions grew and deepened. He was being handed George's flat as a consolation prize.

He did little work that afternoon. He would take the flat sight unseen, he thought: it hardly mattered now. There was, after all, no reason for him to remain in London; indeed, the thought of staying on chilled him. The Englishness to which he had assumed he was heir suddenly seemed to exclude him. Seen down the funnel of his impending departure, his acquaintance seemed to dwindle, his affections to falter. His silent farewell to his daughter – 'Wait for me! Wait for me!' – was, he now saw, a cry of loneliness as much as anything else, as if so simple-hearted was he that he could only be comfortable in the company of a child. He blamed himself slowly for his credulity. The world was, after all, a cold place. He had always known this, but his naïveté or simplemindedness had shielded him from the knowledge. Staring at his hands he determined to leave as soon as possible, before the end of the month. He was now surplus to everyone's requirements. He would meet the Millinships in Paris, staying in an hotel until they went south. He supposed he would get down to some work, although he felt too slow, too discouraged, too futile. Work now would be as illusory a resource as perhaps it had always been.

He was in a mood of desolate calm when he saw Tissy, later that day. The little girl was in bed with a slight cold, for which he was almost relieved; he would have broken down if he had seen her. Tissy received him ceremoniously, her full skirts spread out, her hands folded in her lap like a Victorian child. Her eyes were modestly lowered but he saw that she was now wearing make-up, which gave her fragile beauty a certain brightness, almost a boldness. The lowered eyelids were a greyish-blue and fringed with black lashes, a becoming effect of which she was no doubt aware. Her expression was, as usual, virtuous, as if he were still at fault. She made no attempt to welcome him, apart from a murmured 'Lewis', in a voice that was almost faint, as if he were having his way with her against her will. He felt momentarily sorry for Gilbert Bradshaw, but this was lost in a wave of regret that swept over him, not only for his marriage, but for the whole of his life.

Calmly, desolately, he said, 'Well, Tissy, this is the parting of the ways.'

She was deprived of her usual weapons by this simple statement of fact. He saw that in the absence of reproaches she had little to say. But then he had not married her for her loquacity but for her very silences, her household piety. He had thought them to be two of a kind, as perhaps they were. Perhaps she was the only equal he would ever know, since the way towards a second marriage was, he now saw, subtly barred.

'Tell me,' he said gently. 'Did you ever love me? Don't be frightened, Tissy. I know you'll marry again. But did you ever love me?'

There was a silence. He imagined her to be disconcerted by the very reasonableness of his tone. Finally, 'I was very fond of you,' she said.

Oh, fond, he thought. It told him everything. He was shocked at how little there was to say. So many shocks in one day. He wanted to lay his head in her lap, and say, 'I'm leaving home, Tissy. Do you know what that means, you who have never left home, have never had to? I'm going away. Don't you want to know where I'm going? I wish you could hold me in your thoughts, just for a while. Sometimes I want to stay here, with nothing changed, and yet in my heart I know I must go. And it's time to go, not because I have to, but because nobody wants me to stay. Look after my child. You cannot imagine what agony it is for me to say that. You see, I don't know when I shall see her again, if ever. It feels so final now, what I am doing, as if I shall never come back, never find the energy, the desire, never survive another departure. Tissy, I feel sick at heart. Tell me that you love me, or if not that, which is not true, tell me that you once loved me, even if that was not true either. Tissy, be kind. I can't say I still love you, because I'm not sure if I do. I just know that I regret you. You know, I think I miss you already. That's why I can't say goodbye. I'm too afraid of my own tears.'

Instead, he handed her the piece of paper bearing the name of his solicitor, which she took with her usual expression of maidenliness. She seemed to him to be acting entirely in character. Only her moment of liberation had been uncharacteristic, yet even that had served her well. She was more resolute as a result of it.

He kissed her cool cheek, held her hand for a moment. He tried, and failed, to wish her well, to say something tender and final, to finish the matter with honour. A character in a book would have regarded this renunciation as a great moment, whereas he needed all his strength simply to get out of the house. He was aware of Mrs Harper standing silently in the doorway; she had evidently thought to mark the moment as well. 'Goodbye, Thea,' he said, taking her hand. 'Goodbye, Lewis,' she replied. 'Have you left your address? In case we need you for anything?' No divorce, he thought, kissing her as well, could have been more final.

He telephoned Emmy's flat when he got home, but only heard the answering machine. He told himself that it was just as well: he would only make himself ridiculous, more ridiculous than he already was. He had not realized his disadvantages until he had had lunch with Pen. No doubt she had written him off as a nobody, a simpleton who could not rise to the challenge of making love to her. He could hear the scornful epithets, as if she were discussing him with Pen: *petit bourgeois* would be the least of them. No doubt he had been an object of derision without knowing it. He blushed in the darkness of his room as he thought of Pen and George Cheveley being treated to an imitation of him, with all his scruples mocked and ridiculed. He longed in that instant to get away and to leave them all behind, to vanish completely. He would have left on the instant had he had enough money in his wallet, but in an unusually crowded day he had found no time to go to the bank.

He slept badly, his mind intent on matters of the past which he had consistently misinterpreted. Leaving home, he thought. This is my only resource and I must do it like a man. But he was glad to get up, to bathe and dress, and go to the library. He could not bear the house in the early morning and escaped to eat his breakfast in a coffee bar near the college. He embraced the library, its silences, its sighs, its shining desks and its green lamps, as if he were a monk and this his monastery, or rather as if he were a monk due to leave the monastery to undertake a perilous mission among strangers. Loving-kindness must be his watchword, he thought, still intent on behaving well. Yet he was afflicted with a coldness of the spirit which had him staring at his hands, his pen idle, his index cards forgotten.

Goldsborough would be, if anything, relieved at his departure, since he could now replace him with two or even three recent graduates for the same money. Nevertheless, when Lewis told him that he was going, Goldsborough had the decency to look solemn and even sorrowful, whipping off his glasses to reveal naked childish eyes. They looked at each other in silence. Goldsborough had always been a softie, Lewis thought: trifles made him happy. In that he was innocence itself. 'Do you want a party?' asked Goldsborough, replacing his glasses.

'No, thank you, Arnold,' said Lewis hastily. 'What I should like would be to leave straight away. At the end of this week. I don't think there's much that I could usefully be doing. Not if the computers will soon be here.'

'All right, Lewis. It might be best. Better to take on new staff at this juncture, I mean.'

'Goodbye, Arnold,' said Lewis, holding out his hand. 'You've always been very kind.'

But, 'I hate goodbyes, Lewis,' said Goldsborough, his glasses steaming up. 'Good luck. Don't forget us, will you? All the best.'

So it was Goldsborough, of all people, who would miss him, he thought, walking back to his desk. But the coldness of his spirit remained, although he knew he should be moved. He did a rapid calculation and decided that he would leave at the end of the following week. He could not think of anyone who should know this. In the lunch-hour, he went to a travel agent and bought a ticket for Paris. Pen was absent on a couple of days' leave. For the sake of their old friendship, which now seemed flawed, he would leave a word on Pen's desk, giving notice of his flight number. Perhaps he, and even George, would come to see him off. He did not know how he would manage to go if his departure were not a matter of record.

His coldness enabled him to attend to the formalities of his removal, to discard some books, to pack up others to be shipped to America, to buy new shirts and socks, to have his hair cut, to water the garden for the last time. He felt so estranged that it did not occur to him to say goodbye to anyone: he felt invisible. Yet he performed quite competently in addressing the many small tasks that filled his days, days that were quite empty of human company once he had left the library. On his last evening he sat in the garden until it was dark, watching his roses glimmer and smelling their scent. His bags were in the hall, the taxi ordered for the following morning. A new sympathy told him that this was exactly how patients facing surgery must feel once the preparations were completed and the nurse had left them alone for the night. He even wondered if it were worth it to go to bed and try to sleep, since the silence of the garden suited his condition better than the confined space of his bedroom ever could. In the end he went indoors, gave himself a nightcap, mounted the stairs, and undressed. But sleep did not come, as it had not come for many nights now.

In the end it was a relief to leave. Even the airport was a relief, since everyone there was in the same situation. Every face was strained, anxious. He was now perfectly calm, resigned: the surgeon's knife had been sharpened, the instruments were lying ready. All he had to do was mount the operating table. Now, if ever, was the moment to behave like a hero, to summon up ineffable resources. But he was tired of such fantasies, and when his flight was called he straightened up immediately, picked up his bag, anxious to get it over and done with. Turning round for his last look at England, he saw Emmy, plunging through the crowd, necklaces flying, laughing, swearing, apologizing, and waving her boarding pass in her upheld hand.

ABOUT THE AUTHOR

Anita Brookner is the author of the best-selling *Hotel du Lac* as well as the novels *The Debut, Providence, Look at Me, Family and Friends, The Misalliance, A Friend from England* and *Latecomers*. An international authority on eighteenth-century painting, Brookner teaches at the Courtauld Institute of Art and has also written *Watteau, The Genius of the Future, Grueze,* and *Jacques-Louis David*.

3|90

Sparta Public Library
Sparta, New Jersey
729-3101

RULES

1. Library materials may be kept two weeks and may be renewed once for the same period unless otherwise indicated.
2. A daily fine will be charged on each item overdue.
3. Each borrower is responsible for fines, damages and losses on all materials charged on his card.